'Well, well, how the gods do favour me.'

Giles had managed to escape, then, and had joined up with this English raiding party. Maria was bemused by the encounter, yet there seemed an inevitability about it, as if she had known that the two of them would meet again, that she had doomed herself by that unaccountable decision to turn towards the slave deck that day so many months ago, in order to see a man of her mother's race.

'No word for me? No greeting? No anxiety even to know the fates of your friends at the Residency?'

She chose to reply in Castilian. 'I assume Cartagena will be ransomed and that Don Piero and his lady will be safe from your bully boys, though I understand it is the custom of your piratical dogs to prefer plunder and rapine, even if it means loss of solid gain.'

His grey eyes narrowed and the smile grew less pleasant. 'Perhaps, *muy doña*, I too will prefer to slake my lust and my blood-thirst rather than accept a ransom for you? Who knows?'

Joanna Makepeace has written over thirty books under several pseudonyms. She taught history, English and drama at a large comprehensive school where she was head of English before leaving full time work to concentrate on her writing and research. She was born and continues to live in Leicester with her mother and a Jack Russell terrier named Dickon. Her enthusiasm for the theatre and music is unabated and her greatest enjoyment gained from visits to old houses, ruined castles and battlefields. She began to write when still very young after seeing delightfully romantic historical films which she still finds more exciting and relaxing than newer ones. *The Spanish Prize* is her first Masquerade Historical Romance.

For my uncle, Harry Makepeace,
whose admiration for Dumas, Weyman and Sabatini
is as great as my own.

THE SPANISH PRIZE

JOANNA MAKEPEACE

*Masquerade is a trademark published by
Mills & Boon Limited, Eton House,
18–24 Paradise Road, Richmond, Surrey, TW9 1SR.*

*First published in Great Britain 1990
by Mills & Boon Limited*

© Joanna Makepeace 1990

Australian copyright 1990

ISBN 0 263 12628 5

*Set in Times Roman 10 on 10¼ pt.
08-9007-86834 C*

Made and printed in Great Britain

CHAPTER ONE

THE wind had changed. Maria woke and wrinkled her nose against the insidious stinks which reached her, wafting from the slave deck, and this despite the sprinkling of rose-water and fresh herbs on the bare floor of the cabin by her duenna, Consuelo Henriques. She sat up and reached for her pomander. The clove-stuffed orange failed to keep at bay the stench of sweat, human ordure, tar and bilge-water. It was the siesta hour and the heat almost unbearable. Before nightfall the galleass would be anchored in Cadiz harbour, the captain, Don Esteban, had assured her.

Maria's mouth curved in a wry smile as she turned to where Consuelo sprawled on a cane day-bed, snoring contentedly. Nothing disturbed Consuelo's natural ability to sleep, not even the chaos of their hurried departure from the *estancia* near Malaga and the unaccustomed hardships of the voyage.

Everything had been done to shield Maria from discomfort wherever possible. Don Esteban had immediately placed his cabin at her disposal. It was the least he could do, he said, for the niece of Don Felipe Santiago y Talavera, especially since the journey had fallen so soon on the death of her father, Don Diego.

Maria had observed that her uncle's cabin, close under the forward companionway, was narrow and stuffy. Where the captain slept since vacating his quarters she had no idea. Consuelo made shift with the day-bed in Maria's cabin without complaint.

Her duenna's clacking tongue had softened appreciatively since that terrible day when Don Diego had taken to his bed. On Consuelo's ample bosom Maria had sobbed out her grief, then, true to her upbringing as the daughter of a Spanish *hidalgo* whose blood was as fine

5

as King Philip's, she had managed to hold her anguish under tight control when her uncle, Don Felipe, had arrived to take charge of her affairs.

Her father had prepared her. Even now, as she sat in the airless cabin, she recalled how the sweat had stood out on his forehead in great drops, as, seated in the *estancia* garden, he had grasped her hand tightly within his own.

'Come close to me, *querida*. Sit here, on the stool at my feet.'

She had tried to hush him, horrified by the signs of his suffering. 'You must not try to talk. The effort is too much for you. You are in great pain again, I can tell.'

He checked her gently, one fingertip against her lips. 'You know I have had this pain before, many times. I have always tried to keep it from you. Now—it is neither possible nor practical to do so and there is little time.'

'Father——'

'The doctor tells me it is my heart. I was afraid so. Now,' he shrugged, his narrow, clever face expressing a mixture of satirical good humour and polite regret for her concern, 'a month ago I wrote to your uncle, Felipe. He should be here soon to help you through your ordeal.'

She fought to keep back her tears. 'Surely there must be something the doctor can do——'

'Nothing but ease the pain, *querida*. That he has been doing for weeks now. You will be very brave, Maria. I know you too well to doubt that.'

'I will try, Father——'

'And you will succeed. Maria, I want you to trust your uncle Felipe. You do not know him or your aunt. You will feel very lost, especially——' He broke off and grimaced. 'I have lived here like a recluse for too long since your mother died, guarded you from any threat——'

She looked up at him sharply. 'I don't understand, Father. What possible threat can there be to either of us? We have lived such quiet lives. Who would wish to harm us?'

He sighed heavily. 'You are so innocent, Maria, know so little of the world's sorrow, like your mother. She trusted everyone—me—implicitly, and I was not able to save her.' He gazed beyond her into the distance and Maria saw that his dark eyes were wet with tears.

She said awkwardly, 'How could you have saved her, when God willed otherwise? You must not blame yourself, Father. Consuelo tells me how dearly you loved her and she you.'

He brought himself sharply back to attention, conquering his feelings with a conscious effort. 'Whatever your uncle decides as to your future, you must obey him implicitly. It will be for him to make a suitable match, since I cannot.'

She bit her lip uncertainly. 'You are saying that it will not be easy for him to choose a husband for me because my mother was English?'

Again he turned from her, avoiding her gaze. 'I can see now I have been selfish, keeping you here with me, safe, but too closely sheltered. You are all I had left of her, and it would have broken my heart to part with you, even for a visit to Cadiz where you could have got to know your aunt. She could have introduced you to some kind young man—however, Felipe has already made some enquiries and I hope and pray the outcome will assure your future happiness.'

He had seemed too much in pain to say more then, and later it had been too late.

Maria could not remember her mother, Mistress Mary Gascoigne, who had married Don Diego Santiago y Talavera and followed him to Spain in King Philip's train after the death of the English Queen Mary, to whom she had been lady-in-waiting. Don Diego had loved his English wife passionately and had never recovered from the pain of her death, which had occurred when Maria had been just three years old. He had sought and obtained permission to retire permanently from court and devoted himself entirely to the care of this one child his heart's love had given him.

Maria sat up on the tumbled bed. She saw herself dimly in the greenish reflection which filtered in from the cabin's great stern window. Her eyes were inherited from her mother. Don Diego had told her often that they resembled the tiny English speedwell flower in their depth of blue, the iris circled by a deeper, almost purple line. Her complexion was lighter, creamier than the other girls on the *estancia*. In nearly all else she resembled her *hidalgo* father. Her features were his, the nose high-bridged, nostrils flaring haughtily beneath dark brown, finely arched brows; the mouth too, long-lipped, sensitive, the lower fuller, promising a hint of sensuality when full maturity was reached. Impatiently she put back the loosened waves of her brown hair from the high, broad forehead. Her face was too long for true beauty, oval, a little narrow like Don Diego's. Just now her expression was brooding, melancholy. She sighed. At seventeen one part of her life was over, a door to that joyful, cherished existence on her father's estate near Malaga, with its orange groves and shaded walks, closed to her forever. Even should she visit it after her marriage, life could never be the same again. She would be ruled by a husband, no longer by the gentle, scholarly man who had loved her so.

After the funeral her uncle had expressed his intention to take her back with him immediately to Cadiz. He had not yet broached the marriage plans he'd already embarked upon at his brother's request before the journey to Malaga. The time was not yet ripe. Don Felipe would have all things suitably ordered.

Maria had obeyed her father's dying wish and put herself dutifully into Don Felipe's hands. He was younger by three years than Don Diego, a big, broad man with the blue-black hair and beard of her father but the bluff, hearty manners of a seaman. For ten years he had commanded a galleon under the famed admiral, Santa Cruz. He had greeted her warmly, tried to comfort her, to put her at ease with him. She believed she could trust him to protect her interests, but her grief was too great for her father and it had closed her heart and mind against a warmth for anyone who approached her. She dreaded the coming meeting with Doña Beatriz, her aunt, shying instinctively from the knowledge of that shadowy future which threatened to engulf her in blind terror. Thoughts of that new life she kept grimly at bay while she travelled this strange, half-limbo existence on board the galleass.

A sudden panic seized her in its grip. This breathing-space would soon end. Already this morning she'd heard Don Felipe order the disposal of his baggage, ready for disembarkation. Consuelo had packed Maria's clothing-chests. A bustling house in an alien environment faced her in Cadiz. There would be pious condolences, questions, so many questions.

The still air in the cabin stifled her. She needed to go on deck, feel the salt breeze on her face, cool her heated cheeks. Consuelo still slept soundly. It would be a pity to disturb her and Maria longed to be alone. Soon she would be surrounded by the ladies of Doña Beatriz's household. This was her last opportunity to think quietly of all that was past and to prepare herself for the part of her life to come: womanhood; marriage.

Hurriedly she piled her hair high, securing the luxuriant swathes with ebony combs. Her heavy silk over-gown had been discarded when she'd lain down to rest after the noon meal. Stealthily, so as not to wake Consuelo, she lifted it from the dressing-chest at the foot of the bed and slipped it on, fastening the silver brooch high at her throat. Silver braid edged the front openings and hems, and was repeated upon the slashed roll pads of the shoulders, the only relief from the mourning-black which oppressed her spirits as the heavy silk folds impeded her limbs. She clipped her pomander to the silver chain at her waist. She would need that. As she descended the companionway which led to the poop deck she would be further assailed by the stench from the rowing benches.

If she was fortunate she would find this part of the deck deserted at this hour. Don Esteban had given strict instructions that her privacy must be respected and careful guard was kept on Don Felipe's party from a safe distance. To further enhance her comfort a canvas awning had been erected to shade the passengers from the heat and form a barrier between this part of the ship and that which housed the crew and the slaves. Maria often walked the poop deck in the cool of the early mornings and evenings, escorted by her uncle and with Consuelo in attendance. Now she longed to stand by the taffrail absolutely alone and watch the great sweeps of creamy water part in the wake of the ship's passing.

The sudden chill of the salt breeze halted her momentarily as she mounted the companionstair and she paused halfway, breathing it in with relief, listening to the raucous calls of the sea birds as they circled overhead.

As she had hoped, the poop deck proved to be deserted and she revelled in the freedom to walk unobserved. She stood for a while, arms folded on the taffrail, eyes half closed, watching the shoreline moving ever closer. They were still too far out for individual landmarks to be distinguishable, but Maria could just pick out the dark green of woodland, the brown of coastline and, here and there, the silver gleam of light on water, streamlet and falling waterfall.

The galleass was moving very slowly now, the onshore breeze carrying them on steadily towards the bar of Cadiz harbour. The slaves then, for a short spell, had their hour of respite, as did most other crew members but for those on watch.

The slaves! Again that nauseating stench reached her from amidships. Never, since she had boarded the vessel, had she caught so much as a glimpse of the galley slaves. She had thought many times about those unfortunates, half pitying their terrible, hopeless plight, half acknowledging the need for such punishment. Consuelo had said many of them were pirates, captured upon the high seas in their senseless attacks upon Spanish shipping. Some of them might be English, compatriots of her dead mother. The thought struck her forcibly. Down there, on those hellish rowing-benches, were men who shared her blood. Pirates they might be and heretics, yet the thought of them toiling under the merciless whips of the overseers, so far from the green land her father had spoken of with such nostalgic affection, disturbed her.

She had never met an Englishman. Were they all fair, as her mother had been, or red-haired like their notorious, heretical Queen? Moving strangely, half against her will, she went to the head of the companionstair, descended to the lower deck and turned deliberately towards the rowing-benches. If, indeed, as she suspected, conditions were so horrifying there, she might be able to persuade Don Esteban to ease some part of their suffering.

The overwhelming heat and solid stink of humanity brought her to a standstill, appalled by the sheer horror of the scene.

Two long banks of oars faced her, the rowers chained to the sweeps, slumped forward in attempts to gain some ease from the unexpected rest period the freshening wind had granted them. The hortator's head was well down on the dirty table which faced the rowing-benches. Before him stood the small drum, the beat of which kept the oarsmen strained to their tasks in unity. He, like the slaves, was bearded and filthy. Stentorious snores were being emitted from his half-opened mouth. He moved in his sleep, grunted and settled again on the stool. The rowers also slept the sleep of utter exhaustion.

Maria was unable to withdraw her fascinated gaze from the sight of their misery. All were naked, but for some brief, filthy loincloths which some retained and the iron belts round their waists through the loops of which each was chained to his fellow. The chain ends were secured at each end of the benches by enormous iron staples. The men's hair and beards were so matted, filthy and overgrown as to make them appear animal-like. Chest muscles bulged against the hard lines of their ribcages and she imagined them arching and crouching desperately in the pull, the ceaseless struggle to keep to the hortator's beat. Hour by hour, day by day, year in, year out, they must endure this living hell, chained together in the merciless heat of summer and cold of winter, the overseer's whip encouraging those whose stamina failed to greater efforts until, finally, their hearts gave out under the strain and they gained release from their chains at last, to be cast overside, their sufferings ended, not even granted burial in sanctified ground. Her heart flooded with pity for them, yet they were criminals, pirates, heretics. Maria's faith told her their suffering could be their only means of salvation. Had not the Dominican monks of the Holy Office of the Inquisition fought doggedly to save their damned souls from the pains of Hell? Had not the King, in his great mercy, granted them time for their black hearts to recant, turn from their wickedness and achieve, in the end, some measure of redemption?

Certainly they suffered, horribly. During the days and nights of their journey Maria had heard their screams as the bull-hide whips found their marks on hapless backs as the wind slackened and the hortator's beat quickened.

She stiffened as she became aware that one of the slaves was awake and watching her intently, his head tilted, slightly, as he supported it by a callused palm, his elbow resting upon the stilled, huge oar. Maria's eyes flashed angrily at the insolence of his stare. His bearded lips parted in a grin of pure amusement which brought hot colour flooding to her cheeks. Instinctively she stepped forward slightly to observe him more closely. When she considered her actions later, she could not explain to herself why she did not immediately withdraw. His open defiance was an affront which she deeply resented yet could not ignore.

He stretched indolently. Not for a moment did he lower his gaze and he must have known how he risked punishment for such lack of respect. Even seated at the oar, she could see he was a big man, his hair, though dirty and matted, brownish fair. His eyes were blue, like hers, though lighter, slate-grey almost, and they danced with pure mischief. She guessed he was no Spaniard. Could he be an Englishman, one of those taken on the high seas in an act of piracy against one of His Majesty's treasure ships?

Suddenly infuriated by his raillery, she snatched up the overseer's whip, lying discarded on the hortator's table, and lashed at that smiling face with all her strength.

He made no sound but a little tight hiss and, reaching up, caught at the metal end of the whip and pulled it tight towards him. Maria stumbled off balance and, before she could let go of the handle, found herself drawn to his hard, muscled body. It happened so quickly and so quietly that she had no time to cry out for assistance or to try to hit back again.

He held her pinned against his chest so that the steady beat of his heart stirred her senses and she remained momentarily quite still, held motionless, like a rabbit caught in the deadly, paralysing gaze of the stoat. Like his fellow slaves his body, neglected for months, stank of stale sweat and filth and was iron-hard, not an ounce of spare flesh on his ribs. She could feel them pressing against the silk of her gown. Revolted though she was by such close contact, she could not resist a feeling of involuntary admiration for such magnificent masculinity. He was an animal, true, but a splendid animal. White teeth flashed at her in savage delight at her predicament from that tangled mass of beard.

'Blue eyes,' he taunted, 'no true Spaniard. Now, I wonder who sired you, my proud beauty? Was your sire or dam spawned in the Low Countries?'

He had slackened his grasp on the whip end and she pulled it free and lashed at him again. Bright beads of blood sprang out on his tanned, wind-roughened cheek but he seemed to totally ignore the pain, laughing so loudly that the hortator woke with a great snort of wonder and gazed wildly about him. His horrified eyes lighted upon Doña Maria caught in the frantic struggle with the slave. He jumped to his feet with a great bull-roar of rage and sprang to the rescue.

'Whoreson dog. How dare you so much as look at Doña Maria Santiago, let alone molest her with your filthy paws?'

His bellows roused the other slaves. Instantly aware of their danger, some cried out in alarm, others cringed

back from the oars in mortal terror in anticipation of
retribution to come. Experience had taught each man to
resent the wrongdoings of his fellows, since one de-
faulter could bring down savage punishment on all. Their
persecutors were inclined to hold all of them culpable.

Maria continued to belabour the slave, who merely
laughed the louder. She was too furious and had no
breath to scream out her accusations.

The hortator, almost afraid to touch so important a
lady, reached tentatively to catch at her raised arm.

'*Muy doña*, please, you should not be here. I will
escort you in safety to the stair and call your attendant——'

She was hysterical with rage, unable to hear or answer
the man. 'This dog has insulted me. He——'

'He shall pay for it, *muy doña*, and in full, I promise
you.'

She stumbled backwards and found the slave's dirty
bare foot planted firmly upon the hem of her gown.
Angrily she bent to tug herself free, but the rich cloth
tore as she wrenched at it wildly.

The slave laughed again, impervious to the hortator's
horror. 'Tut, tut. Such fire is only bred in England. My
apologies, my lady. I should have recognised such determined courage. Your mother was a countrywoman of
mine, I imagine.'

He spoke in English and her head jerked in astonishment—before, he had addressed her mockingly in
courtly Castilian. Maria's father had taught her English.
It had pleased him, when they had been alone together,
to hear Mary Gascoine's mother tongue on her
daughter's lips. It had reminded him of those long,
scented nights when he had courted her beneath the
pleached walks of the palace gardens at Whitehall and
Nonesuch.

Now Maria was devastated to hear this devil of a pirate
address her familiarly, as if he had every right to do so.
How dared he make the assumption that the two of them
shared English blood? That his assumption was correct
made the matter even worse in her eyes. For the first

time in her short life she was forced to accept the im-
plication that her mother's blood was that of an enemy
nation. Though England and Spain were not at war, there
had been many incidences of hostility between their
ships, especially within the waters of the New World.
Choked with mortified bewilderment, she turned from
her persecutor, pushed aside the agitated hortator, and
fled past him to the companionway. Once on the stair
she plunged towards the refuge of her own cabin.

The sudden slam of the door woke Consuelo, who
gave a sharp screech of alarm at the sight of Maria,
white-cheeked, trembling, her clothing torn and in
disorder.

'*Querida*, what is it? Where have you been——?'

'Be quiet, Consuelo.' Maria was in no mood for questions or lectures on the impropriety of her conduct. She
began to tug at the torn and soiled gown. 'Order hot
water for me to bathe. Now!' she snapped as the older
woman gaped at her open-mouthed. The too sudden
awakening had left Consuelo temporarily bereft of her
wits.

'Bathe? Now? But, Maria——' Consuelo heaved
herself to her feet and moved towards her charge, her
expression anxious and shocked. 'It is not possible. Don
Felipe told us hours ago we were nearing land. I have
packed your clothes——'

'Then unpack. I need a clean shift, kirtle, gown,
everything.' Maria turned away impatiently as tears of
anger and hurt bewilderment at her own frightened response to what had happened sparked on her lashes.

'If you insist——'

'I do insist.' Maria's foot stamped hard on the cabin
floorboards and Consuelo retreated astonished. It was
so unlike her young charge to be so peremptory.

'What has happened, *querida*? You should not have
left the cabin without me, you know that. You are not—
harmed?' There was desperate concern in her voice.

'No, I am not harmed. I have told you what I need.
Do not stand there arguing. Help me.'

'But how did your gown become torn? Did you fall on the companionstair?' Obediently Consuelo advanced to unhook Maria's undergown, staring incredulously at the great rent in the velvet overgown Maria had flung unceremoniously across the bed.

'Get me some warm water, hurry.'

'I cannot order the men to heat water in the galley, not now when the crew are preparing to reach port. The captain will object.'

'Then I must manage with cold. Pour some of the water from the jug into the basin. I don't care. I must wash—all over.'

Maria tore off her shift, shuddering at the thought of the filthy hands which had mauled her. The green sea light from the stern window played on the beauty of her slender form, shadowing the hollows beneath the taut, youthful breasts, highlighting the curve of belly and thighs. She was tall for a woman, yet, already, her body gave promise of full, rounded splendour to come with aroused womanhood.

She seized a linen cloth from Consuelo, who poured water from the silver ewer on the great travelling-chest into the basin with trembling hands, and began to scrub herself vigorously. She felt utterly defiled by contact with the slave who had handled her, drawn her close to his stinking body. Her flesh tingled beneath her impatient fingers and she shook off Consuelo when she tried to take the cloth from her to take over the cleansing herself.

The older woman was completely bemused and horribly frightened. Her full senses were returning and she cast a hurried glance towards the cabin door. All about them, above, below, men's bare feet pattered on decks and stairways. Commands rang out and muttered replies reached her indistinctly. Was the ship coming into harbour? Was this the cause of the disturbance from the sleepy siesta hours? Consuelo dared not move from Maria's side to look from the stern window to see if they were now close in to land. But if they were not, why the sudden alarms? She ran to unpack a valise and rummaged for Maria's clean kirtle and shift, returning to envelop her charge in a towel, for, despite the heat in the airless cabin, Maria was continuing to shiver uncontrollably.

There came an imperious knock upon the door.

'Maria, I must speak with you.' Don Felipe's voice, not to be disobeyed.

Consuelo's tongue clove to the roof of her mouth. What could she offer in her own defence if she were charged with negligence? Something dreadful had occurred out there on deck and she had lain snoring, unaware that her charge had escaped her vigilance.

Maria ignored the peremptory command but simply held out her hand for her clean shift.

Consuelo managed to find her voice at last. 'Don Felipe, I—I cannot let you in at present. Doña Maria has been resting. She is in a state of undress.'

There was a moment of silence then a whispered exchange outside the door. Consuelo recognised the other voice as Don Esteban's, then Don Felipe spoke again.

'Then, Maria, I must see you the moment you are presentable.' She still did not answer and he rapped out, 'Do you hear me?'

'I hear you, Uncle.'

'Then you will admit me?'

'When I am ready.'

'Then please hurry. The matter is urgent.'

Consuelo held her breath as the sound of booted feet moved away from the cabin door. She hastened to help Maria into a clean gown, her fingers fumbling the hooks in her considerable alarm.

'Mistress, you must tell me what happened,' she whispered, tearfully. 'There is serious trouble. Were you attacked up there? Did one of the crew——?'

'Not one of the crew.'

'But—I don't understand. How——?'

'This is not your business.'

'Maria, it is very much my business.' Tears streamed down Consuelo's plump cheeks. 'It is my duty to guard you constantly. Why, oh, why did you leave the cabin? Don Felipe will be so angry. You are really—unharmed?' There was such emphasis on the final, questioning word that Maria's lips curved into a tight little smile, despite her anger.

'In the sense you mean, certainly I am unharmed.'

'Then——'

'One of the galley slaves dared to insult me. He actually—touched me——'

Consuelo's eyes widened in astonishment. 'A galley slave, *muy doña*? You did not really go near the slave deck?'

'Consuelo, don't act like a foolish old woman. On this vessel it would be hard to avoid the slaves.'

'Sancta Maria,' the duenna murmured. 'Don Felipe will have me beaten. He will cast me off without a crust. He will——'

'Do nothing of the kind. Stop your wailing. You know well enough I would never allow him to dismiss you. Now, tidy the cabin, then go and find my uncle and inform him I am now ready to receive him.'

Consuelo stood for a moment, head tilted to one side, then she gave a birdlike nod, curtsyed and withdrew.

Maria sank down heavily into the tall-backed chair. Her limbs felt trembly still, as if she had been confined to her bed for some weeks. The whole encounter had left her thoroughly shaken. How foolish she had been to go near the slave deck. She knew well enough that Don Esteban had taken steps to ensure that no such unpleasant incident would occur. Yet she had deliberately chosen to go there. Why? These last few harrowing weeks had left her doubtful of her own heritage. Though her father had spoken often of her lovely mother, he had not, until that last revealing moment in the *estancia* garden, suggested that she would ever be considered anything but fully Spanish. But she was not. That hateful slave had immediately jumped to the assumption that she was part English and had dared to taunt her with the fact. Instinctively, she knew that her uncle would be furious, not only because she had not observed the due propriety he expected of the daughter of a Spanish *hidalgo*, but also because this shameful happening had

reminded him of her dubious ancestry, the ancestry which
had made his task of providing for her both difficult and
distasteful. The matter had not been openly referred to.
It had lain like a sword between them since he had arrived at the *estancia*. Now she considered the matter, it
would explain why Don Felipe had not before visited his
brother, and only rarely contacted him. She sat up in
the chair, spine rigid, fingers clutching convulsively at
the carved chair-arms, while she waited for the dreaded
interview with him.

Don Felipe paused in the cabin doorway. His dark
head brushed the hanging lantern suspended above it.
He stooped and stepped unhurriedly inside. Consuelo
hovered uneasily behind him in the corridor.

Without turning he said, coldly, 'Leave us.'

Consuelo looked unhappily from him to Maria and
her fingers caught distractedly at the chain which carried
the little hanging mirror she wore suspended from her
girdle.

Bravely she said, 'Don Felipe, I should be with Doña
Maria. She is distressed and——'

'I said leave us.'

Maria said quietly, 'Do as my uncle says, Consuelo.
You will be informed when to return.'

'But——'

'I am much recovered, truly.'

Consuelo was still undecided, but, catching the sudden
flash of fire in her mistress's blue eyes, she bobbed two
quick curtsys and withdrew, pulling the cabin door closed
behind her.

Maria did not rise; indeed, she felt unable to do so
though strict etiquette bade her show due respect to her
uncle and guardian.

'Forgive me if I do not stand up, Uncle. I am still
upset.'

He stood regarding her coldly, a big, burly figure,
floridly handsome, though he must now be nearing forty
years of age. Like Maria he was dressed in mourning-
black velvet, his doublet and hose slashed with white
satin, his velvet cap adorned with a black plume. There

was the sombre gleam of a ruby at his throat and the same gems studded his black leathern belt. Even the rosettes on his shoes gleamed with tiny ruby hearts. He waited like a true seaman, feet planted solidly apart, one hand resting on the pommel of his sword guard.

'You are excused.' His voice was throaty, a trifle harsh.

Fear tied a hard little knot in Maria's stomach. He was furious with her, indeed, only holding in that deadly anger with a studied show of politeness he would offer a stranger.

She inclined her head slightly, hiding from him the crimson flush of shame which suffused her cheeks.

'Niece, I must ask you to explain. Don Esteban informs me there has been some trouble on the slave deck.' He paused for a moment, then added, still without raising his voice in the slightest, 'Trouble which involved you.'

A pulse beat at her temple. She moistened dry lips, her knuckles strained so tightly on the chair arms the bones showed ivory-white beneath the skin.

'I regret, Uncle, that you should have been embarrassed by my—foolishness.'

'I am waiting for your explanation.'

'I was walking—on the poop deck——' She swallowed, avoiding his eye. 'Consuelo was sleeping.' Then with a rush, 'You cannot blame her. I was headstrong——'

'Certainly you made an error of judgement. Young girls are prone to such wilfulness. I cannot imagine how, from the poop deck, you could possibly have had an encounter with one of the galley slaves.'

'I was merely taking the air. It is so hot in here. Afterwards, as I turned to go below,' she hesitated, 'I thought I would like—I—I knew there were foreign slaves there——' Her throat was husky now with the threat of tears. 'I know it was madness—but I went down to see them. I wanted to know if they were being treated well. I do not like to think of men suffering—even if they deserve to do so.'

'The treatment of the crew and the galley slaves is a matter for Don Esteban.'

'I know,' she whispered miserably, 'it was foolish, I have confessed as much.'

'It was crass stupidity. Don Esteban has taken pains to see you should not be subjected to any contact which might distress you.'

'I know and am grateful.'

'Yet you deliberately sought such an experience. Explain, please, how it was possible for a man who was chained to the rowing-bench to actually be able to reach out and touch you.'

'They all seemed to be asleep, even the hortator, then I saw this man looking at me, so insolently. He challenged me, said something about my eyes, that—that I did not appear to be a true Spaniard. It rankled. I was so angry that I took the hortator's whip and went and lashed out at him.'

Don Felipe raised his shoulders in a meaningful shrug.

'Then, he suddenly pulled on the whip handle and—and dragged me towards him. I was startled. I kept hitting him but he held on. We struggled. It was all so undignified. My gown was torn——' She faltered to a stop, looking down, ashamed, at the polished boards of the cabin floor.

'The man must be punished.'

'Oh, no.' She gave a little shudder of alarm at the flash of anger which emanated from Don Felipe's dark eyes, so like her father's in colour, so unlike in expression. 'I mean—it was I who was at fault, and I lashed him. He was sorely hurt.'

'The dog will suffer further. There'll be scarce an inch of skin to his back when all is over.'

'He did me no harm, Uncle. If he must be beaten as an example to others, and I can see the necessity for that, I would have it remembered in his defence that my wilfulness contributed to his fault and should go some way to mitigate the severity of his punishment.'

'I think you will be reminded of your part in this when you accompany me amidships to see him duly punished.

It will not be pleasant, Maria. I wish you could be spared the sight. Unfortunately that would not be acceptable.'

'You ask me to be present—to witness his flogging?' She murmured the words in a horrified whisper.

'I trust you will not betray weakness. You are the daughter of Don Diego Santiago y Talavera, and my niece. A strong stomach is expected of those who share Talavera blood.'

'When—when is it to be?'

'The moment you feel strong enough to face it.'

'Now?' Her eyes widened incredulously.

'Certainly. Within an hour we shall anchor in Cadiz harbour.' He moved purposefully towards the door and she realised he was expecting her to rise at once and follow.

She swallowed hard and, with a determined pressure of her hands on the chair arms, pulled herself to her feet.

Before they left the cabin, Don Felipe turned, stroking his dark beard reflectively. 'The hortator said the man spoke in a foreign tongue to you. Did he address you in English?'

Her chin jerked in surprise. 'Yes.'

'Did you reply to him in the same tongue?'

'I cannot remember speaking back to him at all.'

'Good.' He gave a quick, satisfied nod. 'I would prefer you not to draw attention to your English blood neither now, before Don Esteban, nor in my home in Cadiz. Frankly, Niece, I suggest you forget your heritage. Your father would have been better to ensure that you spoke no tongue but Castilian. Forget the past. Life on your *estancia* is behind you. Do not refer to your mother. You are Don Diego's daughter—that is sufficient to afford you all the respect that is needed.'

Maria's dark lashes flickered as she veiled her eyes from him. It was almost as if he had struck her. The insult to the memory of her dead mother was so deliberate. Her father had never made a secret of his great love for her mother, yet, after his marriage, he had withdrawn from court circles. Had that action been because

his sympathies were then suspect? Since his death Maria
had been thrown back upon her own thoughts, her fears
of the future. Subtly she had recognised that she was to
be treated as no ordinary *hidalgo's* daughter. Strangely,
now, she began to realise the depth of her reaction to
the slave's challenge. It was as if she had needed to lash
out at him so savagely in order to convince herself of
her loyalty to her own race.

She moved proudly past her uncle into the dimness of
the corridor. Consuelo was waiting, huddled uncertainly
against the door-jamb.

'Go in and repack my valise,' Maria commanded.
There was no necessity for Consuelo to witness the brutal
retribution to be meted out to the slave—it was enough
that she must do so.

The crew was assembled amidships. Don Esteban came
to greet her, his usually kindly face shadowed by his
concern for her welfare. He made her a courtly bow.

'Doña Maria, I cannot express how deeply I am
angered by the affront to your dignity offered to you
aboard my ship. I have striven constantly to keep you
free from such encounters.'

She curtsyed in answer. 'Thank you, Don Esteban. I
am deeply grateful for your continual care of me.'

'This insolent dog must be flogged within an inch of
his life. Once we have anchored, I'll see him hanged.
Unfortunately there are certain formalities to be observed, or he'd be dangling from the yardarm by now.'

Maria said hastily, 'I am sure a whipping will suffice,
Don Esteban. No great harm has been done——'

He bowed again courteously, though firmly ignoring
her protest, and escorted her to a chair placed ready. She
seated herself gratefully as her knees felt decidedly weak.
Throughout the voyage she had proved an excellent
sailor, yet now the movement of the ship left her
strangely sick and dizzy. Don Esteban had ordered a
canvas awning erected to shield her from the afternoon
sun and Don Felipe took up a position immediately
behind her. Deliberately she clasped her hands lightly on

her lap to prevent them trembling and kept her gaze firmly upon the captain.

There was a noise of stumbling footsteps and clanking chain. Two pikemen in morions and breastplates hauled the English slave up from the rowing-deck. Maria turned her head in his direction. She had not meant to do so—an inner compulsion drove her. The nails of one hand dug sharply into the palm of the other, so that she felt the pain of it.

The Englishman stood upright, blinking in the sudden glare. He had been confined so long in the half-light of the slave deck that the sunlight half blinded him. She saw now how big a man he was, taller than her father and Don Felipe. His shoulders were massive and, as she'd noticed before, his physique was still very fine, despite his suffering and neglect. His ribcage arched tautly beneath the tawny gold of the curling hairs on his chest. Under full sunlight his matted hair now appeared fairer than she had first thought. She wondered how much longer it would take for that superb body to waste and fail in the primitive conditions aboard the galleass. He was still young, probably younger than he looked beneath that tangled mass of hair and beard. She drove her thoughts from regret that he must die so young and horribly, for she feared her pleas on his behalf would go unheard. She told herself that fate might prove more merciful than to allow him the slow, long drawn out torment of continued existence on the rowing-bench.

There was no hint of subservience in his mocking half-bow in her direction, then to the captain. She bit down savagely on her bottom lip as she encountered the cool amusement still mirrored in those slate-grey eyes.

Don Esteban made a brief movement of his hand and the Englishman was impelled towards the grating which had been strapped tight up against the mainmast. Maria lifted her pomander to her nostrils, hiding her face, as he was lashed to the frame by wrists and ankles. He made no sound, no plea for mercy nor any curse or snarl of fury.

The men assembled on deck were very silent. It seemed to Maria that each fixed a pair of accusing eyes upon her. In theirs she read no trace of pity for the prisoner, but each had known the bite of the lash or seen it administered. She was aware of their contempt, as if it struck her physically. She had brought this about by her foolish and wanton curiosity. She tilted her chin and outfaced them. They should not have the satisfaction of seeing her quail from the ugliness which was about to take place.

The boatswain stepped forward. He was a barrel of a man, so short as to be almost deformed, yet with muscles as taut and developed as those of the slaves below. He uncurled a long bull-hide whip, its tip sheathed in iron.

Maria caught back a little hiss of despair. As the prisoner had passed her she'd noted the lash wounds she'd already dealt him besides the scars of others habitually dealt by the guards. Dried blood stood out starkly on that weathered skin. Those marks and those he would now receive would remain with him forever. She pursed her lips at the disturbing thought that that might not be for long. Those already half-healed scars on his tanned back told her his insolence had not been directed at her alone, for she could not imagine his tremendous strength failing him and needing the encouragement of the overseer. No, he was not yet subdued nor resigned to his lot. But after this further savage punishment, what then? Could he endure it? What if he died under the lash? Overwhelming pity surged through her and caused sudden bile to rise in her throat. Yet she was powerless to prevent this.

The whip sang through the air and reached its target with deadly accuracy. The blow seemed to thud on Maria's own body and she flinched visibly, despite her effort to remain motionless. The Englishman made no sound but his body arched in agony. Again the whip curled and fell. This time there came a sharp exclamation, as of an indrawn breath. Maria was conscious of no one else but herself and the slave. Even the whip appeared to her bemused senses to be wielded by some totally mechanical hand. She felt deadly sick, her whole being tense and strained to feel the reverberation of every succeeding blow.

Why didn't he cry out? Scream? The effort to hold in such pain was superhuman, yet she knew he would strain every nerve to remain silent in her presence.

Despite his resolve, there came a thin, high-pitched cry.

Maria's determination to stay calm in her seat, outwardly unmoved by the dreadful thing which was taking place before her eyes, faltered. She turned beseeching eyes to Don Felipe but his attention was fixed impassively on the slave. There was to be no help from him. She switched her gaze to the captain, Don Esteban, and found his dark eyes watching her intently. The whip flew again through the air and the slave gasped once more in pure agony.

Maria forced her knees to obey her as she stood up from her chair. 'Don Esteban, please,' she whispered hoarsely, 'the man has suffered enough.'

Her tone was imperious, and the captain bowed and snapped out an order to his boatswain. 'Wait.'

The man drew in the now bloodstained whip, gave a grunt of compliance and stepped back from the prisoner.

'Maria,' her uncle's voice grated unpleasantly, close to her ear. 'Don Esteban knows what he is about. The slave is being punished for his gross insult to you. Without such a show of severity how could the captain keep discipline on board? It is not for you to interfere.'

She ignored him, deliberately did not look at him, though she was trembling again, violently, and afraid her voice would fail her. 'Don Esteban, I—I—I know the man is aware of his fault and—regrets it.'

She was sure this was untrue. Though the slave's features were turned from her she was convinced his lips were twisted in a contemptuous rebuttal of her defence of him, yet she pressed on determinedly. 'I beg that—he be spared further punishment.'

Her eyes pleaded with those of the captain that he would understand, recognise that she could bear to watch no more.

Her uncle's hiss of fury was not lost on her. Not only had she embarrassed him by flouting convention and venturing on to the slave deck as no well-bred girl would do, but now she was exhibiting weakness in her inability to watch the slave's punishment without showing distress. This was not the behaviour he expected of his niece.

The captain bowed again and snapped out a further command. The two pikemen moved to the grating and released the prisoner, who slumped to the deck. Only now could Maria allow herself to withdraw her gaze from the torn, mangled body and the ominous stains upon the deck.

Don Esteban was bowing. His words came to her as if from a great distance and she was incapable of comprehending their meaning. Her uncle took her arm and steered her towards the companionstair. The grip of his fingers was steely. There would be bruises later. Clearly he feared she might faint or further disgrace him by yet more unwary expressions of sympathy for the graceless slave who had dared to lay hands on his niece.

Her thoughts raced chaotically as she walked, head high, oblivious of the staring crewmen.

She prayed the slave remained unconscious for a while at least. No one, not even a heretical Englishman, deserved such inhuman punishment. But steps would be taken to revive him. He would recover his senses quickly because he was a strong man, and he would suffer accordingly.

Hot tears pricked at her lashes. She, and she alone, was responsible for this.

Don Felipe bowed to her stiffly at the door of her cabin. He did not speak, but she could feel the cold ferocity of his disapproval. She curtsyed dutifully and, as he released her and turned his back on her in the dimness of the corridor, she caught fiercely at the cabin door for support.

Once inside, she stood with her back to the closed door. Tears rained down her cheeks, then her stomach heaved and she gagged. Consuelo cast her one startled glance, then drew her hurriedly to the basin, holding her head and stroking her hair while she was horribly sick. The duenna made no complaint, not even when she was once more forced to unpack the valise for yet another gown.

Maria lay on the bed sobbing uncontrollably. Consuelo crept quietly about the cabin completing her final tasks before disembarkation.

'There, *querida*,' she said gently. 'It is over now. You must not think about it any more.'

'It was terrible, Consuelo. The flesh was torn from his back and he was so brave. He made no sound at first until——'

'Whatever he suffered, he deserved it,' Consuelo said stoutly. She had heard of the encounter on the slave deck from Don Esteban's page and burned with indignation for the slave's temerity.

But Maria could not be comforted. She was hardly aware of the noise of the galleass docking, the patter of crewmen's feet above her, the drawing in of sail, the clank of hawsers, or even the merciful cessation of the hortator's beat and the resting of oars on the slave benches. The galleass was at anchor. Maria could give no thought to the new life which faced her. She prayed only that the Englishman she had all unwittingly brought to such dire straits would be spared the chokes of a hempen collar about his neck in the morning.

CHAPTER TWO

MARIA could remember little of her arrival in Cadiz. Crewmen efficiently handled their baggage and a ship's officer helped her down the ladder into the waiting boat. She spoke no word to her uncle as they were rowed ashore.

The harbour was crowded with vessels. She saw the glint of the now westering sun on white-painted buildings, a riot of tall masts, hawsers and capstans, bales and packages littering the waterfront. The noise of rattling chains, raucous voices uplifted in sea songs from the harbour taverns, curses, wheels rattling on cobbles, failed to bring her fully from her self-induced stupor.

The Talavera carriage was waiting on the quay, a splendid equipage, the paintwork on doors and wheels picked out in gilt. Maria was glad to take her seat on the fine leather cushions and pull the scarlet leather curtains across the windows. Even here, among men and women who did not know her, she felt an embarrassed flush dye her cheeks.

Soon the carriage was turning from the crowded narrow streets into pleasanter thoroughfares. High walls protected the houses of the *hidalgos* from the curious gaze of the common people. The vehicle swept along a shaded drive and came to a halt before a massive, studded door. Talavera grooms rushed to hold the horses' heads. The carriage steps were let down and Don Felipe descended, then helped Maria down and escorted her into his home.

The scent of waxed wood and jasmine teased her nostrils. The hall was high and cool, the floor elegantly tiled. Serving wenches and henchmen curtsyed and bowed, then hastened outside to deal with the baggage. Maria was led into the rear parlour. A woman rose from a high-

29

backed chair near the window where she'd been busied with her embroidery and came towards them, her hand outstretched in greeting.

'Maria, *querida*, how good it is to have you here with us at last.'

She brushed Maria's cheek lightly with her lips and stood back to survey her niece.

Maria returned the scrutiny. Her aunt was still a handsome woman. Her modish gown of black silk was worn over a wide satin underskirt which was heavily embroidered in silver. Her padded sleeves were slashed in white and silver brocade and her undersleeves and partlet embroidered in the same colours. Her silver lace cap and wristbands were embellished with seed pearls. Her figure was Junoesque, the facial features good, though too heavy for true beauty. Her eyebrows were thickly marked and raised now in interrogation. Maria mistrusted the thin line of her rouged lips.

'You must be weary and sickened by these long hot days on the ship. You will find it restful here out of the bustle of the town; I imagine you will prefer to remain secluded for a time while your grief is still raw.'

Maria curtsyed dutifully. 'It is kind of you to make me welcome. I do not know what I should have done without my uncle to help me when——' She broke off, a catch to her voice.

Doña Beatriz gave a little trill of laughter. '*Querida*, we are both glad to be of service.'

She cast Don Felipe an inquisitive glance and he shook his head very slightly. Maria felt a stab of misgiving. Doña Beatriz was enquiring if she had already been informed of the plans made for her.

Her uncle said, a trifle curtly, 'Maria should go immediately to her chamber. She is feeling unwell.'

Doña Beatriz shuddered slightly. 'I am not surprised. The stench from those galleys must be nigh unbearable——'

Don Felipe cut across her diatribe. 'We could not bring a maid. There was no room on the galleass. Send one of the maids to help Señora Henriques, Maria's duenna, unpack.'

Doña Beatriz herself escorted Maria up the white-painted stairs. The chamber assigned to her was at the rear of the house. Two very young maids rose from their curtsys and withdrew under the steely gaze of their mistress.

'I hope you will be comfortable. Now the sun is down the air from the garden will refresh you. You have only to ring for whatever you want.'

Maria thanked her. Again she lightly brushed Maria's cheeks with her lips and was gone in a rustle of silken skirts, leaving behind her the cloying, heavy scent of musk.

Consuelo arrived from another door as Maria thankfully flung back the wooden slatted shutters, drawing in the sharp fragrance of citrus fruit and more elusive scent of jasmine.

'Consuelo, keep the servants away for the present. My head is splitting.'

'Most likely from the sickness. Lie down and I'll bathe your temples with rose-water and order a soothing tisane.'

Consuelo drew off Maria's gown and she lay down in her shift, staring up at the bed's brocaded tester. Her uncle lived in some style. The hangings and carpets were over-bright for her taste, but the house was luxurious compared to the simplicity of furnishings at her *estancia*.

She began to feel better after Consuelo's ministrations. The duenna pressed her to eat.

'It would choke me.'

'You must not distress yourself over the fate of that heretical Englishman.'

'Who told you the slave was English?' Maria sat up sharply.

Consuelo shrugged. 'What does it matter? I know you are blaming yourself for his punishment.'

Maria balled tight fists. 'Naturally I am sorry he suffered so, but why should I be blamed because the insolent oaf took it upon himself to insult me?'

Consuelo's eyes narrowed shrewdly. 'Then you should be sufficiently recovered to eat supper with your aunt and uncle.'

Maria nodded, frowning. She had intended to excuse herself from table tonight but Consuelo was right. Don Felipe must, even now, be relating to Doña Beatriz the tale of her shameful conduct, and she would not skulk away in her chamber as if she were admitting her fault. Her uncle must be made to understand that she was not to be cowed into subservient obedience.

She lay, eyes half closed, while Consuelo went off to order a tub of heated water to be brought to the chamber. Consuelo's assertion that she was unduly upset by the slave's flogging rankled. He had deserved it, though the memory of the savagery of it made her shudder again. She had no cause to pity any Englishman. They were piratical dogs who preyed upon Spanish shipping and the settlements of the New World.

Yet the whole incident had left her thoroughly shaken, the first thing to touch her since the death of her father. The very contact with the man's unwashed body had so affronted her that she had needed to scrub away at her own flesh until she was sore. Even now, as she thought of it, her skin tingled and crawled. It was the man's assumption that she was a countrywoman of his which had infuriated her—'Such fire is only bred in England.' Did he believe all Spanish noblewomen were tame cats to be pampered and stroked into compliance? Worse, he had implied she should feel some responsibility for the plight of her own people, or so it had seemed to her.

They were not her people, she told herself fiercely, only her mother's people. Loyalty to the English crown had ceased for Mary Gascoine when she had given her heart and her hand to Don Diego Santiago y Talavera.

Her scented bath seemed to finally dispel all lingering thoughts of the Englishman's touch. She donned clean shift and kirtle and waited while Consuelo tied in place the whalebone farthingale and corset over which the silken petticoats were fitted. She had already ruined one of her mourning gowns and her wardrobe was not extensive. Only one was left, a simply cut black satin gown, low at the corselet, its sleeves tight-fitting, relieved by a white gauze partlet and high starched ruff. She would appear dowdy by her aunt's standards, but that could not be helped.

Consuelo was searching frantically through Maria's jewel chest.

'The silver brooch you wore this morning, I can't find it.'

'Oh?' Maria's eyes widened. 'That is strange. It must have been on the torn overgown. Do you remember putting it away after I changed? It would set off this ruff opening well, particularly as it is silver with just one single pearl.'

Consuelo shook her head. 'We were so confused. I wrapped the overgown up quickly and stuffed it into one of the still opened chests—I can't remember which. I could see at once that you will never be able to wear that gown again until it's expertly repaired.'

'The brooch is perhaps still attached. Don't fuss, Consuelo. The little pendant cross with the pearls will do just as well.'

Fleetingly she wondered if the silver pin had fallen to the deck in her struggle with the slave. If it were found, doubtless Don Esteban would have it returned to her.

Doña Beatriz greeted her with a kiss, though Maria had suspected she would have preferred for her niece to sup tonight in her own room. There was an air of restraint in her uncle's dealings with her, and she was now sure she had been the subject of their talk before she'd entered. She ate sparingly. Her head still ached but pride kept her seated at her uncle's side, her head high.

No mention was made of Maria's recent bereavement. She half listened to her aunt's gossip until one phrase brought her sharply to attention.

'We have so little time before you sail that I shall be hard put to it to adequately oversee the furnishing of your dower chests. There must be gowns for later, when your mourning is over——'

'Before I sail?' Maria's fingers fumbled her wine goblet and she righted it hastily.

Doña Beatriz looked anxiously at her husband and gave a little hiss of concern. Don Felipe sighed heavily. 'I had hoped for a more propitious time to inform you of the plans I've made for you.'

'Marriage plans?'

He inclined his head. 'Plans, I hasten to add, which your father fully approved.'

'Felipe, this talk of marriage settlements must be very disturbing. Maria is over-weary——'

Maria interrupted her curtly. 'I am anxious to hear who my future husband is to be.' Her challenging eyes met her uncle's dark ones.

He cleared his throat. 'It is natural you should want to know the details now the matter is settled.'

'He is here in Cadiz?'

'Alas, no. Don Luis Ortego y Castuero is the only son of a very good friend of mine. His father, Don Alonso, is high in favour at court. Luis is almost twenty. I think you will find no fault in his appearance. I have a miniature which I will show you after supper. At present Luis is in the household of the governor of Cartagena. For reasons which I will not dwell on now, it was your father's wish that you do not, at present, live in Madrid and become involved in court affairs.'

'You mean there would be hostility towards me because of my English blood?'

He nodded. 'Affairs between the two countries are now critical. In a year or so difficulties will be resolved, your future assured. As the wife of Don Luis you could assume your place at court when he is recalled to Madrid.'

She thought for a moment. 'I take it Don Alonso's financial affairs are not in the settled state he could wish. My dower will serve to put the matter right.'

Don Felipe's cheeks crimsoned and his dark eyes sparked with anger. 'I have done the best possible for you, in view of the circumstances. Your father was determined that you should not be sacrificed to some elderly lecher, not even to ensure your acceptance at the Escorial.'

Maria's lips trembled at mention of her father's love and concern, and she took a sip of wine to hearten her.

Her uncle continued. 'I have not been in Don Luis's company for some time but I have heard no ill reports of him. It is true that Don Alonso has had some ill luck recently. His estates have become impoverished due to some mismanagement. Don Luis's grandfather was profligate and the family fortunes became considerably diminished before his death. Don Alonso is, however, a more careful man, but much at court. I have every expectation that Don Luis will inherit a much greater inheritance than his father did.'

'But he needs my dowry urgently.'

Don Felipe hesitated. 'The King holds Don Alonso in great regard but is in no position to grant financial favours at present. Don Luis has been placed in a position where he can further his own and his father's interests. There are gold and emerald mines in New Spain and expedient native labour. Don Alonso needs only the money to invest and to furnish ships and crew to transport the wealth of the colonies home to Spain. I have taken all possible precautions for you. The marriage settlement allows for the customary dower rights, one third of your husband's total property to enjoy throughout your lifetime in the event of your husband's death before your own. The settlement also, naturally, safeguards your rights should the marriage be declared null and void for any reason whatever. You would retain your own *estancia* and some proportion of your husband's wealth, though the initial dowry would, of course, become Don Luis's the moment the marriage is solemnised.'

'Uncle, my father and I were used to straight talking. We never fenced with words. I understand the bargain; my dower for Don Luis's name and protection. I'm sure we shall make an agreeable couple. So I am to join him very soon?'

'Within the week. The *Santa Isabella* sails for Cartagena in convoy on Wednesday. It would be fully six months before another suitable passage could be arranged. I would have preferred to keep you with us during the next months, but it has not proved possible.'

'I understand.'

'Don Alonso is in Madrid, so——'

'I shall not be received by my future father-in-law either, before I sail. I see.'

The coolness of her tone was not lost on him.

'I wish I could escort you to Cartagena personally, but I have urgent duties with the fleet and in Madrid. Don Carlos de la Cosa, the Visita, is sailing on the *Isabella* on a tour of inspection of His Majesty's colonies and he has agreed to escort you. He was a close friend of your grandfather and of myself and your father also. Though you will not remember him he saw you often when a child, and was present at your christening. He has great affection for the family and will see to it that you have every comfort and protection throughout the journey. His presence in the colony when you are married to Don Luis eases my mind of any concern regarding your welfare. I am sure you will prove obedient and show him the respect his office merits.'

Don Felipe fixed her with a stern gaze and Maria swallowed uncomfortably. He was reminding her that there must be no repetition of the wilfully unconventional behaviour on board the galleass. He need not have worried. Even now her body trembled at thought of the punishment she had brought upon the English slave. The sight would remain with her throughout her life.

Looking up, she encountered her uncle's hard eyes and resisted the impulse to beg him to send to Don Esteban aboard the galleass and request him to pardon the man and return him to the rowing-bench. Not now, in her aunt's presence. She must find a chance to speak with her uncle privately. She must do her best for the slave, though it would not be easy—her uncle's attitude was most uncompromising. There was so little time for the Englishman——

She lowered her gaze again, her fingers clutching the slender neck of her wine goblet. 'Consuelo goes with me, of course?'

'Naturally, and if you also need the services of a maid——'

'I think it better if we manage alone. Some untried girl could prove an encumbrance. I will speak to Consuelo, but I am used to making shift for myself. We did not live in grand style on the *estancia*.' She dabbed at her lips with her napkin. 'If you will now excuse me, I would like to retire.'

Don Felipe rose courteously and escorted her to the door. 'If you would wait in the parlour for a moment, I will bring you Don Luis's miniature.'

When he returned and handed her the small, ivory-backed portrait on its heavy gold chain, she fumbled it awkwardly, unwilling to look on the painted face of the man who would soon order her life.

Don Luis was remarkably personable. His hair was dark and curling, his beard trimmed to an elegant point. The features were gentle, the nose well shaped, the eyes half hooded. Maria wondered if the chin beneath that curled beard was weak, for there was little sign of strength in that handsome face. Momentarily she contrasted it with the weathered features of the English slave, that contemptuously smiling mouth, the grey eyes which had mocked at her in the face of impending suffering.

'He is a—handsome young man.'

'Then you are satisfied?'

She made a little murmur of acquiescence, shrugging slightly. 'You appear satisfied by his credentials, as, apparently, my father was. I must be guided by your judgement.'

'Good. Keep the miniature. I had it painted for you.'

As he escorted her to her chamber door, she made her plea for the slave. 'Uncle, I must again express my regrets for what happened on the galleass.'

'We'll say no more on the matter.' His tone was brusque, not a promising sign.

'I brought the house of Talavera into some disrepute and, worse, I brought disaster to that unfortunate slave.'

'I would hardly deem the piratical dog "unfortunate", since his flogging was curtailed at your request.'

'Don Esteban has threatened to hang him.'

'Indeed. The sight of his body dangling from the yardarm should prove a deterrent for others who might so far forget themselves as to dare to lay hands on a Spanish noblewoman.'

Maria moistened dry lips. 'Yet it was my fault. Uncle, I beg of you to send to Don Esteban and ask for mercy for the slave.'

'Maria, such a course would be unthinkable.'

'For my sake, Uncle. I shall be gone soon from your house and will never ask other favours of you.' Her blue eyes swam with tears as she put her hand pleadingly on his arm.

'I understand your womanly compassion but I cannot order Don Esteban to pardon the fellow, and I doubt if any intervention on my part could make any difference to his decision, but I will send a message informing him of your concern and distress for the man's fate. Now try to rest. You must be exhausted. Your aunt will be anxious to plan your wedding garments with you in the morning.'

Consuelo had not sat at Don Felipe's table. Maria knew that she must feel somewhat resentful. On the *estancia* Consuelo had always been treated as an equal, eating with the family and present when guests were invited. Now, as she helped undress her mistress, Maria informed her of the marriage plans and showed her Don Luis's miniature. Consuelo examined the likeness thoughtfully.

'He is certainly an attractive young man, *querida*. Your uncle has chosen well.'

'If the young man's disposition matches his appearance and if the painter has not too greatly flattered the sitter,' Maria commented drily.

'Are you concerned at being packed off to the Indies so quickly?'

'Since I have no say in the matter, I must be content. Apparently it was my father's wish that I should live away from court.' Consuelo glanced at her sharply and Maria shrugged. 'I doubt if we can be ready on time. Doña Beatriz says we shall be busy buying silks and gowns over the next few days.'

'The whole plan seems over-hasty,' Consuelo grumbled, but she did agree that it would be better for them not to be accompanied by some green girl who would possibly prove more trouble than she was worth.

Despite her utter weariness it was a long time before Maria slept. She could hear the shrill sound of cicadas and the faint rustle of leaves in the garden. Deliberately she held her mind from speculating too long on what life would be like in Cartagena. There would probably be as much jockeying for power in the governor's household as at the King's court in the Escorial.

What of Don Luis? Maria had had no sisters or companions with whom she could have discussed the doubts and fears which beset all on the brink of womanhood. Consuelo had been married young and widowed within the year. Her husband had taken a summer fever and died of it. Her baby son had died soon after and she had been free to wet-nurse Don Diego's daughter and had given her all the love and care she would have lavished on her own child. Maria knew she would prepare her for marriage when the time came but, instinctively, she shied from pressing her duenna to discuss such delicate matters.

Her lips curved into a little derisory smile. She had caught snippets of talk from the serving girls. They had hushed, blushing poppy-scarlet, when she had come on them unexpectedly. Though she had not been allowed to be present when her father's hound bitch was mated nor when she littered, she could not be ignorant of what took place. The thought of surrendering her body to this unknown young *hidalgo* was both distasteful and alarming.

CHAPTER THREE

GILES NORWOOD caught back a gasp of pure agony as he forced himself to a sitting position, his back against the dank wooden wall of the ship's brig. His throat ached as if someone had poured a firkin of salt-water down it and his back was a fiery torment. God's wounds, how could he manage to stand unaided, let alone move about? Yet walk he must, aye, and swim too, if his neck was to remain free from the choke of a hempen collar.

He allowed himself a moment to rest, stretching his arms and legs experimentally, wriggling his shoulders, despite the spasms of pain which shot through him at the slightest movement of his neck and back muscles.

It was almost pitch-black in the brig, apart from a sliver of light coming through the gap of the ill-fitting door. He sniffed curiously, then leaned back, breathing steadily, evenly. They were at anchor. He was sure of it, for he could smell the harbour stinks, carried offshore by the breeze, and hear the slap and slither of water rats on the anchor chain. How long he'd been unconscious he couldn't tell. When he'd come to himself, he'd been face-down in bilge-water. It was a mercy he hadn't drowned. He reasoned that most of the crew had gone ashore apart from the guard watch. Before long someone would take it upon himself to see if the prisoner still breathed, and decide, if he did, whether it was worth the trouble of feeding him before he was hanged in the morning.

Norwood swore beneath his breath as he swallowed again, painfully. At this moment he would give a week of his life for a tankard of good English ale to assuage this tantalising thirst.

Doggedly he fought the overwhelming longing to slip into a pain-fogged stupor. He heaved against the slippery wall with his arms till he was standing upright, but the effort had cost him dear, for he was deadly sick and faint.

Fiercely he told himself he had no time for such weakness and fished carefully within the folds of his filthy loincloth, allowing himself a faint hiss of triumph as he found what he sought. Surely Dame Fortune was with him, for such a small implement could so easily have fallen and been lost to him during the agonising business of his flogging or afterwards, when he'd been dragged below and thrown into this dark hole below the water-line.

The silver brooch pin gleamed in the faint light from the door-jamb and Norwood gave a quiet chuckle. The pin was solidly made and strong and would serve his purpose if he was granted the time. He prayed he would be, for he'd suffered dearly to get it.

Movement still made him catch his breath with pain but he turned towards the door and felt for the lock. Thank God it had a lock, and wasn't simply barred from the outside. Possibly one of the galleass's captains had kept valuables inside which would not have remained safe from a thieving crew by such a clumsy device as a bar. He listened carefully.

Someone moved on deck above, gave a shout to a shipmate, then settled again.

Skilfully Norwood worked at the lock. A less experienced man would have damaged the pin within the first sweating moments of haste, but Norwood did not allow himself to lose patience or panic. He had been trained in a hard school. Walsingham had neglected no aspect of his education in skills which would enable his chosen agent to perfect his art. He gave a grunt of satisfaction as he felt the lock give beneath his careful manipulation. His palms were sweating now, his heart beating uncomfortably fast. Now was the moment of testing. The cautious Don Esteban might well have ordered a bar thrust across the outside of the door as an extra precaution.

He waited and summoned his strength, then, leaning one sturdy shoulder against the jamb, he pushed steadily.

The door gave outwards but he was ready for it and let the weight rest on the balls of his feet, his body crouched. There was no one on guard in the dim passageway. The only light came from the iron grating situated above the companionway. The lantern swinging on its hook above his prison door had not been kindled. He had no idea of the time. It was too dark below to judge the hour, but he must have lain unconscious for some time, since the ship had anchored and he presumed most of the crew and the passengers had disembarked.

His lips curved into a wry smile as he thought of the passengers. Don Felipe Santiago y Talavera was one of His Majesty's most trusted captains, serving under Admiral Santa Cruz himself. So why had he absented himself from his duties with the fleet at so critical a time? Obviously the girl was a close kinswoman, not a daughter. There had been a restraint between them which suggested their acquaintanceship had not been long; a niece, perhaps, or cousin. Both had worn mourning. So Don Felipe had travelled to Malaga to escort the bereaved lady to his home in Cadiz. What a beauty she was, with the aristocratic features of the finest blood in Spain and those eyes as blue as a June sky in England. Of course he had seen blue-eyed women in Spain, known some of them intimately, though the colouring was more rare than the brown or black-eyed *señoritas*. Her grandmother or grandfather might have been fair, like the King himself, yet he had thought she had understood what he had said to her in English. She had been incensed by his challenge. He chuckled softly. What fire she had, what passion. There had been an inner strength too, a determination he had not met in other Spanish ladies, who were always so closely guarded by their parents and duennas that not one of them would have so much as thought of venturing to the rowing-deck, let alone dared to do so unescorted.

It had been long since he'd felt the soft, yielding flesh of a woman against his body. For moments, as he'd held her close, his senses had been stirred, despite the urgency of his need to secure that tantalising pin he had glimpsed on her gown.

He wondered what she had felt when she'd witnessed his chastisement. There had been no flicker of regret in those blue eyes as he'd been dragged by her towards the grating. She'd stared directly at him, her lips tightly compressed, her chin tilted arrogantly. Reading in her gaze contempt and disgust for his impudence, he'd determined she should not have the satisfaction of hearing him scream. He knew he had not been able to keep that resolve.

It seemed an age while he crouched near the grating, listening intently for the least betraying movement above, then, hearing nothing but the usual sounds of a ship at anchor, he advanced to the stair. Once braced for action, he managed to put aside bodily weakness and pain and moved easily and silently. Stiffness would set in later, when he allowed himself the benison of rest.

As he'd surmised, there was only one guard on watch. Norwood lingered just below deck at the head of the companionway, his eyes narrowed against the suddenly blinding crimson glow of sunset. At last he became sufficiently accustomed to the light to be able to pick out the dark form of the crewman who guarded the ship's boarding ladder. The slightest movement amidships would alert the man to his presence. He might simply call a greeting, thinking Norwood a comrade, but it was more than likely he would turn to acknowledge him.

Norwood could not afford to wait until the man was joined by a companion. He moved silently to the stairhead across the deck and had broken the fellow's neck before he could so much as grunt. Gently Norwood lowered the body to the deck and armed himself with cutlass and dagger. It was the work of moments to slip quietly into the water with scarcely a ripple of sound.

Before him the prow lantern gleamed, casting golden, fish-like scales across the water. A man was singing somewhere in the stern and, since the song continued, Norwood judged his comrade's death had still not been discovered.

The salt-water stung his raw wounds, but he swam strongly towards the bobbing lights of the harbour. Already the red orb of the sun was sinking below the horizon; it would be full dark by the time he reached land. He allowed himself to drift with the current, which carried him north of the town.

Finally he made for a fishing vessel lying close in-shore. The ship's hull would afford him shelter and he clung to a projecting bulkhead, giving himself respite while he considered his next move.

How was he to swim ashore without arousing undue notice? The harbour would soon be swarming with humanity, those denizens of the brothels and taverns whose business was best concluded at night. In his present state and sorry garb he would be taken within the hour and returned to the galleass. He needed food and clothing urgently before risking himself in open country.

He knew Cadiz well enough, both from personal experience before he was arrested and from the perusal of Walsingham's charts of the town. He would wait his opportunity, scramble from the beach north of the harbour and make for the more secluded part of the town where there were the walled villas of the wealthy *hidalgos*. Among them was the house of Don Felipe Santiago y Talavera. It seemed fitting that he should choose the lady's house to supply him with what was needed for his escape. She owed him that. Some groom or stableboy venturing to the outbuildings could be made to part with shirt and breeches, and, if necessary, silenced as simply as the guard on the galleass. He would climb the wall and wait. If Dame Fortune was with him still, he might even be able to catch a glimpse of the lady who had cost him so much, yet, without knowing it, provided him with the means of his salvation.

Maria woke suddenly and completely. It was still dark and she could hear Consuelo's even breathing across the room, so it was no movement of hers which had woken her. She sat up and listened intently. There was no other sound but the monotonous chirp of the cicadas, not even the hoot of a hunting owl. Maria sighed. She missed the country sounds. The very quiet seemed oppressive. She lay down again, pounding the pillow in an attempt to force sleep, but it was useless. Something had disturbed her, but, try as she might, she could not sleep again.

The same restless urge which had led her to the deck of the galleass was upon her now. Visions of the English slave imposed themselves starkly upon her wakeful mind. She shuddered as she saw again, more vividly, the bright drops of scarlet falling from the whip's lash, and she covered her ears as if, even in imagination, she would hear again that final, single scream of pure agony.

What was he feeling now? Had they shackled him to the rowing-bench again, or did he lie in some foul prison in the ship's hold? Was he, too, wakeful, counting the hours till sunrise, knowing this would be his last night on earth?

This was ridiculous. She sat up in the bed angrily. Why should she agonise over the man's fate? He had deserved it. What right had he to draw her close to his stinking flesh? She must forget him, put the incident firmly behind her.

Her eyes were becoming more used to the darkness and she could see the faint bars of moonlight across the wooden floor, made by the open slats of the shutters. She climbed from the bed and moved to the window. Far off she could hear the murmur of the sea, and her teeth bit down savagely upon her nether lip as the disturbing thought of the coming voyage was borne in on her. Sudden tears welled in her eyes. She needed time to mourn. Too soon she was being thrust into the strong tides of life. Perhaps, after all, her uncle did know best. The strangeness of her life in New Spain would overwhelm her, prevent her thoughts turning sadly back time and time again to her loss.

She would have liked to walk alone in the garden as she often had done at home, on the *estancia*. There she would have received only a mild scolding from Consuelo or from her father. Doña Beatriz, she was sure, would be scandalised by such wayward behaviour. She could not bring further disgrace on the hapless Consuelo by her unconventional wish to wander about in her night attire. Sighing, she turned back into the room and prepared to face the long, sleepless hours until the household roused.

Her ears caught again the rustle of movement behind her, which could not be accredited to the normal sway of foliage and branches in the breeze. A marauding cat? Possibly.

She stiffened, unwilling to turn, the hairs on the nape of her neck lifting slightly.

The attack, when it came, happened with such speed she had no means of countering it. A hand clamped above her mouth from behind, a muscular arm held her tight against a hard, bare body. Horrified, she felt the cold kiss of a dagger blade against her throat. She could not have screamed, even if that nauseating hand had not stifled all sound; her vocal cords were paralysed by sheer terror.

A voice spoke very softly, close to her ear—in English.

'Make no sound. Don't try to free yourself. I shall not hesitate to use this. Do you understand?' The dagger blade was drawn caressingly against the flesh of her throat so that she felt the pressure of it nicking the skin. Surely there was a thin line of blood seeping, or was that the agony of fear which constricted her breathing?

Frozen with shock as she was, she managed a faint nod of her head.

'Walk with me, then, back towards your bed. I shall withdraw my hand from your mouth, yet you will not cry out?'

She shook her head again and allowed herself to be pulled further from the window.

Her captor halted for a moment in the middle of the room and listened. Held tight against him, Maria was conscious of the quickened beat of his heart.

'Your attendant sleeps with you?' The whisper was urgent, as the dagger pressure was again increased.

'Yes.' She answered him in English.

Even in her stark panic and bemused by the speed of events, she knew to whom she spoke. Yet how could he

possibly be here, within her own chamber? Had he
sought her out to revenge himself? Escape from the galleass was surely impossible. Conflicting doubts and fears
jostled together in her shocked brain.

'Wake her.' His tone was as grim as it was peremptory. 'But—quietly. Remember, it would take but a
moment to kill you both.'

He hustled her in front of him to Consuelo's truckle-
bed. Trembling, Maria bent over her duenna's sleeping
form. How could it be done without frightening
Consuelo so that she did not wake too suddenly and
scream in panic?

'I must kneel down, touch her, warn her.' She wasn't
sure if her words were couched as an entreaty. They
sounded husky in her own ears.

He released her, yet stood so close in the darkness she
was aware of the rank stink of those galley rags and the
odour of human sweat made sharper by tension.

She knelt down, one hand gently reaching out to
Consuelo's hunched shoulder. She shook her duenna
gently but urgently.

Consuelo came awake with a sudden snort, as she often
did. 'What is it?'

Maria's arms held her firmly down in the bed. 'Listen,
Consuelo,' she implored in a whisper. She had reverted
to Spanish, but was sure that the Englishman understood every word. 'Lie very still and silent.'

Consuelo tried ineffectually to struggle up. Fearfully
her eyes encountered the huge bulk of the galley slave
looming out of the shadows, and Maria hurriedly placed
trembling fingers across her duenna's lips before she
could so much as gasp out her shock and horror.

'He has a dagger. He'll kill without pity. We must do
as he says.'

Consuelo's struggles subsided and she gently pushed
aside Maria's restraining hands and sat up. 'Give him
your jewel chest and let him go.' She reached for Maria's
hand, squeezing it hard in a comforting grip.

'It's not such a simple business, *señora*,' he retorted
grimly in Spanish. 'My needs are more specialised. You

will find me food, clothing, and,' he grimaced, 'a razor. You'll do it quickly and without rousing a soul in this house, for I'm sure you're aware what will happen to your mistress if you disobey me. Be assured I'll use the dagger on her without a qualm if my freedom is threatened. They can but hang me once.'

'This house is strange to me, *señor*. I cannot——'

'I had a wet-nurse who used to remind me constantly that such words as "cannot" and "won't" do not exist, or, at least, have no significance to a determined person.'

'It will take time, *señor*.'

'Not too much time. You'll appreciate your charge is at my mercy and hurry back to her, I'm sure.'

Consuelo shuddered and he laughed quietly, the laugh of a man without a trace of real humour or vestige of compassion.

Consuelo turned appealingly to Maria. 'I won't leave you alone with——'

'You must. Do what he says.'

'But——'

'Please, Consuelo. Despite his threats, he'll not dare harm me. I am too useful as a hostage and he desperately needs what you will bring back for him.' She flashed a scornful glance at their captor. 'In his present guise he would not last an hour on the streets of Cadiz once the sun is up.'

He jerked her closer to him so that, again, she felt the sting of the dagger blade on the side of her neck.

Consuelo gave a strangled gasp, then, as he made a menacing movement of his dagger hand, she caught up the hem of her night-rail and ran to the door.

Maria's heart beat more painfully fast as she knew herself alone with the man, and in spite of her brave words to Consuelo she was deadly afraid.

He turned and smiled at her, but there was no warmth in the parting of the lips and flash of white teeth in the bearded face. It was the grimace of a badly used animal, snarling at bay.

'Now, you, go and sit on the bed.'

The dagger was removed from her throat and she half stumbled, then, as he brutally impelled her towards her own bed, she recovered herself and obeyed him, shrinking back as he came close.

'Don't be afraid, *señorita*,' he sneered. 'I've no time for the kind of dalliance you have in mind—at least, not yet awhile.'

He went to the dressing-chest where there was water in a large jug, poured it into the basin, splashed face and chest vigorously then came to the bed again, drying face and arms upon one of her finest towels. Flinging it from him, he stood, arms akimbo, watching her, his grey eyes narrowed.

'You are wondering how I managed to find you. Not difficult, *señorita*. Your kinsman is an officer of the fleet, well known to all galley slaves. As you observed just now, I dare not venture on the streets in full daylight as I am. I had to risk breaking into someone's house, preferably one with stables and outbuildings where I could rest up for the night, hide, until some hapless groom arrived and I was able to persuade him to provide for my needs, as I have your duenna. Any nobleman's house would have done, but I decided it was meet it should be your kinsman's. You owe me a debt, *señorita*,' he gave a yelp of grim laughter, 'though, indeed, I had not really expected Dame Fortune to actually allow me to find you alone and unguarded in the window. You do seem to make a habit of evading your duenna, and at such unfortunate moments. I've no time now to take due payment, but this favour will do on account.'

She registered the implied threat, and he continued. 'You'll be glad to know that it was by your assistance I managed to escape from the galleass.' He held up the silver and pearl brooch torn from her overgown. 'I saw it. It offered hope, slender, but a hope, and they are few on the rowing-bench. With it I hoped to work away at the wood round the bolt which held my waist chain, while our kindly hortator slept, of course. As it happened, your desire to see me flogged helped my cause further.

It was even simpler to pick the lock of the brig where they flung me to await the gallows.'

She was about to retort that, but for her intervention, he would have suffered more hardly on the captain's orders, but thought better of it. Clearly he had fainted towards the end and knew nothing of her plea to Don Esteban to halt the whipping.

She was shocked to see the terrible open wounds on his back and said, a little gruffly, her voice still refusing to obey her in its normal register, 'Your back needs attention. Sit down here, on the bed.'

She stood up quickly as he stared at her, his slate-grey eyes widening in astonishment. She gave him a slight push. 'Sit down, I say. How can I tend you if you stand towering over me?'

He was too surprised to prevent her as she moved past him and began to rummage in one of the still open travelling-chests.

'What are you doing?' He half rose, his voice sharpened with suspicion.

'Do you think I conceal weapons among my personal linen?' she snapped. 'I need cloth to bathe your wounds and a pot of salve from my medicinal herb chest.'

Her fingers were clumsy in her haste and fear of him but she eventually found what she needed and returned to him, tearing a linen napkin in two with her teeth.

'Now, turn your back.'

As he opened his mouth to protest, she snapped again, 'Put down that stupid dagger. If you kill me, Consuelo will rouse the household and you will be taken in moments. We both know that, so why pretend?'

'If you believe that, why do you not summon your kinsman's servants?'

'Don Felipe is my uncle and it is perhaps because I have more regard for my reputation than to be found with an escaped slave in my chamber—or possibly I have other reasons.'

'Name them,' he challenged, his grey eyes twinkling now in sardonic amusement.

'As you said earlier, I have no time for pointless argument. Now hurry and do what I say and keep your voice low. This apartment is well away from those of my uncle and aunt, but you could still be heard if you continue to bully and threaten.'

He shrugged and allowed the dagger to fall beside him on the bed coverlet.

It took all her courage, despite that, to turn her back on him to go to the basin of water and soak one of the cloths, then form it into a pad for bathing.

His eyes went to it and he grimaced, knowing the pain her touch would cause him, then turned obediently to allow her to begin the work. She felt him stiffen under the touch of her fingers as they encountered the torn flesh of the still open wounds, but he gave no gasp or moan.

'The salve will sting,' she warned, 'but it contains tansy and will cleanse and heal, so you must endure the discomfort.'

He gave a muted snort of laughter and she dashed away from her lashes angry tears. How foolish she was to talk so to him who had experienced constant pain during those endless days and weeks on the rowing-bench.

The bathing completed and the area dabbed gently dry with a towel, she opened the salve pot and smeared her fingers with the rich green ointment. She had often tended servants on the *estancia*, but she felt a strange reluctance to allow her flesh to come into actual contact with his, and paused for a moment, uncertainly. He twisted round to peer at her intently and she flushed darkly.

'Turn round again. I—haven't finished.'

His eyes held hers for moments, then he nodded slightly and turned away from her again.

His shoulder muscles rippled and tautened beneath her touch. What a fine animal he was! A rush of anger coursed through her. He must not be taken and returned to the galleass to face certain death, for she distrusted her uncle's word that he would send to Don Esteban and plead for his life. Fury for his tormentors turned to pity as her questing fingers smoothed edges of the raw scars and also found older, more puckered ones. He moved slightly, whether from pain, she could not say, then, as he heard a sudden slight sound from the corridor, he was up on his feet, watchful and lithe as a cat, his eyes fixed on the closed door.

Maria stood, her hand raised, her eyes wide in fear of discovery, and her panic was not merely that the Englishman would harm her in his rage, but for him, too. The door opened very slightly after a faint scratching sound that told her Consuelo had returned, and much sooner than Maria had dared to hope was possible. She appeared to have been successful in her quest, for she put down a loaded tray upon the dressing-chest and flung a bundle of clothing on to the bed.

'Fortunately for all of us the turnspit slept soundly in the kitchen. Also I found these, airing on a line. The Virgin knows who will be blamed for their loss in the morning—the wretched boy, most likely.'

'I see you managed to recover your tongue along with your courage once out of my sight,' he returned cheerfully, pulling the tray towards him, 'and whetted the edge of it. Don't get over-confident, old woman.'

Consuelo's button-black eyes flashed angrily but she flounced well away from him while he wolfed down the broken meats and coarse bread she'd brought.

'No wine? Ah, well, it was to be expected that you'd not cosset me, *señora*.' He chuckled as he gulped down the remaining water in the pitcher. 'Sea-water increases a man's thirst and stings at his wounds.'

Maria sorted out a fine cambric shift from her travelling chest and tore it into long strips with fingers and teeth.

'We must bandage those wounds of yours or blood and grease from the salve will seep through to your shirt and betray you.'

Scandalised, Consuelo made to protest at such outrageous behaviour on the part of her charge, to say nothing of the ruin of an expensive shift, then, noting the expression on Maria's face, went meekly to sit by the bed, averting her face while the Englishman divested himself of his tattered and filthy loincloth and donned the frieze galligaskin breeches she'd brought in the bundle. Maria bound the improvised cambric bandage into place over his back and shoulders, trying the knots with her stiffened fingers while he stood docilely. Finally he put on a rough, homespun shirt of linsey-woolsey, wriggling his shoulders experimentally.

Maria silently winced as she thought what pain the movement and the scratching of the coarse wool would do to those wounds, but he gave her an unaccustomed bright smile and nod.

'That feels fine. The bandaging is cushioning the wounds and the salve easing the sting already.'

Consuelo snorted again in disgust.

Maria went to the bed to gather together the discarded pieces of cambric and Consuelo mouthed, 'Is this the man—the one who—I mean the man from the rowing deck?'

For a moment Maria was startled that Consuelo would doubt the fact, then reminded herself that her duenna had not seen him. She nodded. Her ears were strained for any sound outside the door or from the garden. She dared not ask if Consuelo had managed to alert some servant in the household. It seemed incredible that they could be here, prisoners in her own chamber, and no one of her uncle's household aware of their plight. Yet she was sure Consuelo had been too frightened for her safety to bring men to the chamber. The duenna knew only too well that the slave could have cut Maria's throat as simply as shelling a pea pod as help arrived and men burst into the room. Easier than shelling peas, Maria thought grimly; a pea pod sometimes offered resistance if tough, and she had dared to make none.

Though one practical part of her longed for someone to come, pound on the door, raise the alarm, she realised, as she had told the Englishman so curtly, that as well as danger to herself and Consuelo it would be far better if the man were not discovered and trapped here. She would be utterly compromised and her uncle furious. If gossip got out, as it was prone to do however sternly servants were sworn to silence, and reached the ears of her intended father-in-law, he might refuse to allow his son to proceed with the marriage, despite the richness of her dowry. As for Doña Beatriz, the knowledge that a man had invaded her niece's chamber would have had her fainting with shock and humiliation.

'No razor?' The Englishman's voice was harsh, yet carried an underlying note of grim amusement.

'Did you wish me to wake Don Felipe and demand to borrow one?' Consuelo snapped.

He chuckled again. 'So astute and so sour. Well, my dagger must suffice. Already I am beginning to look at least half human again.'

The two women watched him as he moved nearer to the window, carrying with him Maria's small travelling-mirror. She had kindled one small candle by the bed after Consuelo had left her, but it gave little light and the grey whiteness of early dawn was already paling the dark sky. Seating himself cross-legged, tailor fashion, before the mirror on the floor, he began to scrape at the bushy growth covering his face and, very carefully, to trim his beard.

When he rose to his feet again Maria saw that, certainly, the shave, wash and trim, however inexpert, and the servant's garb made a great difference to his appearance. He was fair, true, but such colouring, though rare, was not unknown in Spain, especially in a main port such as Cadiz, and his complexion was dark enough after the long months under blistering sun and spray at sea. Now he resembled some perfectly respectable serving man and should be able to pass in the streets in the morning without causing undue notice.

He seated himself on the bed—while the shocked Consuelo hastily removed herself—and pulled on the accompanying coarse woollen hose, wriggling his toes in grim amusement.

'I take it the unlucky turnspit was still wearing his shoes?'

'He was indeed, fortunately for him,' Consuelo retorted.

'Then I must manage to steal some shoes. That shouldn't be too difficult. Stable lads are prone to leave muddied boots outside lest their ears are cuffed by an outraged cook.'

Consuelo affected a confident air she was not feeling. 'Now you'll rob us and leave us, I trust.'

His grin faded and Maria waited, dry-mouthed, for his answer. Now he had all he required it was likely that he would quietly murder them and make his getaway.

'Aye, I'll take one or two baubles. Needs must. I'd prefer not to risk further thefts.'

Angrily Consuelo thrust Maria's smaller jewel chest under his nose. 'Take what you want and let's be rid of you.'

He sorted out various small trinkets, thrusting them deep into the pockets of his galligaskins. 'Doña Maria won't want me to starve.'

'Doña Maria hopes to see you hang, as I do,' Consuelo snapped.

'There's always a good chance of that.' Grey eyes regarded Maria dispassionately and she shivered, not sure if he was mocking them still or shrewdly weighing his chances of escape against the likelihood of Consuelo's summoning help the moment he left. It would simplify the situation if he murdered them, Maria considered again. He could silence Consuelo before she could give little more than a squawk of alarm.

He shrugged, then gestured Consuelo with an imperious wave of one hand towards her own bed. 'Get some sleep.'

Consuelo was affronted by the suggestion. 'Not before you've gone. I'd not rest easy——'

'Easy or otherwise. Go and lie down.' His tone was menacing.

The duenna stood uncertainly. Maria longed to be able to order her to obey him. Their safety lay in the older woman's hands and Maria feared that in her blustering temper she would fail to realise the reality of their danger.

There was a silence while slave and duenna outstared each other, then, muttering darkly beneath her breath, Consuelo flounced away into the shadows. Maria heard the heavy creak of the truckle-bed's leathern strappings as her duenna lay down, as bidden.

Maria's relief was shortlived for, suddenly, the Englishman snatched up his dagger and motioned her to her own bed.

'You, lie down also.'

'What——?'

'Lie down, I say, and lie still.'

Heart pounding again, she obeyed him. He was not to be trusted. Like the caged animal he had resembled, his mood was unpredictable. For a while he had seemed amused, sardonic, but his fear of capture overrode any other considerations. She realised that fully when he moved to the woven curtains at the bed foot and cut through the silken rope which held them back. Returning to her side, he knelt close on the bed.

'Put your wrists together behind you.'

She rolled over and did as he bade her while he secured her wrists and then her ankles with sections of the rope.

'I am truly sorry, sweeting,' he said sternly, 'but I must ensure your silence also, otherwise I would not cause you such discomfort, but my life depends on it, you understand that?'

Unresisting, she allowed him to use one of the discarded cambric strips from her torn shift to gag her. Lying helpless, she was unable to gauge his next move until, to her horror, she felt the heavy sag of her own bed strappings as he laid himself down beside her.

He chuckled softly in the darkness. 'Be easy, sweeting, I'm only waiting for full day. I don't wish to be challenged by the night patrols. The moment I think it safe I'll be off and mingle with the crowds on the harbour front.'

She forced herself to lie still beside him, though her body was drenched in the ice-cold sweat of terror. He eased himself into a more comfortable position and hot blood raced to her throat and cheeks with the sudden closeness of their contact. Would she ever feel truly clean again? If she admitted the truth, his body no longer stank unduly. He'd swum ashore and his servant's clothing was not unclean. There was about him a homespun scent of new-washed wool mingled with the not unfamiliar odours of saddle soap and oil. He moved slightly, grunted and cursed softly in his own tongue. His wounds evidently pained him and she strained away. The sight of that merciless flogging and the wounds she had dressed would haunt her all her life.

It seemed that the small hours dragged on into infinity. After a while Maria caught the sound of Consuelo's renewed steady breathing. Despite her fears, the duenna had managed to sleep. There was no such relief for Maria. She lay in mental and bodily torment. Once she moved, in an effort to ease her cramped limbs, and felt the cold kiss of the dagger. She flinched and he roused instantly, starting up to peer around him. Just as suddenly he relaxed against the pillows and she guessed he was husbanding his strength for the hazards of the escape.

Full dawn finally thrust spears of grey light through the wooden shutter bars and Maria strained to catch the sounds of movements in the house. On her own *estancia* servants would be up by now and beginning their early morning tasks. There came the noise of a door opening and closing somewhere but all went quiet again. As if the Englishman heard it too, he stirred again at her side, lay still for a moment, listening intently, then the bed supports creaked under his weight as he sat up. Maria released a pent breath. Now, please the Virgin, he would make his escape into the gardens.

She froze as he loomed over her and she felt his warm breath fan her forehead. Clammy sweat drenched her hair. She was desperately afraid. He'd accomplished his aims. What was there now to prevent him plunging his dagger into her heart as she lay bound and gagged? The cold, early morning light glinted on the dagger blade in his raised hand and she closed her eyes, believing her final moment had come, then, miraculously, the nauseating pressure was released on her mouth and the gag fell away.

She took great, welcome gulps of air, her eyes staring up, unbelievingly into his.

'You will not cry out,' he murmured, softly. 'To do so would bring you as much harm as capture would to me. I gagged you throughout the night only for fear you called out in sleep or on waking too suddenly. Wish me well, sweeting. For your sake it will be better for me to get clean away. Ask your duenna as to the truth of that.'

She knew he was right. Disgrace would be a hard price to pay to witness his capture, and she was by no means certain that she wished him to be caught. For the moment her jaws were too bruised and stiff for her to reply to him. She lay still, her heart pounding in her breast, and he bent and kissed her hard on the mouth. Feebly she tried to resist, but his grip on her arms was iron-hard and she was still bound. It was a brutal, savage assault, and her tortured lips moved frantically under his. She felt he was suffocating her, drawing her very soul from her body. Then she was released and he sprang away towards the open shutter.

It seemed an age before she could manage to croak out a cry for Consuelo to come to her help. How could the woman sleep so soundly while they had both been in mortal peril? Even later, when her voice was returning to some semblance of normality, she dared not call too loudly for now she was sure the household was rousing. A dog barked somewhere in the stables, doors and shutters were flung wide and a woman's voice called querulously to a serving wench to build up the oven fires.

At last Consuelo woke. Maria had struggled to the bed's edge, her wrists and fingers bruised and sore after her frantic efforts to free herself. The duenna came clumsily in haste to the bed, then brokenly whispered her charge's name.

'Maria, *querida*, forgive me. How could I have snored like a drunkard——?'

'Don't struggle with the knots. Fetch my embroidery scissors. Quickly.'

Consuelo was gasping and sobbing together as she sawed away at the confining linen strips in her haste to free her mistress.

'That's better.' Maria flexed her fingers as the blood coursed agonisingly through the cramped veins. 'Don't cry, Consuelo. He's gone. We're safe—and my aunt must not know. Hurry, cut my ankles free. We must tidy the room.'

Freed at last, Maria tried to get to her feet, but Consuelo caught her by the shoulders, staring deep into her eyes.

'Tell me, *querida*. You can trust me. Did he—did he——?'

'He did not harm me.' Maria's lips curved into a grim little smile. 'To him I am just an enemy, and one to be scorned.'

'A man like that, without a woman for so long.' Consuelo shuddered and mouthed the words fearfully. 'The Virgin be praised you're untouched.'

'Indeed, and now let us make sure I am not disgraced.' Once more, at Consuelo's words, Maria felt herself defiled by the Englishman's touch. When her duenna turned away, she surreptitiously scrubbed at her lips as if she would burn off the feel of his passionless kiss by scraping off the skin itself. There was no time for her to bathe, as she would have wished to do. The torn linen must be hidden away, the bed tidied, before the serving girl knocked on the door with fresh hot water for her toilet.

As Consuelo drew a clean nightshift over her head, Maria shook back her hair impatiently. Her thoughts conjured up a mental picture of her aunt's reaction if any disclosure was made at her uncle's table of the happenings of the night. Certainly the marriage plans would have to be postponed, if not abandoned entirely.

Her eyes met Consuelo's troubled ones and she shook her head in silent entreaty.

No word would be said. The Englishman would escape his hanging because it was in her best interest to see that he had every opportunity to do so.

CHAPTER FOUR

It was well into November that the *Isabella* navigated the dangerous waters off the coast of New Spain and dropped anchor in the harbour of Cartagena. Consuelo was in a fever of impatience during the final days of the voyage and Maria was amused by her excited twittering as she peered from the stern windows over to the white-painted buildings of the town.

Maria had surveyed it earlier from the poop deck. She had leaned eagerly over the taffrail, Don Carlos de la Cosa, His Majesty's Visita, special official to New Spain, an imposing figure at her side. His elegant purple doublet was heavily gold-braided, and his shrewd dark eyes under bushy white brows were fixed attentively, as hers were, on the light native canoes which circled their vessel, paddled by the naked brown bodies of the Indians.

They had sailed from Cadiz almost three months ago to avoid the westerlies off the coast of Portugal, and had been becalmed for days at a time in the great sea of weeds called the Sargasso. Maria had gazed down in amazement at that choking waste of weed while Consuelo had hastily crossed herself, muttering darkly about the works of the devil, before she had scuttled off to the comparative safety their luxurious stern cabin afforded.

After long, uneventful days at sea it seemed the harbour was a hive of frantic activity and the houses, taverns and quay glittered and wavered before Maria's eyes in the perpetual, harsh light. Behind the town she could just glimpse a vista of dark green forest, mahogany, cedar, ebony and rosewood, the rich woods of the New World, and behind that grey-purple hills. The sea was the same heavenly blue she had become accustomed to in the Caribbean.

She had forced herself to put behind her the harrowing episode in Cadiz, though, try as she might, she couldn't prevent her thoughts dwelling on the Englishman. How had he fared? Had he managed to escape from the harbour?

There had been no fuss over the clothing Consuelo had been forced to steal from the kitchen, or, if there had, it had not reached Maria's ears. The incident now took on the unreal aspect of a dream. Had she really lain for hours, bound and gagged, on her bed with the English galley slave at her side? Her cheeks burned when her thoughts raced ahead to the imminent meeting with Don Luis, so soon to be her husband.

A cannon salvo of salute to the Visita and the armada was fired from the Governor's fortress. Overhead she heard the flurry of activity associated with arrival, shouted commands, the creak and pull of heavy ropes as the longboats were lowered to convey the passengers ashore. She took a final glance around the cabin which had been her home for the last months. Her heart thudded uncomfortably. Very soon now, an hour, perhaps less, and she would be surrendering her hand to her betrothed to kiss.

She was about to move to the cabin door when a trumpet call halted her and she looked enquiringly towards Consuelo.

The duenna shrugged. 'Perhaps the Governor is coming aboard to welcome Don Carlos.'

It was likely. Unwelcome as the Visita's presence would be in the province, courtesy demanded that he be greeted with the formality and respect due to His Majesty's representative. And with the Governor would be Don Luis Ortego y Castuero? Maria looked hurriedly down at her mourning gown. Within her travelling chests and trunks were the clothes hastily bought and altered during her brief stay in Cadiz before she had embarked on the *Isabella*. There were rich silks, brocades and velvets in bright colours, as well as the more subdued ones meant to be worn before her marriage. On the voyage she had continued to wear her mourning, but she had hoped for an opportunity to bathe and change into less sombre attire before being presented to her betrothed. Foolishly, she now conceded, she had expected to be installed within her own chamber in the Governor's residence before being formally introduced to Don Luis.

Consuelo grumblingly voiced her doubts. 'There, I told you we should have been more prepared. First impressions are so important. The Governor and his lady would be more impressed if they saw you first in a brighter gown.'

'It cannot be helped now. I've no wish to parade myself in peacock colours. The months of my mourning are not actually completed,' Maria snapped, tartly.

There was a polite tap upon her cabin door and she nodded to Consuelo to open it and admit whoever stood outside. Don Alfonso, the *Isabella*'s captain, bowed and stepped aside.

'Allow me, Your Excellency, to present to you my other distinguished passenger, Doña Maria Santiago y Talavera. His Excellency, Don Piero Fernandez del Busto, Governor of Cartagena.'

Maria kept her eyes modestly lowered as she curtsyed. She was drawn instantly to her feet and a hearty kiss of greeting bestowed on her cheek. She was startled and not a little dismayed.

Don Piero was a huge man who dwarfed all others in the narrow confines of the corridor. He was smiling warmly and his plump, beringed hand held hers longer than the dictates of courtesy necessitated. Maria's first hasty glance took in a bluff, open countenance, red cheeks badly at odds with his doublet and hose of vivid carmine. His thighs and legs straddled the boards of the cabin floor like some Colossus. Try as she might, Maria was unable to see beyond his gigantic figure to the two or three attending gentlemen behind him, standing, as they were, within the deep shadow of the between-decks corridor.

'Welcome, my dear child, to Cartagena.' The Governor's voice was as deeply pitched and mellow as his stature dictated. 'My lady, Doña Serafina, is eagerly waiting your arrival at the Residency and everything is prepared for your comfort. It is not every day we have the great pleasure of greeting a bride, eh, Don Alfonso?'

His huge paw squeezed familiarly over her small hand as he half turned, not an easy movement for so huge a man in so confined a space.

'But it is not me you are so anxious to see, eh, *querida*. Here's one who has first claim on your attention. Come forward, Don Luis, you young dog, and greet your lady.'

Don Luis was as tall and slim as his superior was immense, and was almost effeminate in build. Foppishly clad in blue and silver, he was more suitably attired for some formal occasion at court than this meeting in the between-deck corridor of a merchant ship in New Spain.

His grasp of her fingers was entirely formal, as was the light brush of his lips upon her fingertips. It was as if a moth had touched her briefly with its wings in passing, and, just as if she had been dealing with the irritation of such a creature touching her, she felt an equal desire to brush away his contact with her flesh.

Handsome he was, as his miniature had revealed, perhaps even more so, for the artist had failed to catch the immature roundness of the features, the perfection of the lips, parted now in a smile of welcome which was not echoed in the eyes. Maria found her gaze drawn to those eyes; they were large and luminous, with a cold ferocity of stare which made her blink in astonishment.

'The time has hung heavily since I was informed of your embarkation, *muy doña*.' His voice was soft, almost caressing in quality, belying the chilly hauteur of his expression. 'It is my very great happiness to see you here, at last.'

She curtsyed once more and made to withdraw her fingers from his grasp. He made no attempt to detain them, bowing stiffly in courtly fashion. It was as if he was repeating, dutifully, some phrase he had been taught. His gaze passed over her, taking in the sombre dullness of her gown, the slightness of her youthful form. The smile had vanished now and she had no way of assessing whether he liked what he saw or was disappointed. There was an icy quality in his whole manner she found completely unnerving. She hesitated, uncertain just how to proceed, but the Governor took the initiative.

'Well, now, *querida*, we'll have you rowed ashore. It's only just past midday and the sun at its height. A good siesta in a shaded room is what you need, what we all need, eh, before we can think of any further business.'

He turned aside and moved ponderously back to the companionstair. Maria turned to Consuelo, who hugged her silently. It was a comforting gesture after the stultifying encounter with the man who was soon to be her husband.

As she sat in the boat, shaded by a canvas awning, she told herself fiercely that her reaction to the meeting was exaggeratedly alarmist. It was natural that Don Luis should be reserved in his manner. He had been bred in Madrid where court formality was strictly observed. There would be time in plenty before the marriage ceremony, time to probe behind that rigid mask. Chaperoned by Consuelo and the Governor's lady, she would have opportunity to become thoroughly acquainted with her betrothed. He was showing her due consideration, had greeted her so, out of respect for her mourning. Of course she could not expect that he viewed this coming match with any more enthusiasm than she did. He had been commanded by his father to wed her, this was a perfectly normal meeting of two complete strangers, yet she could not dismiss the feeling that there was something more than formality behind his oddness, a distaste, almost a decided antipathy towards this marriage. Why? She was not unattractive, even dressed sombrely and behind the fashion as she was. Maria had no foolishly false modesty. Men had looked on her with scarcely restrained desire. She was young and wealthy. What more could Don Luis reasonably wish for? Maria gave an angry little hiss, and, looking towards the harbour front, made a determined effort to dismiss the unpleasant forebodings from her mind.

Doña Serafina, the Governor's lady, appeared to be as delighted by Maria's arrival as her husband had promised. She was diminutive and pretty, and at least thirty years younger than Don Piero. Maria considered that her gown of emerald-green satin was gaudy and over-decorated, and dismissed the notion as uncharitable. Doña Serafina, so far from Spain and the court, had few ladies of taste to guide her in her choices and Maria suspected that her gowns were admired by the elderly Governor.

The Residency was partially stone-built, white-painted, and fine, though all the outbuildings were wooden. Maria was impressed by the house's fashionable furnishings and tapestries, obviously imported from Spain.

Her hostess chattered volubly as she conducted her through the spacious hall, up the ornate staircase to the small suite of rooms which had been prepared for her. The largest of the two bedchambers was more sparsely furnished than her own room on the *estancia* but light, airy and exceedingly well kept. Consuelo expressed herself as satisfied with the smaller room she was to occupy.

An Indian servant girl who came in answer to Doña Serafina's summons on the bell pull was very young, dressed respectably in plain cotton dress and wore a rudely carved wooden cross on a string round her neck, which pronounced her a convert to the Catholic faith. Maria had averted her eyes from the naked Indian men and women she had seen in the boats earlier and won-dered, fleetingly, how much pressure was put upon these Indian house servants to become Christians. The girl ap-peared to understand Spanish, so long as she was given only simple commands.

A light repast was sent up and later a tub of scented water was provided. Maria sniffed appreciatively at the unfamiliar fragrance, assuming the oils had been dis-tilled from some bloom native to New Spain.

Consuelo insisted that she put aside her mourning for the evening meal and, reluctantly, Maria donned a white satin gown with wide puffed undersleeves slashed in black, and a deep ruff, also edged with black lace. Her demure little cap, which hid almost all of her hair, was similarly ruched with priceless black lace. Consuelo clicked her tongue approvingly as she fastened round Maria's waist a golden chain with its bejewelled crucifix.

'Your betrothed will doubtless be dining with the Governor and Don Carlos. This gown makes just the right impression, tasteful, elegant but modest.'

The Governor's lady, dressed in gold and white brocade and an outsized ruff of gilded lace, kissed Maria warmly on the cheek as they prepared to enter the dining-room.

'*Querida*, how very lovely you look. Don Luis is a fortunate young man.'

The Governor kept some state and the table napery was of the finest damask; candlelight glittered on silver and Venetian glass. Maria was relieved to find Don Carlos, the Visita, present and he rose gallantly to greet her. Don Carlos had been like a father to her throughout the voyage, indeed, his gentle courtesy and entertaining talk had made the journey tolerable. He had prepared her as much as he could for her new life and she would be unfailingly grateful to him forever for his constant care of her. After the chilling reception at her uncle's house, the old man's simple kindness had been balm to her hurt mind. Maria was bedazzled by the splendour of silks and jewels as attendant ladies and gentlemen took their seats. Doña Serafina had placed Don Luis opposite to Maria, but she kept up such a constant stream of inconsequential chatter that Maria was hardly aware that her betrothed, clad tonight in the traditional black and silver of the Spanish *hidalgo*, said barely one word to her.

She found herself watching him covertly. His table manners were faultless and he ate and drank sparingly. At the close of the meal, when the ladies withdrew to the inner coolly shaded solar, he hastened to attend on the Governor. His eagerness to be out of her presence was hardly flattering, she thought wryly.

The ladies' talk was all of domestic matters. They might have been sitting in a room in Madrid or Cadiz. No mention was made of the very real threat of war, or

the danger to Spanish shipping from English ma-
rauders, not even of the undertones of the Visita's visit,
which might well uncover some corruption in the
province and cause one of their husbands disgrace or
worse. Maria was forced to hide her bored half-yawns
behind her fan and was amused to catch Don Carlos's
sardonic glance when he returned with the other
gentlemen.

Don Piero's unctuous tones cut across the soughing
of fans and mutter of small talk. 'Luis, my boy, time
you became acquainted with your betrothed. Why not
escort her on a tour of the gardens? It is pleasant now
the sun has gone down. You are excused further attendance.' He laughed. 'In my young day I'd not have
needed to be reminded of so pleasurable a duty.'

Don Luis was immediately by her side, bowing over
her hand. 'Doña Maria, may I have the honour of
showing you the beauty of the Residency gardens?' His
tone was as coolly impersonal as it was formal.

Maria rose and, curtsying, surrendered her fingers to
him. Consuelo closed in, watchfully, behind.

Once in the scented garden, lit by flaming sconces
along the walks, he instructed her in the names of unfamiliar trees and shrubs. Everything here, in the New
World, grew in super-abundance; great gaudy blossoms,
flowering trees and shrubs, palms, rattan, so she was
amazed by it all. The orderly correctness of a typical
Spanish garden made this place a primitive, splendid
jungle, by contrast, yet, for all of it, she saw evidence
of skilful planting and pruning as well as excessive
watering.

'Is the gardening done by slaves? I see the Indians in
the house are all Christians.'

He halted in mid-stride and stared at her in astonishment. 'Slaves or Indians, it's all one. Labour is plen-
tiful in New Spain and easily replaced.'

She made a further attempt to keep his attention. 'I
regret I was unable to be presented to your parents before
I sailed. The arrangements were all so hurried.'

'I understand my father is at present in attendance on the King at the Escorial,' he said quickly. 'As for my mother,' he shrugged, 'her health is indifferent. She keeps to her own chamber most of the time.'

'Have you brothers and sisters?' Maria was anxious to hear more of his family.

'I have two sisters. One is preparing to enter the novitiate of Benedictine nuns in Madrid. The other is still a child.'

He appeared little interested in them, did not so much as volunteer their names, nor did he ask her about her own family or life on the Malaga *estancia*.

As they returned to the house she spoke warmly of her kindly reception by the Governor and his lady. 'I am anxious to explore the town and discover more about the people here.'

'Doña Serafina will see to it that you are presented to all the ladies of note in the province.'

'Yes, I am sure, but I was referring to the natives. Their customs are new and fascinating.'

He frowned, gazing haughtily at her down the length of his aristocratic nose. 'It is not necessary for you to concern yourself with such matters. Doña Serafina will instruct you in the business of handling the house slaves. In all else you will live exactly as you did in Spain.'

He parted from her in the same attitude of icy politeness as he had shown towards her all evening.

Consuelo commented, as they prepared to retire, 'He has little conversation, this high-born betrothed of yours. He is very handsome, yet you are very reticent about your feelings towards him. Does he disappoint you?'

'His manners are good, but I am at a loss to understand his attitude. It is as if he had downright contempt for me. I know this match was forced on both of us, but his icy formality is like a slap in the face.'

Consuelo nodded sympathetically. 'At least you are unlikely to find him—importunate.'

Maria gave a harsh little laugh. 'That will be a mercy indeed.' She gave a shiver of distaste. 'Handsome or no, I find him almost—frightening.'

Her duenna shot her an alarmed glance.

'It seems he will not be in haste for the wedding ceremony. At least I shall have a respite.'

At breakfast next day she was informed that Don Luis had accompanied the Governor and Don Carlos on a tour of inspection around the colony which would be likely to keep them away from Cartagena for some weeks. She was hard put to it to hide her expression of relief.

Giles Norwood stood amidships with the other sail trimmers, his eyes narrowed to watch the approach of the advancing galleon. His lips parted in a grin of wry amusement, pure irony that his efforts to reach his homeland seemed destined to put him in danger from his own countrymen. He was reasonably sure that the vessel even now bearing down upon the Portuguese merchant ship bound for the Low Countries, was, indeed, built in an English shipyard. Her long, projecting beakhead and low forecastle, set well back from the bows, the graceful, sleek lines of her, was as familiar to him as his own manor in North Yorkshire. The flag of St George flew proudly from her masthead, yet Norwood's teeth were bared still further, as he noted the distance narrowing between the two vessels. He thought he knew her, and her captain.

Around him the sullen muttering of the Portuguese crewmen told him he was not alone in the thought.

El Draco, the notorious English pirate, surely aided by the Devil himself.

Already the captain had prepared the ship for action. Two bolts of canvas had been erected around the merchantman's waist to afford the men some protection from possible fire from the enemy vessel. Gunports had already been lifted, cannons run out. Gunners waited, nervous as cats, spitting on their hands in readiness for action.

The grey-beard at Norwood's side cupped his hands to his mouth to hiss in his ear over the din of shouted commands and the wild trampling of bare feet as men rushed to their battle stations.

'All useless.' He spat downwind, disgustedly. 'I've seen it all before. Look at the lines of her, the sheer manoeuvrability. What chance have we got? We'll be boarded and captured in less than an hour. Better to allow the cursed English dogs to grapple and sack us, then let us sail on.'

Norwood nodded abstractedly. Even now he was busy sizing up the possibilities of evading action himself. It would be dangerous in the extreme to jump overside and swim towards the enemy craft. If he was not picked off by one of the English marksmen, he certainly would be by one of his former Portuguese shipmates recognising betrayal. He gave a little hiss of breath. His muscles were already tautened, his brain alert, trained to the familiar thrill of threatened danger. The feeling was not unpleasant. While he accepted the exhilaration of excitement, he was not one to relax his guard. He would fight, if fight he must, with the Portuguese crew, if he felt it necessary to save his life, but he would infinitely prefer that such an unpleasant eventuality be removed from him by his captain's decision to capitulate.

A warning shot crashed across the Portuguese merchantman's bows. An English voice barked out a command to lower the flag and surrender.

His fellow crewman spat again. 'He'll not see sense. The Virgin protect us from young sprigs of captains with mother's milk scarce dry on their lips.'

A whip cracked across the oldster's shoulders together with an order to trim the foresail. Norwood leaped to obey, while his mind still teemed with conflicting ideas.

The forward culverins barked and smoked, but, despite their longer range, the English galleon swung into the wind, easily avoiding their crippling fire. A splintering shot from one of the Englishman's bombards struck the mizzenmast with devastating effect. Men below Norwood, in the ship's waist, screamed in agony as falling spars of timber and rigging trapped them beneath the blazing debris. A trumpet blared out a call to clear the deck.

Norwood sprang nimbly from the shrouds, slipping in spilt blood, and rushed to the assistance of his comrades. All about him men pleaded desperately for help to pull them free, alternately babbling prayers or curses. Norwood tugged vainly at a cable wedged across his friend's legs. They had forged a rough companionship during the short voyage from Lisbon.

The old man caught at Norwood's hand, clawing frantically. 'Give it up, friend. The pain's too great. There's nothing you can do. Pray for me for a moment, then get yourself below, if you can.'

Norwood bent his ear to the other's lips, as the man hoarsely whispered an act of contrition. He stayed for a while, even after the grip on his wrist had slackened.

A trumpet shrilled again and Norwood staggered up, as the dull thuds warned him that boarding hooks were locking the two vessels together in the final throes of mortal combat. He looked quickly round for some hiding-place which would make it possible for him to keep clear of the slaughter of close-handed fighting amidships.

A ship's officer summoned him imperatively to the poop deck where another officer had been laid low by the splintering bombard shot. Impassively Norwood helped convey the stricken man below and lingered while a blood-smeared ship's carpenter gave the wounded man a cursory examination.

All hell was let loose on deck by the time he reached it again. The English boarding party was making short work of the Portuguese crew's resistance. Finding himself surrounded, Norwood drew his cutlass and fought his way towards the poop deck. He checked at sight of the young Portuguese captain ringed round by the enemy. At swordpoint the debonair young nobleman ordered his trumpeter to sound surrender. Norwood watched as cutlasses, swords, belaying pins and all other weapons were thrown to the deck and the Portuguese crew rounded up in the ship's waist. He joined his companions as a bosun's whistle announced the coming aboard of the English captain.

Norwood grinned. He had not been mistaken. The square-built man with the jutting forked beard and the rolling gait of the English sea-dog was, indeed, Francis Drake. Norwood made no immediate move to make himself known to his countryman. Drake cocked his head to one side as he surveyed his captive. The captain's helmet and cuirass had been badly dented and his clothing was dishevelled, an occurrence unusual for the noble young dandy. Blood smeared his face and hands.

'Is there an interpreter? I speak few words of Donnish talk.'

The crew remained sullenly silent and Norwood, recognising his opportunity, moved to Drake's side.

'Can I, perhaps, be of assistance, Frank?'

Drake swung round, his eyes widening. He put both hands on his hips and leaned forward to peer intently into the darkly bearded face. 'An Englishman? God's blood, surely not. Yet someone who appears to know me well.'

Norwood chuckled. 'A compliment you don't return, Frank. Look again and ignore the black hair. It's not my usual colour. See my eyes, man, or, if that's no help, perhaps I can prod your memory with an incident one night at Hampton when you were so drunk you almost stepped into the ornamental pond in the Great Court. Would have, if my arm hadn't checked you.'

Drake's bearded mouth opened in wide astonishment as he continued to stare, then he leaned back and gave a great bellow of laughter. 'Great God in heaven, it can't be, but it is, sure. Giles Norwood?'

Norwood reached out to take the proffered hand. 'Giles Norwood it is, and thankful to hear his own tongue from the lips of an old friend.'

'Great Harry, man, what are you doing aboard this Portuguese?' Drake waved a hand impatiently. 'But that can wait. Inform this coxscomb I'm confiscating his cargo and all hand weapons and shot. When we've done, he's free to sail to the Devil for all I care.'

Norwood translated in faultless Castilian for the Spanish captain's benefit. The man stared insolently at him, then at Drake, shrugged, and snapped an order at his bosun. He demanded to be allowed below.

Drake made no objection, signalled to his second in command and gestured Norwood to accompany him overside to his own vessel.

Drake's crew needed no prompting. They had these situations well in hand, were trained to cope with them swiftly and efficiently, and Drake retired to the *Elizabeth Bonaventure*'s main cabin with his newly rediscovered friend. He waved to a side table laden with Venetian decanters and wine goblets.

'Help yourself, man. If you've a thirst, later, for good English ale, there's plenty of that on board.' He called to a youthful page to help him unbuckle his steel cuirass, stretched, scratched himself in comfort, and, finally, flung himself down in a padded armchair.

Norwood downed a goblet of excellent malmsey, as he looked appreciatively round the sumptuously appointed cabin. 'You live like a king, Frank. Her Grace would not approve.' He perched on the table edge, smiling down at his friend.

Drake gave a rumble of belly laughter. 'She'll not complain while she shares the proceeds of my nefarious activities.'

'You admit they are nefarious?'

'They're profitable.'

'Precisely. That's why I request permission to join your crew.'

Drake's bushy eyebrows were raised expressively. 'Without enquiring my destination?'

Norwood grinned back at him. 'So long as I share the profits of the voyage, you can sail to the mouth of hell itself. I take it, though, you're bound for New Spain and the Antilles.'

'You surmise correctly.' Drake indicated a decanter and Norwood pushed it over towards him.

'So you'll take me?'

'Why not? You're your own master or—are you Walsingham's dog?'

'I was Walsingham's dog. After eight months in a Spanish galley, I feel I'm entitled to a measure of freedom and suitable compensation.'

Drake whistled soundlessly. 'So you were taken? What of your mission report?'

'Sent long ago overland by reliable messengers. I informed Walsingham I would make my own way home and in my own time.'

Drake gestured for him to be seated more comfortably. 'The galleys, eh? At the oars? You were lucky to escape burning in an *auto de fe*.'

Norwood seated himself in the second chair and leaned back his head, stretching his long legs out before him. 'My faith is my own business. Even Walsingham acknowledges that and does not question my loyalty. The Spaniards had no reason to charge me with heresy.'

Drake regarded him warily through narrowed eyes. If Norwood was, indeed, a Papist, that was his own affair, as he had said. Northern gentlemen, Drake knew, held strange opinions and loyalties, and Norwood's manor was in the Yorkshire Dales.

Norwood looked up from his wine as if he read what Drake was thinking and said, abruptly, 'Yes, I am of the Old Faith, as my father and grandfather were before me. My grandfather took part in the Northern Rising, the so-called Pilgrimage of Grace, in 1536. He was lucky to escape with his life and to retain the manor. Henry pardoned him but he was heavily fined and the estate burdened with debts ever since.'

'And your father?'

'He remained a true son of the Church and was one of the first men to offer his support to Queen Mary in 1553 during the difficult days of the Northumberland Rising and the abortive attempt to place Lady Jane Grey on the throne. My father was with Queen Mary when she rode triumphantly into London on July the nineteenth.'

'So your fortunes were restored on her accession?'

'My father was restored to favour. The Queen granted him no financial benefits. He was pleased to attend on her at court and was delighted by the Spanish Marriage, hoping it would restore the true faith to England.'

Drake nodded grimly. 'It certainly accomplished that.'

'My father married in 1555. My mother, Anne Scrope, was descended from the Scropes of Bolton, through a lesser branch of that great family. She was a true Northern lady. I was born the following year, baptised in the Faith and with a priest for tutor.' Norwood smiled briefly. 'My father's attachment to King Philip's train brought him into contact with several *hidalgos* attendant upon His Majesty. He made many Spanish friends, learned to speak Castilian passing well and to read the language. He came to admire many Spanish customs and to appreciate Spanish music. I learned very early to speak the Spanish tongue and earned my father's approval by speaking it often with him long after the Queen's husband had left England.'

'So that is the reason you passed so easily as Spanish, a very useful accomplishment for Walsingham's purpose,' Drake commented drily.

Norwood made a wry grimace. 'But, for all my father's allegiance to Queen Mary, and he never faltered in that— she was Henry's true heir and he insisted we acknowledge the fact—he became sickened by the cruel persecutions of Protestants. His presence at the burning of Archbishop Cranmer was the final disillusionment. Soon after, he asked leave to withdraw from court and retire to our Yorkshire manor at Askrigg. My father was a very gallant but truly gentle man.'

'And you, too, are disgusted by the excesses of the Inquisition?'

Norwood inclined his chin briefly. 'I hold to my faith— privately. My father talked often of the horrors he had seen at Smithfield and, since my capture, I, too——' He shook his head almost angrily. 'Yet God is not responsible for the cruelties and injustices perpetrated in His name. I shall never recant, but I do not attend mass. Of course we in England have had little opportunities to do so safely, but, even if it were possible, I doubt if I would do so. My feelings are strangely mixed but my al-

legiance, as my father's was to Mary, is to our Queen
Elizabeth, her sister. I pay my fines as a recusant and
do not attend our parish services.'

Drake was silent, his eyes thoughtful.

'And now you are wondering how I became
Walsingham's man.'

'It has occurred to me, you, a gentleman born——'

'Living the life of a spy?' Norwood's lips curled sardonically. 'How gentlemen hate that designation; almost
as much as you dislike the term "pirate", I doubt not,
Frank.'

Drake laughed heartily. 'Giles, you wrong me. I know
more than the next man how essential it is we have information regarding Philip's state of readiness for war.
And no man more than I recognises how dangerous your
work is. The Queen should be made aware of it and
reward you fittingly.'

'Aye, but I doubt if she would. Like her sister, Mary,
she inherited her closeness of the treasury purse strings
from her grandfather, Henry the Seventh, who was never
noted for his generosity. Well, as to my association with
Walsingham. My father sent me to court, knowing
Elizabeth's propensity for youthful and adventurous
spirits about her, with the hope I might catch her favour.
I was overheard speaking Castilian with a gentleman in
the Spanish ambassador's train.'

'And recruited by Walsingham.'

'Not without some misgivings, but, whatever you may
think of Walsingham, he has the Queen's welfare and
the safety of the realm truly at heart. He convinced me
of the real need for a gentleman traveller in Spain and
the Netherlands, one who could listen to the natives talk
and not be noted too closely as a foreigner.'

Drake nodded. 'So you went abroad immediately. But,
no, I saw you frequently at court.'

'Walsingham saw to it I was trained well. I have all
the accomplishments of a successful spy and a pick-
pocket, too.' Norwood's eyes twinkled. 'Had I not, I
might now be swinging from the galleass yardarm, for
the crows to pick. He also sent me to sea, that I might

know the sailing and handling, aye, and the design of ships, for he believed our greatest threat comes from Philip's intensive ship-building programme. I occupied my first year in Walsingham's service learning your trade, Frank, and, at the same time, helping to fill our empty coffers at Askrigg.'

'Yet Walsingham is so rabid a hater of all Papists——'

'Aye; as I said, if he suspects my religion, he has never put it into words, and I believe he trusts me implicitly in my allegiance to Her Grace, the Queen.'

'And are the details of your escape your own business and not for the telling? They would make a fair tale, I wager.'

Norwood nodded. He sat silent for a moment, then poured more wine, holding the priceless goblet up to the light from the stern window, admiring the ruby glow of the precious liquid. 'I had the assistance of a countrywoman.'

Drake's hand stilled in the movement of conveying his own goblet to his lips. 'An Englishwoman, on a Spanish galley?'

'Half English, I suspect. Hair as brown as nuts and eyes the colour of an English June sky.'

'You always had an eye for a comely wench, Giles.'

'Comely she was, yes—accommodating, by no means. She was so incensed by my insolence in addressing her in English, she had me soundly flogged for my pains.'

He related the story while Drake listened in mounting amazement.

'And the house you robbed? You chose it deliberately, putting yourself in more danger? You took a big risk, Giles, on the chance you'd see the wench again.'

Norwood shrugged, expressively. 'I knew she was a kinswoman of Don Felipe Santiago y Talavera. He's one of Santa Cruz's most noted commanders. The garden of his house was easy of access. I desperately needed a change of clothing and somewhere to lie low until I dared mingle with the morning crowds.'

'There was no hue and cry after you?'

'Not that I heard. I didn't wait to find out, I assure you! I left just after sun-up and made for Lisbon where I felt I'd find it easier to melt into the cosmopolitan atmosphere of the harbour front. I darkened my hair and beard en route and signed on the Portuguese craft where you found me. It seemed the fastest and safest route home. We were bound for Flushing. From there it would not have proved too difficult for me to make for France and home.'

'Hmm. Fortunate we boarded. We've saved you some inconvenience. You say Walsingham should have received your report?'

'I dispatched it before I was taken. A good thing, too. I had no incriminating papers on me. I was judged to be a simple seaman, shipwrecked and adrift in enemy country, accused of piracy and finally condemned to the galleys.'

'Were you betrayed, do you think?'

Norwood's face darkened. 'It would seem very likely. I was arrested in a raid on a harbour tavern with other foreign seamen. Once the authorities had assured themselves I was no heretic and no concern of the Holy Office, my sentence was merely a matter of form.'

Drake's genial face was unwontedly grave. 'Did you discover what we've all feared—evidence of impending invasion?'

'Nothing so definite, but Santa Cruz is building his fleet, and treasure ships from New Spain are adding considerably to Philip's coffers, so making it easier for him to arm for war.'

Drake's teeth bared in a wolfish grin. 'Then it's patriots we find ourselves to be, Giles, my boy, for relieving the Dons of so much of their ill-gotten gains.'

'Better far, if the Queen could be brought to see our privateering ventures in this light.'

'In private she does, Giles. I'm sure of it. It's the greybeards in her council chamber who advise caution.'

'And Elizabeth herself is no hothead, despite that flaming hair of hers.'

Drake was about to question Norwood further when his sailing master arrived to report that the *Elizabeth Bonaventure* was now ready to sail, her prize cargo duly stowed in her holds.

Drake rose to his feet. 'I must be off to the poop deck. Make yourself at home, Giles. There's clothing in the chest there, some of it acquired on one of our ventures so you should find something to fit. I'll send the boy down with a jug of hot water from the galley. Later, we'll sup. I have a proposition to put to you.'

He departed and Giles Norwood moved to the stern window as grappling hooks were disengaged and the slapping of bare feet on the deck above him told him sail trimmers were running to the stations aloft. The *Elizabeth Bonaventure* would sail south, leaving the crippled Portuguese vessel to limp into the nearest friendly harbour. He stretched and smiled. For the first time in months he would be able to relax his guard. He was among friends, he could sleep without fear of betraying himself by some incautious muttering, aye, and stuff his belly too. He'd been on short commons too long.

Drake's page arrived with the promised ewer of water steaming hot from the galley cooking-fire. Norwood dismissed the boy's offer of assistance, stripped to the buff and thoroughly cleansed himself. He shrugged on velvet trunk hose, amused to note that some dandified *hidalgo* must have been pained to lose such elegant garments, for those and the doublet were in fine blue figured velvet, slashed, padded in the height of fashion, and elaborately embellished with gold braid. He was about to don a fine cambric shirt when he caught his reflection in Drake's travelling-mirror. There were ugly purple welts still marring his shoulders. He turned to view the scars more closely and those clear grey eyes became suddenly steely.

It had never been his way to make war on women. He'd never known the need. Even in his privateering days they had come to his arms fast enough when he'd had time for them. This Spanish woman had been different and her uniqueness did not lie in her possible mixed blood. He smiled grimly as he recalled the naked fury which had blazed in those blue eyes of hers, the flaring arrogance of those aristocratic nostrils. Yet she had shown him some care when she'd a need to rid herself of him. Many times on board the merchantman he'd fallen asleep with the teasing scent of her healing salve reminding him sharply of the night he had spent in her chamber.

He had had opportunity to take payment in part of the debt she owed him, but he had felt a strange reluctance. He had told himself that he had spared her, not for her sake, but his own. He had been spent and to have taken her then, ravished that white flesh he'd glimpsed beneath the flimsy nightshift, bruised and marred that slender body, would have endangered him further, distracted him from the clear thought-out plan for escape. Yet he was aware that his forbearance was moved by something stronger than his own native caution.

He'd heard snatches of talk on the harbour front. The lady was to sail on the *Isabella* for Cartagena. She was promised to some young sprig in the household of the Governor.

He tied up the shirt fastening and put on the fashionable doublet, smiling confidently at his reflected image. The smile betokened ill for his lovely adversary. Fate would bring him within her vicinity, and, if he knew Drake, the rich plum of Cartagena would fall ripely into his hands.

Drake commented pithily on his changed appearance as they supped together later that evening. 'I see you're the Queen's courtier once more. You're sure you'd not prefer to take ship for England from the Canaries where we refit, and ruffle it at court again?'

'Not until I've prize money enough to ruffle it suitably.'

Drake grinned. 'I think I can promise you that. I took a prize galleon some weeks ago. She's being careened off Cape Verde. I need an experienced captain for her.

We rendezvous with the rest of my fleet there. If we can agree on suitable terms, concerning any prizes we take, I'll make you a present of her.'

Norwood's eyes glittered as he reached for an apple. 'Why honour me with your choice?'

Drake lolled back comfortably in his padded chair. 'I want a man who'll strike hard at the enemy. You are that man. You've much to repay.'

CHAPTER FIVE

MARIA found the weeks leading up to the Holy Season of Christmas both fascinating and rewarding. Unused to the extreme heat, she was glad to rest well into the evenings. The siesta hour in Spain did not take its toll of energy as this enervating, oppressive air of New Spain. The Governor's lady proved an amiable companion but, as Don Piero and his staff continued to tour the plantations in attendance on the Visita, she saw nothing of her betrothed.

The Governor's party arrived home on Christmas Eve and the festivities were celebrated in style, Maria involved with Doña Serafina in all the preparations. She had dreaded her meeting with Don Luis again, but the days passed with little opportunity for them to be alone together.

It was on Twelfth Night that Don Carlos broached the matter she feared above all else.

'And when is to be the nuptial day?' He beamed in Maria's direction. 'I had hoped to be present and must sail for Spain in early February.'

Don Piero had appeared more relaxed, positively jovial again since he had returned to the Residency. Apparently Don Carlos had given him reason to suppose that his tour of inspection had proved satisfactory and the Governor had no need to fear the Visita's report to the King.

He nodded, smiling. 'Only this morning Serafina and I discussed the matter and determined to put it to Doña Maria, that the end of this month would prove suitable.'

Don Luis studiously avoided Maria's eye. 'When it pleases Your Excellency. We shall be honoured by the presence of the King's Visita.'

Maria's fingers trembled on her drinking goblet.

'Well, Doña Maria, you must put this impatient dog out of his misery. He's waited, conscious of your mourning and your need to acclimatise yourself to life here in New Spain. Can we call Father Rodrigo and settle on a day prior to Don Carlos's departure?' The Governor was smiling at her benignly.

Maria turned challengingly to her betrothed. He met her gaze unwinkingly and inclined his head in a little authoritative gesture. 'Whatever is convenient for Don Luis and Father Rodrigo,' Maria said quietly.

So it was settled. The priest appointed the fifth day of February. Doña Serafina was anxious for time for the household to catch its breath after the Christmas festivities before being thrown once more into preparations for another ceremonious occasion. Maria was thankful that she still had a respite of almost a month.

In the following days Don Luis paid her considerable attention, squiring her in the Governor's carriage on visits to some of the province's most notable families and to the famous pearl fisheries where he made her a betrothal gift of a single magnificent string of matched pearls, rose-tinted in colour and very rare.

Don Luis occupied rooms in the Governor's Residency and it was decided that, for the present, the newly married pair should be provided with a larger suite there until Don Luis could arrange to have a house built for himself and his bride. Doña Serafina generously donated some of her own finely crafted furniture and arras newly shipped out from Spain. For the rest, native craftsmen were set to work to fashion side tables, chairs, stools and chests from local woods. Maria had brought her own bed-hangings, linen and even one or two tapestries, so, when completed, her new apartments would be comfortable and luxurious.

Cartagena's cathedral was a fine building, white-washed within and richly decorated with wall paintings and gilded wood. The altar vessels of precious metals set with gems were scarcely less impressive than those to be found in the churches of Malaga and Madrid. Her

wedding would be a splendid affair, but, as the time drew
nearer to it, her mind quailed at the thought.

One morning in early February, needing to be away
for a while from the flurry of wedding preparations, she
requested permission to ride out of the town to view the
sea coast and plantations behind the harbour. Don Luis
instantly placed himself at her disposal, and, with
Consuelo in attendance, they set out early before the sun
became too gruellingly hot.

Once clear of the town, Maria revelled in her explo-
ration of the terrain. Always before she had been seated
in the Governor's carriage and, though its shade had
been welcome, she enjoyed this morning the advantage
of a clear view of the harbour and plantations ahead of
them. The native trees and plants overawed her with their
size and luxuriant growth: logwood, bamboo, the
feathery foliage of palm. Already settlers had cultivated
the indigenous cacao, coconut, tobacco and sweet potato
as well as imported crops such as sugarcane and the
various citrus fruits. Soon the wealth of the New World
would be as deeply rooted in the fertile soil of these
plantations as in the gold and emeralds from the Peruvian
mines and the pearl fisheries along the coast.

Consuelo complained bitterly of the mosquitoes and
sandflies but the constant irritation of these insects, together with the more serious threat from hidden snakes
in the undergrowth, failed to counter Maria's fascination with the verdant growth, the beauty of the hum-
mingbirds and flamingos, even the gaudy plumage of
the raucous parrots.

As usual, Don Luis seemed as bored and reticent as
Maria was enthusiastic. He answered her questions po-
litely but she sensed some undercurrent of passion she
could not fathom. Once she caught him staring at her
so intently that she immediately dropped her gaze in
confusion. In that smouldering stare she read a mixture
of reluctant admiration and blatant desire.

Now they were away from the Residency she hoped
she might talk with him more freely, gain a new understanding and respect. The wedding was so close on them

now, her need to feel that her husband would not despise her or treat her with open disdain was becoming desperate.

Eventually Don Luis turned his mount inland between lanes of high-standing sugarcane, and made for a knoll of higher ground, where there was an excellent view of the bay. He dismounted, then came to lift her down and did a like service for Consuelo. Here there was a little wayside shrine and Don Luis made a reverent obeisance, which she and Consuelo copied. He moved to the edge of the hill and she paced silently at his side. Consuelo drew apart, watchful, aware how necessary it was for her charge to have serious talk with her betrothed.

Maria stared thoughtfully at his frowning countenance, then said deliberately, 'Don Luis, clearly my presence displeases you. You have made that very obvious. Was the report of my appearance unduly flattering, so that now you find yourself saddled with a bride you cannot warm to?'

He frowned disdainfully. Obviously her plain speaking both embarrassed and infuriated him. 'You are as lovely as I was promised; more so, if that were possible.'

'Yet you are displeased by the match. Since it seems inevitable, can we not be friends?'

He stiffened and turned to face her directly. His mouth was working and that strange glitter in his eyes was now almost frenetic. 'Friends? You and I? My father has commanded this marriage. I am a dutiful son and will obey, but do you think I should find it pleasurable to be matched with the daughter of a condemned heretic?'

She flinched as if he had struck her. 'Heretic? I fail to understand you, *señor*. My father——'

He made a derisive flick of his fingers. 'Your father? Who talks of your father? It was your mother, that bitch of an Englishwoman, who confessed her heresy in the prison of the Holy Office at Malaga and blatantly refused to be won from her stubbornness. She died in her black obduracy and was damned for it.'

It was as if someone had tightened a metal band round Maria's chest. She felt suddenly that she could not breathe, let alone reply.

Don Luis had moved from her as if to put distance between them and was staring down over the harbour.

'I cannot bring myself to forgive such arrant wickedness. The King will never be brought to accept us at court.' His voice had lost some of its thickness as if, already, he was shocked by the force of his own revelation. 'He is a pious son of Holy Church. He will hold me in contempt for accepting you in marriage. How can my hopes of preferment ever be fulfilled? You are the stumbling block. My father selfishly sacrifices my ambitions for his own present financial difficulties.'

Since she made no reply he turned back to her accusingly.

She could find nothing to say. Her tongue froze to the roof of her mouth as her thoughts raced. This, then, was the reason why her father had wanted her out of Spain. She had known she was different, had considered her mixed blood had made her ineligible for a position at court—but this... She could not believe it. Her mother had been one of Queen Mary's ladies and Mary had burned heretics, even princes of the Church—and her father had done nothing? He had loved her mother so, yet he had done nothing? Her mind shied from the terrible thoughts of what her mother had suffered in the prison of the Holy Office. She had heard snatches of talk about others who had vanished from sight. Her father had always discouraged such gossip, any speculation concerning their fate. Had Consuelo known? Surely she had done so, she had wet-nursed Maria from her birth, been with her mother when the soldiers had come for her—yet——

Maria turned to where Consuelo knelt by the shrine. She made some inarticulate sound, as if she would alert her duenna to her side, but her mouth was still dry.

'Doña Maria.' Don Luis spoke gruffly and she turned back to him, her lips parting soundlessly. 'Please, I

should not have spoken. It seems you were not aware—
we should return to the Residency.'

She shook her head and he moved to take her hand.
Instinctively she lashed out at him with her riding whip
and he recoiled.

'You are upset, angry. This has been a shock. When
you have had time to talk to your duenna—please, Doña
Maria, you must say nothing of this at the Residency.
Don Carlos must not be told that I have spoken out.
My father would be furious——'

'And your father's anger disturbs you more than this
imminent marriage with the daughter of a heretic, it
seems.' She had found her voice at last and contempt
edged her tone. 'Or is it that you, too, find the contents
of my dower chests sufficient to lessen the intensity of
your disgust?'

He took one more step towards her.

'Don't touch me,' she snapped.

Consuelo rose, startled by the vehemence of Maria's
tone. She raised a hand and started towards the two.

Maria had no desire for her duenna's presence either.
Like a wounded animal, she wanted only to crawl away
by herself, and suffer this terrible blow alone. Her
mother, a condemned heretic? The thought could not
be borne. They could not meet, not even in heaven, for
heretics must dwell forever in purgatory, forever bereft
of God's love. Don Luis had said she had refused to
recant. Had she burned at the stake, and no one had
dared to tell Maria?

Don Luis signalled to Consuelo to approach. He recognised the need for Maria to be away from him. He
said sullenly, 'I will help you to mount your horse.'

'Don't touch me, I said. Lead him to a rock. I will
manage.'

Consuelo approached timidly and reached for Maria's
arm. '*Querida*, what is it? He has not offered you some
insult?'

Maria gave a harsh laugh. 'Oh, no, Consuelo. Don
Luis would do nothing so ill-bred as to offer me dis-
courtesy. He merely tells me he has no wish to marry

the child of a bitch of an Englishwoman who was condemned for heresy. It is bad for his hopes of royal favour.'

Consuelo's eyes widened and she turned to where Don Luis was leading Maria's horse to a convenient flat rock which might form a mounting block.

'*Querida*——'

'You knew,' Maria mouthed, and there was hatred in her eyes for the older woman.

Consuelo recoiled from her as Luis had done. She opened and closed her mouth like a startled fish. '*Querida*, you must understand——'

'I understand only that I was ill-prepared for this dishonourable match, and deliberately kept so.'

'Oh, no, *querida*, not dishonourable. Don Luis is——'

'A pious son of Holy Church who despises me,' Maria finished, bitterly. 'I cannot marry him.'

Consuelo let out a wail of distress. '*Querida*, consider——'

But Maria had walked past her to her waiting mount, and, shrugging off Don Luis's hand to assist her, climbed into the saddle.

He went to lift Consuelo on to her own mount and Maria turned from both of them. Tears of bewilderment and anger were welling up in her eyes and they must not see them.

He rode up to her, his eyes sliding unwillingly from meeting hers. 'Then we will start back?'

She inclined her chin in a stiff gesture of assent. He lifted his riding crop to point the way.

Suddenly, from the harbour, came the deafening bark of a cannon.

Maria's mount sidled wildly, its eyes rolling in alarm, and she fought briefly to keep her seat. Don Luis gave a muffled oath and reached across to once more seize her bridle rein. He led her to the head of the knoll from which they had a clear view of the harbour beneath.

Maria followed Don Luis's gaze, her horse now under control but still skittish and moving uneasily. He was a sensitive animal and had already been disturbed by her awkward efforts to mount, and sensed all was not well with his rider. Consuelo, at her side, moved her mount nervously some way from them.

Even from this distance, where people were moving about like ants, Maria could see something was wrong on the harbour front. A puff of smoke drifted across the clear blue of the sky and two ships, clearly etched against the horizon, could be glimpsed approaching the harbour mouth.

Don Luis spoke curtly, his breath rasping with shock. 'Someone's firing on our defences. *Santissimo*, pirates, Englishmen, most probably!'

Again the thundering roar of shot resounded across the bay.

'Can you be sure? Could it not be some sort of salute, for the Visita? Visiting ships, perhaps?'

'No, look, they're running out the fortress culverins.'

She stared open-mouthed, astonished as the frenzied activity intensified below. It seemed that, for moments, none of them could find a will to do anything but watch in horrified bewilderment. Consuelo gave a little quiet moan of terror.

Maria said desperately, 'But the fortress and harbour watch must already be alerted. Surely our defences are adequate?'

Don Luis ground his teeth in fury. 'These dogs of Englishmen have the Devil's own luck as well as some hell-spawned skill at arms. It's likely the fleet put in elsewhere along the coast and have taken us by surprise. I can see only two ships but there'll be more standing further out. We can but hope and pray. If they loot the town——' He shrugged expressively, then, without warning, he leaned across to bring his riding whip hard down on Maria's horse's withers.

'Now, ride like the wind for the Residency!'

She tried to cry out some protest, some alarm for Consuelo, whom, in his panic, he appeared to have forgotten, but her horse gave a terrified snort and went off at the gallop, and the breath was torn from her mouth.

Maria was a fine horsewoman but she found it hard to stay in the saddle. The frightened beast slithered and scrambled over stones and out-grown roots in its headlong plunge downhill. She lost her riding hat in the first minutes and her hair, torn free of its pins, streamed in a heavy brown cloud round her shoulders. Once her horse reared, frightened again by some small animal in its path, and she kept her seat only by clinging frantically to its mane. Her heart was thudding wildly and her eyes blurred with sweat and tears. Grimly she held on, not knowing if Don Luis still rode by her side or Consuelo had followed. She had no time now to fear what was happening in the town. All her attention was fixed on staying safe throughout this terrible ride.

It was only to be expected that her mount could not continue to stay safe on so difficult a terrain and in such a lather of sheer terror. It jarred abruptly to a sickening halt and Maria was flung to the ground. She heard herself scream sharply as if from a distance. The breath was jolted from her so that, at first, she could hardly breathe at all. Fortunately she had fallen in open ground, so had not encountered a rock or tree trunk. She lay stunned, gasping like a landed fish, unable to move.

Don Luis rode up and stared down at her wide-eyed. His nostrils were flared, his lips drawn back from his teeth in a tight grimace. He mastered his own mount only with difficulty.

'We must reach the Residency. If we are cut off in the town...' His voice was sharp with panic.

She forced herself to move, struggling forward on to her knees. She must have struck her head, for her vision was impaired and there was a blinding pain across her right eye.

Astonishingly, he made no move to dismount, as she managed to stand and stumble towards her own horse. Obviously it was injured for, otherwise, it would have taken off without her for the town. She reached blindly for the trailing rein and managed to pull herself fully upright on to her feet.

'Don Luis,' she begged, 'you must help me to mount.'

He shook his head impatiently, his staring eyes intent on the carnage below them, then, suddenly, he whipped up his mount and took off without a backward glance.

Maria leaned against her horse's sweat-stained shoulder. Her vision was clearing but she was too shocked and numbed to do anything but garner her strength. Even now she could not really believe that Don Luis had abandoned her in such a cowardly manner. She could hear the pounding and scrabbling of his mount's hoofs in the wooded terrain ahead of her, then nothing but the terrified whirring of wings as the birds overhead wheeled and darted, alarmed by his desperate passage.

The numbness was beginning to leave her and she was conscious of pain as the sprains and bruises acquired in the fall made themselves felt. She could stand, walk, thank the Virgin, and she had broken no bones, but her head wound oozed blood and the pain intensified, and her right shoulder was now a torment. Experimentally, she moved the fingers of her right hand and gave a great gasp of relief to find she had not been mistaken. There was a bad sprain but no fractured bone.

She gave her attention then to the lathered and trembling horse. If he had broken a leg, what could she do? She had no pistol to put him out of his agony and, in all events, she flinched from the necessity of such a task. She had been thrown before, of course, but never so heavily, and had always been on her own *estancia* where assistance had been readily available. Gently she examined the horse's left foreleg. The animal shied nervously but she persisted. There was a bad swelling above the fetlock but she believed that the horse, too, had escaped the fatal tragedy of a broken bone, but clearly it could not proceed at any speed. It seemed unwilling or unable to put weight on the injured limb. She patted its shiny neck encouragingly.

'There, fellow, you will be well soon. You must find your own way home or––God willing––I will send a groom to fetch you.'

It was then that she heard Consuelo calling her name, her voice shrill with terror. She called back and soon the duenna rode up and stared down at her charge in horror.

'I could not find you and this son of Satan seemed to have a will of its own. I couldn't manage it,' she panted.

'What is it, *querida*? Where is Don Luis?'

Maria shrugged. 'I took a fall. My horse is injured. Don Luis rode off.'

'He left you?' Consuelo's tone rose to a shriek of anger. Never in her life had she encountered such contemptible conduct. 'I was astonished at the little consideration he bestowed on me, leaving me to fend for myself like that. I imagine he knew I would follow but— to leave you, a lady, and his betrothed——'

'It is no matter,' Maria said wearily. 'Doubtless he considered it more essential to reach the Residency and get help for me.'

'But——'

'And that must be your first consideration. No, don't dismount. You will find it difficult to get up again without a groom to help. You must follow the path down, Consuelo, to the town. There'll be men-at-arms there. You can help me most by bringing one back with a spare horse.'

'I won't leave you——'

'Consuelo, you are slower on foot than I——'

'But you are hurt!'

Maria's need, now, was to persuade the older woman to go. It would be pointless for them both to be in peril and Consuelo must reach the Residency. Luis's fear had been real enough. The town would be looted. Consuelo would be in far greater peril than Maria. Her breathing was not easy. She carried too much weight and, if caught, she would be summarily dispatched. Who would want an elderly, plain serving woman for entertainment or ransom? She cut off Consuelo's wails of protest and assumed her most imperative attitude.

'Did you hear me, Consuelo? I need an escort. I order you to go, immediately.'

As Luis had done to her mount, she struck Consuelo's horse a stinging blow with her whip. The beast whinnied and reared and Consuelo cried out fearfully, but Maria was not to be gainsaid. She struck out at the beast again and it took off with Consuelo clinging on for dear life, her wails cut off by the wind.

Maria turned back to her own mount and patted him once more. The sun would soon be fully up. She must not stay here, exposed, in this barren terrain. First she must lead the horse into the shaded scrub ahead, get her second wind, then struggle on foot down into town.

CHAPTER SIX

MARIA could hear the screaming even before she caught her first sight of the harbour. She checked in her weary tramp to pause and take breath.

Since entering the area of dense vegetation, the view of the town had been lost to her, but now she was approaching the outskirts and the din and confusion of battle preparations met her.

She had sense enough to realise that she could be in real danger of molestation in the town. She was without escort and, looking down ruefully, she saw how torn and dust-stained her riding dress was, her hair dishevelled and still streaming over her shoulders. Her appearance would undoubtedly cause some disquiet when she arrived at the Residency. She considered if her best plan might be to remain here for a while, just outside the town, in the shade of the trees, well hidden, and hope the emergency would soon be over.

Despite Don Luis's despicable panic, she was confident that Don Piero had the defences of the town well in hand. She had heard Don Carlos explain that the entrance to Cartagena harbour was difficult for shipping. The currents were unpredictable, and only shipmasters well acquainted with this part of the coast found it practicable to navigate there. Cartagena stood on a sandbank protected on two sides by thick mangrove swamps. The harbour fort had been built strategically on the narrow spit of land which effectively divided the outer basin of the harbour from the inner. This was why, so far, Cartagena had proved less open to attack from piratical vessels. Surely, then, it would not be so difficult for the colony to fight off this challenge.

Over the last week Maria had heard talk of a possible attack, though discussions had been hastily cut off when the ladies were present. Only a few days ago, the colony had been heartened by the arrival of a Spanish vessel with news that another galleon would soon be dispatched from the home country to add to the strength of the squadron which guarded the Indies.

Don Piero was no fool despite his jovial manner, and he had already made extensive preparations. High barricades had been built along the length of the stone causeway, the Caleda, which linked the promontory with the town, and a heavy chain had been drawn across the inner basin to the harbour, where an armed galleass and two galleys had been placed on alert.

During their ride from the town, Don Luis had pointed out the lines of poisoned stakes which had been erected along the shoreline against the possibility of an attempted landing. Yet he had so needed to reach the protection of the Residency that he had ridden off in a sweat of fear, leaving Maria and Consuelo to fend for themselves.

Though she dreaded the walk through the town, Maria decided it would be best to follow his example without delay, so she gritted her teeth and struggled on. From time to time she heard the booming of cannon, so shots were being exchanged between ships and shore.

As she entered the outskirts of the town itself, a party of Indians fled by her towards the mangrove swamps and plantations—slaves, most likely, making their bids for freedom. That could not last for long; they would be rounded up easily once the troubles were over and returned to their masters.

This part of the town was deserted. The civilian occupants of the shuttered houses and shops were huddling inside, hoping the disturbances would leave them and their property untouched. It could not be far now to the Residency. When she reached the harbour front, she'd be in sight of it. Perhaps one of the defending officers from the fort would be freed from his duties to escort her to safety. Her shoes were almost in ribbons and her feet were rubbed sore. The aching of her shoulder had certainly not lessened.

As she approached the main square she saw that the corsairs had breached the fortress and the causeway defences, for pirates and defenders were engaged in bitter hand-to-hand fighting. Maria drew back in horror against the adobe wall of a shuttered *posada*, or tavern. The attackers appeared to have the advantage, at least to Maria's bemused eyes. They were brandishing long pikes and clad in heavier armour than their opponents. The sunlight glanced off polished helmets and cuirasses. The Spanish defenders, used to the hotter climate, had come to war in their quilted cotton jackets, which, though light, could still deflect cutlass and pike thrusts. The Spanish musketeers fired a volley. Through the clearing smoke Maria glimpsed the white, grey and brown habits of Dominican monks and friars among the ranks of the colonists. The corsairs fell back before the superior gunfire, but were soon joined and thrust forward again by numbers of whooping pirates from the waterfront barricades and the Spanish flanks were turned and broken.

There were hysterical screams and shouts that the town had already fallen to the enemy. 'Fly for the mangrove swamps and scrubland!'

One wall of the unfinished church crumbled before her eyes, and oaths, screams and moans told her that the shot had taken its toll of lives. She whimpered, averting her eyes from the horror of the sight. Reason told her she should run, yet her limbs seemed frozen to the spot. Her fear was mounting moment by moment and she knew she must make the effort to reach some safe shelter.

The breach in the harbour defences had given rise to sheer panic. Men thudded past her, deaf to the shrieked commands of their desperate officers. Maria's foot slipped in spilt blood and she caught back a scream. A man lay sprawled beneath the masonry of the ruined church—half his body must have been crushed. Unable to help him, she swallowed down a sharp rush of bile to her mouth and whispered a prayer for his soul.

She pushed and clawed her way through the fleeing soldiers and townsfolk down towards the waterfront. Hesitantly she put out a hand to delay a running guard officer. Impatiently he beat her hand from his sleeve.

'Please, will you help me to reach the Governor? I am Doña Maria——'

'Not now, *señorita*. Get back to your own house. Can't you see that the pirate dogs will soon be looting the town?'

He cupped his hand to his mouth to bawl urgent commands to the gunners, still frantically manning one of the harbour culverins.

Maria drew back from him. It was clear she could expect no help from that quarter. A brawny auquebusier thrust her unceremoniously from his path.

Now she could see what had caused this mass desertion. The great foreign ships had drawn in closer. They were draped funereally in black, a sight to send a *frisson* of cold terror down her spine. As Luis had surmised, there was a whole fleet of them.

There came a deafening, explosive roar from the harbour's inner basin and Maria saw one of the defending galleys break up in a sheet of flame. Even from this distance, she could hear the frantic screams of crew and galley slaves. Men scrabbled helplessly in the water, some still chained to sections of the shattered oars. The second galley began to move slowly towards the narrows near the fort, apparently in a desperate bid to escape the punishing shot from the corsair pinnaces, now moving inexorably closer in to harbour. Maria closed her eyes and swallowed. One of their last hopes was gone. The defensive chain across the inner basin must have been lifted to allow the vessel's escape. The town and harbour lay now entirely at the mercy of the looting corsairs.

The water of the basin seemed now to be filled with small boats. Some had already made fast to the causeway and men were scrambling ashore under intermittent continuing fire from the fort. Many fell to a hail of pistol shot. A shower of arrows sped harmlessly by one group of attackers. A round shot from a nearby culverin narrowly missed another boat from which men jumped, waist-high in water, to reach the harbour. To Maria's terrified gaze, nothing seemed to deter them. They were yelling and singing, armed with pistols and cutlasses, most of them naked to the waist, their hair caught back from their brows by colourful bandanas. Still they came on and those who were left of the hardy Spanish defenders fell before them.

Maria was unable to tear her shocked gaze from the savage hand-to-hand carnage. Common sense told her she must get back the way she had come, but she could not summon the strength or the courage. These fearsome men would give no quarter and all women would fall easy prey to them. She must run now, hide with the others who'd already taken flight within the plantation fields. It was her only hope. Yet the solid press of bodies continuing to flee in panic was now too great to allow her passage. A remnant of the defenders fought on doggedly, but many of the rank and file were beginning to desert and further shots from the leading pinnace crashed into a house behind Maria, damaging buildings on either side of it. The inhabitants erupted into the street as the roof and walls began to collapse. There were women among them and a sortie of pirates, seeing them, gave great whoops of delight. One of the younger women, recognisable as being well-born, for her gown was of silk and richly decorated with silver braid, was scooped up by one grinning corsair, his arms bloodied to the elbow. A desperate attempt to prevent him by a slightly built youngster who might have been her brother was foiled by a cutlass blow to the face. The stripling gave a shrill scream and dropped like a stone.

Maria hid her face against the rough wooden support of a house, and covered her ears as the girl was borne off, begging and screaming, by her triumphant captor.

Maria's delay was to cause her own downfall. She experienced an agonising pain as her long, flowing hair was yanked hard from behind and a stained, bloodied hand forced her chin round, so she might see her attacker.

He was a big man, fully dressed in loose canvas drawers and a torn shirt, a red woollen seaman's cap perched askew on his head. He kept his painful hold on her, while he thrust his reddened cutlass through the leathern sheath on his baldric.

'Well, my pretty *señorita*, it looks as if you might be worth any loot I might lose by attending to you.'

He spoke in English. So Don Luis had been correct: these attackers were English cut-throats out for rapine and plunder. She made no attempt to fight him. He was not young, and his paunch and flabby muscles made for his size rather than brawny strength, but to struggle free from him was beyond her puny ability and she knew it. Proudly she stared back into his bronzed, rat-like features, and when he threw back his head and bellowed with laughter she spat at him in fury. His response was to force back her head so hard she was afraid he would break her neck.

'Little Spanish puss 'as sharp claws, 'as she?' he grated. 'We'll soon clip 'em, never fear that.'

He was about to drag his prize into the privacy of some deserted house when an authoritative voice halted him in his tracks. 'Evans, let the woman go. You heard the orders. Get on to the Residency.'

'Aye, aye, sir, but the girl——'

'Take her to one of the boats, then. She can be kept under guard there.'

Obstinately, Maria's captor kept his tight hold on her hair. 'She's mine,' he snarled. 'I'll not have her taken by——'

The corsair officer menaced his inferior with his drawn cutlass. 'You'll do as you're ordered, damn you.'

Respect for his superior apparently prevailed, as well as a healthy regard for his own skin, for the seaman jerked Maria round in the direction of the waterfront.

'Come on then, my pretty. I'll have to wait, it seems, to see what you're made of, but what's good'll stand waiting, won't it?' He delivered her a snag-toothed, wolfish grin.

Half sick and dazed with terror, Maria allowed him to propel her towards the ships' boats now moored to the causeway. She was so relieved that her immediate peril was over that she stumbled along without protest until another pair of brawny arms seized her and forced her into the stern of the nearest jollyboat. There was a shouted exchange between captor and her new guard. Her arms were roughly forced behind her and secured with a length of tarred rope. Then she was flung on to her face, retching weakly at the pain of the blow which had sent her sprawling and the stink of tar and bilge-water which threatened to overwhelm her. She lay still, hoping her new guard would deem her unconscious.

Her head ached abominably, yet her thoughts raced, horrific images forming and reforming in her tortured brain. There seemed to be no defence against these seamen from hell. The town must fall and the fate of that poor girl she'd seen captured would be the lot of all women here in Cartagena. If she could bide her time there might yet be a chance to escape, but, with her hands bound, she'd hardly be able to scramble from the boat and the corsairs would mount guard on their only lines of retreat. But to wait, passively, for her fate to catch up on her—she murmured a sobbed entreaty to the Virgin to save her. These pirates would be bent on acquiring loot, primarily. They would demand a ransom from the Governor for the town itself and for the more wealthy and important captives. If she could convince one of the ships' officers of her identity and her coming marriage to the Governor's aide, she might escape ravishment.

The sun was high overhead now and it became punishingly hot in the boat. Maria tried to wriggle into a more comfortable position which would shield her eyes from the glare, for she had managed to scramble on to her back again now, but her movements were hampered by her pinioned wrists, and she blushed to think how undignified she must appear with her skirts askew, displaying her sprawled legs to the eyes of lascivious seamen. The guard, whom she had not seen clearly, seemed to have moved away some distance from the boat for his tuneless whistle could not be heard. The shots and shouting appeared to be coming now from further off than formerly. She managed to struggle up until her back was partly supported by the boat's gunwhale and drooped her head on her chest.

Misery and exhaustion had their way and, finally, she fell into a part doze and part stupor.

She came to herself with a sudden start, as the boat moved suddenly under her and heavy articles were dumped unceremoniously into the stern. The corsairs were moving back from the town towards the harbour, then. She could hear them yelling triumphantly in their heretical English tongue. The raid had obviously been successful, beyond their wildest hopes. A renewed stab of fear shot through her. What of the Residency and the town? Had the English fired it? What of Don Luis? Had he managed to make good his escape or had he been attacked within the Residency? And Consuelo, how had she fared? Maria's heart contracted painfully as she wondered if she had done well to send her duenna off ahead of her. Yet how could it have served either of them to stay together? Consuelo would have been taken with her or dispatched as of no use to her captors. Consuelo had been everything to her since childhood—nurse, companion, confidante. She loved the older woman as a mother. Even if Consuelo had escaped harm and managed to flee with some of the other women to sanctuary in the plantations or mangrove swamps, who would care for her later if Maria was not by to ensure her future?

There was a murmured word of command and heavy bodies descended into the well of the boat. Oars were unshipped and the line to the causeway cast off. Someone seated himself and stirred the shapeless bundle lying in the stern. Maria ineffectively tried to turn away her face. She was ashamed and embarrassed more than she was truly afraid.

A voice which sent cold shivers of terror down her spine, a voice she recognised only too well, said, 'Ralf, you dog, what have we here? You know I made my orders very clear. No women, until the success of the raid was assured and I gave word for men to enjoy shore leave.'

'She ain't mine, Captain. Josh Evans, he brought her down to the boat. Mr Swift's instructions. Evans, he weren't best pleased.'

There was a chuckle. 'I can imagine. Well, she'd best come aboard with the rest of the loot and Evans can claim her then, if and when I say he can.'

'Aye, aye, Captain.'

'In the meantime, let's examine the goods and judge their quality; that will decide Evans's fair share of the prize in the share-out.'

Strong fingers turned Maria's chin inexorably, so that she was forced to gaze into a pair of slate-grey eyes she had last seen appraising her in her own chamber at her uncle's house in Cadiz. She gave a little sob of despair.

He threw back his head and roared with laughter. 'Well, well, how the gods do favour me. Doña Maria Santiago y Talavera herself, and I've come half across the world to find her again.'

Her eyes widened in astonishment and he laughed again.

'You are wondering how I knew where you were, *muy doña*. I have my sources of information. After our last meeting, which was exceedingly pleasant if rather hurried,' he bowed his head in a gesture of mock courtesy, 'I asked on the harbour front what was known of Don Felipe's niece at whose house I had been so fittingly entertained.'

The grey eyes danced while her lips trembled.

'I was told of her intention to travel to the New World on the next ship to marry her betrothed, aide to the Governor of Cartagena, so you see we had an assignation, you and I.'

She closed her eyes to block out that amused stare.

'Indeed, I have only just now been enquiring about you at the Residency. Don Piero could not enlighten me as to your whereabouts. Your betrothed, the illustrious Don Luis, did not seem sure either, nor was he unduly concerned. Yet, according to Don Piero, you had ridden out together. I thought the glances he cast his aide were less than favourable. Now I find you conveniently fallen into my lap.'

She stared back defiantly into his jubilantly mocking countenance, unwilling to give him the satisfaction of hearing her voice tremble if she attempted to reply.

He had prospered, obviously, and he looked tolerably well groomed, even after the exertion of battle. His tall figure had filled out. His golden beard was now exquisitely cut and pointed, his hair bleached even lighter by the sun than she remembered it, his complexion healthily tanned. There were powder smudges on one cheek and on his shirt of fine linen. She looked hurriedly away from the ominously reddish brown stains on his right arm, bared to the elbow, where he had rolled up his sleeves for the combat ahead.

He had managed to escape, then, and had joined up with this English raiding party. She was bemused by the encounter, yet there seemed an inevitability about it, as if she had known that the two of them would meet again, that she had doomed herself by that unaccountable decision to turn towards the slave deck that day so many months ago, in order to see a man of her mother's race.

His eyes continued to mock her. Then he released his hold on her chin and leaned back in his seat to let his gaze take in fully her dishevelled state. His bearded lips parted in a wolfish smile. 'No word for me? No greeting? No anxiety even to know the fates of your friends at the Residency?'

She chose to reply in Castilian. 'I assume Cartagena will be ransomed and that Don Piero and his lady will be safe from your bully boys, though I understand it is the custom of your piratical dogs to prefer plunder and rapine, even if it means loss of solid gain.'

His grey eyes narrowed and the smile grew less pleasant. 'Perhaps, *muy doña*, I too will prefer to slake my lust and my blood-thirst rather than accept a ransom for you? Who knows?'

She went white to the lips at his jibe, but stared proudly beyond him to the two sturdy oarsmen who were steadily

rowing the boat towards its mother ship. 'Yet surely, by
the strange rules of your kind, I belong to my captor.
Is not that the way of your piratical brotherhood, that
he who takes keeps his own plunder?'

'Not usually,' he returned mildly. 'Often the sum total
of the loot is assembled and shared out between members
of the crew according to their share of the action and
the state of any injuries they might well have sustained
and need to be compensated for. You think you would
fare better with Evans?' The tone of the question was
coolly contemptuous. He continued to address her in
English, whether to enable his men to hear and understand his words or to force her to accept the truth of
her own descent she could not say, but a further shiver
of apprehension went through her.

Her flesh crawled at the thought of the rat-faced man
who had captured her and yanked at her hair so cruelly.
She swallowed painfully at the memory of his fetid breath
hot on her face. She could not repress a shudder of
horror.

He saw it and laughed. 'Don't be afraid, Doña Maria.
I'll save you from him. Evans is no fool. He'll accept
the price I'll pay him in compensation for his lost—
pleasures, shall we say? We'll be equals at last, you my
slave, when I was once, and so recently, yours.'

'You were never my slave, *señor*.' She was stung to
answer him this time in his own tongue. 'It was never
my wish that men should suffer so at the oars of our
galleys, even though you deserved your fate as a thief
and a pirate.'

There was a roar of mirth from the oarsmen and her
face flamed. He seemed unconcerned by his men's impudence and made no effort to silence them.

The boat grounded against the stern of the parent
vessel and the men held her steady for their captain to
mount the ship's ladder to the deck.

He bent and lifted Maria into a sitting position. She
flinched as he drew his dagger and the blade glistened
in the rays of the dying sun.

'Be still, now. I only want to free your arms. You will find it difficult to mount the ladder with your wrists bound.' He sliced through the confining rope and the blood raced back into her tensed fingers. She had to catch back a gasp of pain. Her pride refused to allow her to reveal her fear to these men. The thought of mounting that swaying ladder terrified her, but she allowed him to turn her body so that she faced the ship's side.

'Can you manage, or shall I carry you?'

The humiliation of being carted aboard like a sack of grain prevailed over her terror. She shook off his hand on her arm and began to climb.

Willing hands from above drew her on to the deck and she shook herself free of them the moment she could and stood, staring woodenly ahead, ignoring the openly salacious glances from the little knot of crew members who had been left aboard to guard the ship.

The captain's voice was peremptory, not to be disobeyed. 'Get to work, you men, there's baggage to be stored.'

'Aye, aye, Cap'n.'

Maria's arm was taken and she went, unresisting, towards the steep companion ladder which led below decks.

Even here, at anchor, reflected green light from the stern windows kept the master cabin cool. Maria took a step inside and let out her breath in a little sigh, glad of the relief from the unrelenting glare of the late afternoon sun outside.

The ship's captain moved by her towards a table by the bulkhead. 'You'll have a raging thirst, no doubt. Sit down before those trembling legs of yours give way beneath you.'

Her cheeks flamed at his imperious tone, but she was glad to obey him. There was a leather-backed chair by the bed and she sank thankfully into it.

She had expected the cabin of this corsair ship to be raffishly and opulently furnished from the stolen plunder of countless Spanish and other merchant ships, but it was comfortably though sparsely furnished; a bed, a table littered with the impedimenta of seamanship, compass, charts, cross-staff, which she knew was used for navigation from her questions to the *Isabella*'s captain. There were also two chairs, a stool and a sturdy sea-chest. The place had been scrubbed clean and the glass in the window and in the hanging lantern gleamed bright, but there were no luxurious hangings or carpets. The leathern jack of wine he thrust into her hand was serviceable, without ornamentation. Perhaps, as yet, this captain had taken little plunder from which he could enrich his surroundings.

She drank gratefully. The wine was of the finest. In this, at least, he didn't stint himself.

His bearded lips parted in a smile as, trembling, she wiped her lips with her fingers after draining the jack.

'Thank you. I—I was a long time in the boat in that sun.' She watched as he drained his own jack and, taking hers from her, put both down on the table.

'What, *señor*, do you intend to do with me? There will be a ransom, at least——' She swallowed painfully. Could she be sure of that? Would Don Luis take this opportunity of ridding himself of her? There was no binding responsibility encumbent on Don Piero as to her welfare.

The English captain was regarding her quizzically, one fair eyebrow raised. 'You think they might not consider you worth the sum we ask, these fine *hidalgo* friends of yours?'

Feeling the warning of tears smart her lashes, she looked hurriedly away from him.

'If he does not, your betrothed is a bigger fool than I first thought.' The Englishman's tone was mocking, but Maria detected a sharper note to his next question. 'He takes exception to your English blood. Is that it?'

'My mother was, indeed, English,' she snapped, 'though how you can be aware of that——'

'A guess only,' he said, putting up a hand as if to restrain her from further argument. 'Your English is exceptionally good and your colouring might suggest a dilution of pure Castilian blood.'

'My parentage is none of your business, *señor*. My loyalties have always been and will always be to Spain.'

'Your mother is dead?'

The question was softly put and yet it touched so shrewdly upon the terrible revelation Don Luis had made earlier that she was hard pressed to prevent tears coming at full flood.

'Yes.' Her answer was whispered and he was forced to bend close to hear it.

'In a Spanish prison?' Her eyes opened wide in shocked bewilderment at his knowledge and he nodded grimly. 'Accused of heresy?'

'How could you know?' Her voice was hoarse with the full force of her suffering. His probing had opened the terrible wound Don Luis had dealt her which, during the terrible hours of the attack on Cartagena, she had been forced to thrust to the back of her mind.

He shrugged. 'That fate has overtaken others.'

'She was no heretic. I will not believe it.'

'Yet your father was, apparently, unable to save her.' His tone was dry.

'No.'

'How bravely your Spanish grandees protect their own.'

'How dare you impugn my father? He, too, is dead. If he were not, he would take you to task for daring to suggest he—did not love her. I know——' She broke down then and he waited for the storm to pass.

'I'm sure he did everything he could.' His tone became brisk again, businesslike. 'I shall be gone from this cabin for some time. You had best get some sleep. I'll lock the door, as much for your protection as for your restraint, as I am sure you will realise.' There was a savage gleam of mockery once more in his slate-grey eyes. 'I'll send up my cabin boy with some food. He has a key but you can trust him.'

Her eyes went fearfully to the bed. She longed to take his advice. She was physically and mentally exhausted by all the terrible events of the day. He strode to the sea-chest and, throwing back the heavy lid, rummaged about inside. 'Here, you'd better put this on for now and this for later.'

Two bundles of silken garments landed on her knee. She touched one in outraged horror. It was in garish red silk. Without even examining it, she guessed it to be outrageously low at the corsage. Her protest died on her lips as he said, cuttingly, 'You can hardly continue to wear your present attire.'

Shamed, she followed his critical gaze down the length of her riding habit, filthy and so badly torn as to be hardly decent.

He waited for no more but hastened from the cabin.

She sat, bemused, until the click of the key in the lock and the sound of feet on the companion ladder roused her to awareness that he had mounted to the poop deck.

She laid out the red gown on the bed and found that the second garment was an undershift, soft as thistledown and beautifully embroidered. He had not, then, kept entirely aloof from the pleasures of looting. These garments had either been taken as plunder or left behind by some dusky beauty who had warmed his bed. She felt a deep aversion to wearing them, but necessity would force her to do so.

She waited till a knock on the cabin door and the light voice of a boy requested permission to enter.

The lad was perhaps thirteen or fourteen, lanky, tousle-haired but clean enough. He looked at her with frank curiosity as he put down a tray holding a platter of cold meats and bread and a pewter jug and tankard. He touched a forelock respectfully.

'Cap'n Norwood says he'll dine with you later, mistress, and begs to suggest ale'll best go down with bread and meats, but there's wine on the table if'n you'd prefer it.'

'Thank you.' She answered in English and in as firm a tone as she could manage. 'You can go now,' as he hovered uncertainly.

His eyes wandered to the garments on the bed and her own flashed sapphire fire at him. He backed hastily to the door. 'Never you fear, mistress. I'll lock up safe.'

There was water in a big ewer and she stripped and washed herself, shivering at the icy touch of it on her flesh but anxious to cleanse herself of the dirt, sweat and smell of fear. The shift was clean and smelt vaguely sweet and spicy. Noises on deck were subdued by distance and she climbed into the bed and allowed herself the luxury of closing her smarting eyes.

It was full dark when she woke and she shrank back against the bulkhead in terror as she realised someone had entered the cabin while she slept.

'Who's there?' She spoke sharply in Castilian.

Captain Norwood answered her in her own tongue. 'It's the captain. I tried not to wake you, but, since you are awake now, I'll strike a light.'

His bearded features loomed above the feeble glow after he'd done his work with tinder and flint and the candle on the table lit up the cabin.

'What—what do you want?'

'At present nothing more than to dine. It's later than I thought and, finding you asleep, I was about to join my men. However, you must be hungry too. We'll summon Jem and order him to serve us here.'

'No, I'm not hungry.'

'But I am. Come, mistress, get up and dress.'

She clutched the coverlet to her agitatedly, aware that her loosened hair streamed to her shoulders in disarray and the finely woven shift must reveal the contours of pale flesh too clearly for her comfort of mind.

He waved a hand impatiently. 'Get up, I say, unless you would prefer that Jem served us as you are. I could join you in the bed——'

'No,' she gasped in sudden panic. 'I'll get up at once, if—if you will leave me.'

That mocking fair eyebrow rose again and the bearded lips broadened in a wide grin. 'Leave my own cabin, mistress?'

'Just—just while I dress.'

'That will not incommode me.'

She reverted to English, haughtily. 'I presume, by your speech, you were bred a gentleman.'

'A dog of a pirate?'

Her colour rose. 'I take nothing back. If you were not a pirate, you would not have taken part in the attack on Cartagena.'

'True.'

'Yet——'

'I am a pirate, have attacked Cartagena, and see no reason which compels me to humour your whims, mistress. Dress or join me at table as you are. I care not a whit.' He seated himself in the armchair and stretched out his long legs. 'Oblige me by sounding the little bell, there on the table by the bed. Jem will come at once.'

She flashed him a vitriolic look and turned her back on him. The red gown, which she'd lain on the chair when she'd climbed into bed, landed with a sudden flop on the floor near her, where he threw it, and she slipped aside the bed coverlet without climbing from the bed.

'You'll need to get up, sweeting,' he drawled. 'Come over here and let me do up the laces. I'm found to be a tolerable tiring maid at need.'

Seething with fury, she was forced to obey him, anxious that he would not summon the cabin boy before she was fully dressed.

Mortified, she submitted to the cool touch of his hands on her shoulders. If she rebelled, her struggles could only arouse his lust. She knew that well enough. He released her and she sought and found her hair combs, biting her lip in futile effort to restore some order to the tumbling masses and pin up the heavy dark tresses.

His expression was openly appraising. 'Leave it so, loose. It is not the first time I've seen you like this, remember?'

Memory of that second encounter between them, in her uncle's house in Cadiz, flooded over her, leaving her in a cold sweat of terror. He had lain by her side for hours then, and she had been pinioned and gagged, unable to call to servants so close at hand. He had had her at his mercy then and spared her. Would he do so again? This time she was totally helpless and he was not at the disadvantage of having to flee into a hostile town.

The boy, Jem, served them deftly. This time he did not allow his eyes to roam over her. Grimly, Maria noted the control which Norwood exerted over him and was grateful for that. Did it extend to the rest of his crew? She thought so.

She found herself unexpectedly hungry and ate with relish. Once she paused to find Captain Norwood regarding her with sardonic amusement. Hastily she wiped greasy fingers on the napkin provided and lowered her gaze to the spotless napery of the table's appointments. Now, it seemed, Norwood was ready to display his looted treasures: Spanish silver and plate, Italian glassware. The meal was well cooked in its sauces, though obviously drawn from the casks of salted flesh in the hold. The wine glowed golden and superb. She drank sparingly, but still found its fiery strength flowed through her. The stresses of the day had taken their toll. She told herself that she needed to eat and drink well, strengthen herself for the ordeal that might face her, but knew, shamed, that she was actually enjoying the fare far more than she thought she ought to do in such compromising circumstances.

Jem was summoned to remove the dishes. Maria lingered at table. Her heart was pounding and she recognised the increased dryness of mouth as a symptom of her returning fear.

The captain leaned back in his chair, smiling, his fingers playing appreciatively over the crystal of his wine goblet. When his chair scraped back from the table, she flinched instinctively. He rose and bowed courteously. 'If you will excuse me, *muy doña*, I have duties on the poop deck.'

She swallowed hard and nodded.

At the door he turned back to her. 'I suggest you get to bed.'

She swallowed again and forced out the single word, 'Here?'

His expressive eyebrow swept up in amusement again. 'Where else?'

She found it hard to move from the chair, even after he had left her. Where else indeed? Would she be any safer anywhere else on this ship but in the master's cabin? She shuddered. Undoubtedly she could fare far worse at the hands of his crew. Yet, remembering what had passed between them, could she expect their captain to be any more restrained, or, if the worst happened and he decided to forgo his demand for her ransom, as he had suggested, more gentle with her?

She slipped off the flamboyant red gown after some struggle with the laces and laid it, distastefully, over the back of a chair and climbed reluctantly into the bed, once more pulling the coverlet up to her chin. Even in the pleasant warmth of the evening, she found herself shivering.

He returned more quickly than she expected. She forced herself up to a sitting position, cowering as far from him as possible.

His grey eyes dwelt mockingly on her tumbled brown hair and the pale marble of her superb shoulders gleaming softly golden in the lantern-light.

She watched, horrified, as he stripped off sword belt and baldric, then bent to kick off his shoes. A pulse beat agitatedly in her throat and she found herself unable to say a word.

He straightened and smiled at her. 'Comfortable?'

'I—I . . .' She summoned up some remnant of dignity. 'Thank you, yes.'

He moved towards the seaman's chest and she leaned forward to see what he needed, then he was close by the bed.

I will not plead with him, she told herself firmly. It would be to no avail and the daughter of a Spanish *hidalgo* will not stoop to such craven behaviour.

'Very lovely,' he chuckled. He was speaking in English again. She noticed that he was prone to do so when he wished to discomfit her. 'What a pity that I must think of the ransom.' He reached out and cupped her chin in his hand. 'The only other safe place for you, my beauty, would have to be the brig. I couldn't guarantee that my men would obey my orders else, talk of ransom or no. By the way, I have had to compensate Evans, your captor, and extremely well for such a lost prize. I know you will be grateful for my generosity.'

She forced herself to reply to him in an even, steady tone. 'I am sure that my ransom will compensate you adequately for that, sir.'

'Perhaps,' he murmured, one finger lightly tracing the line of her lips, 'but hardly enough.' Stooping, he kissed her with quickening passion, bruising the soft flesh of her lip against her teeth. She lay very still and closed her eyes, though she felt he must be aware of her rapid heartbeat.

'You will not begrudge me that for my reward. I think even Don Luis would not, considering the limit of my forbearance. Can you imagine, *muy doña*, how much and for how long I felt the need of a woman on that hell of a galley?'

She made no reply, not even turning her head from him.

Again he chuckled, low in his throat. 'I can wait. Who knows, *muy doña*, it may be that your betrothed will not be prepared to pay the sum we ask? Then I'll not need to be so forbearing.'

She felt him move from her, away from the bed and, only slowly, opened her eyes.

There was a little swishing sound and she saw he had strung a hammock between two hooks in the timbering above them. The Visita, Don Carlos, had told her on the voyage out how the seamen had willingly adopted this comfortable form of bed from the Indians as an alternative to hard lying on the boarded lower decks and as a means of saving space. She heard the soft plop as he slipped his body into its strong supports, and then there was silence.

She lay, staring upwards, her teeth clenching hard on her lower lip. He had left the lantern glowing softly on its swinging hook. To reassure her? Or to ensure that he could see more easily if she made any move to leave the cabin?

At last her breathing quietened, but every muscle in her body remained tense.

She had slept earlier, the sleep of utter exhaustion, but now she must endure the long hours of darkness while her tortured mind turned on the horrifying events of the day and the desperate fear that neither Don Luis nor Don Piero would wish to take the responsibility of providing the sum demanded for her release.

CHAPTER SEVEN

MARIA woke with a sudden start to find Captain Norwood leaning down across the bed, watching her intently. Dappled sunlight was playing across the crumpled coverlet. Obviously she had slept late. She gave a little muffled cry and reached for the sheet, pulling it well up to her throat.

He threw back his head and laughed. 'Your modesty is very touching, *muy doña*, if a little misplaced. I have been feasting my eyes on your charms for quite some time.'

This morning he had dressed for work above deck in wide canvas trousers like a crewman, though his shirt, opened almost to his waist, was of the finest quality. His sleeves were rolled high for action. Clearly his night in the hammock had not disturbed his rest. He looked ready and eager for the day's activities. Maria looked angrily from his slate-grey eyes, alight with the now familiar mocking insolence.

Determined to nettle her further, he said, suavely, 'You appear to have slept soundly despite my hated company.' He stood up and gave her an exaggerated bow. 'Breakfast has been brought for you. Come to table, please, and eat.'

She clutched the sheet more firmly to her breast. 'I—I am not hungry, *señor*.'

He had addressed her in English and she replied in Castilian.

He ignored the fact and continued in his own tongue. 'I hope we will not have the nonsense we had last night. It is well into the morning. Of course you are hungry. Come and eat. I wish to talk to you.'

116

'I have nothing to say to you, *señor*.' Angered, for once she laid aside her intention to speak to him in Spanish and snapped back at him in English.

White teeth flashed in a smile of triumph. 'Good. I've no wish to hear complaints. I said I want to talk to you. You have only to listen.'

'Then I can do that from the bed.'

The good-humoured smile faded and she was astonished at the way his lips set in a hard line and the grey eyes narrowed in anger. 'You will obey me.'

'No.'

She thought to outface him, but decided better of the idea. Hitching the coverlet round her body, cautiously aware of it trailing awkwardly round her ankles, she left the bed and took the seat he indicated.

She had been brought a tankard of ale, meat and a bowl of fresh fruit which could only have been obtained from the town. The thought struck her forcibly that she had slept unharmed while the citizens of Cartagena suffered. She dared not think too intently of how the women, decent, well-protected women, daughters and wives of merchants and plantation owners, had suffered at the hands of the undisciplined rabble of sailors once the town had fallen. Anxious he should not read her thoughts, she lowered her gaze to her plate and forced herself to eat.

He leaned back in his chair opposite and poured ale for himself. 'So, I see you have recovered your appetite.'

She ignored the jibe.

'Well, as to what is about to become of you.'

Still she remained silent, unwilling to give him the satisfaction of recognising her growing dread.

'For the present you will remain here on the *Gloriana* and you will continue to stay within my cabin. You will never leave it without my escort. I shall see that at the appropriate times you have the necessary air and exercise. You will not attempt to suborn the cabin boy or even speak with any other member of my crew unless I am present and give you leave. You understand me?'

She nodded, dry-mouthed.

'Good. Then, for the moment, you have little to fear.' A wintry smile crossed his lips. 'Except from me, of course, and I am a hard man to cross.'

'Then you intend to keep your word and ask ransom for me?'

'I made no such promise,'

'But——'

He shrugged. 'Decisions as to important prisoners must be made by agreement among all members of the Brotherhood. It will be for Captain Drake to set terms for the town and I go soon to a meeting aboard his flagship.'

'You said that Don Piero, the Governor, was unharmed.'

'And you will be relieved to hear that the admirable Don Luis suffered not so much as a scratch.' The hard lips parted in a mockingly sweet smile again, as if he was aware of the contempt she felt for Luis.

'You will be meeting with members of the Residency household?'

'Yes. I shall accompany Drake ashore later with the other officers.'

She swallowed, hating to ask even the slightest favour of him. 'Would you—would you ask after the welfare of my duenna, Señora Henriques?'

'Ah, I seem to recall the lady who did me the favour of obtaining a change of clothing for me—under compulsion, of course. Yes, certainly, I shall be glad to make enquiries about her.'

'Do these arrangements take long? I mean——'

'You wish to know how long you'll be forced to endure my hospitality? That, *muy doña*, will depend entirely upon the sense of responsibility and the generosity of those who had charge of you.'

She watched the closing door with the accompanying click of the lock with increasing agitation. Her emotions overwhelmed her so that she found herself unable to think coherently. Captain Norwood both fascinated and terrified her. Her heart pounded uncontrollably when he had forced her to leave the bed and go to the table. That drawing together of the brows and the hard, grim line of his lips had sent a cold chill down her spine. He had said he was a hard man to cross and she believed him. Don Piero must agree to pay the ransom, yet, if he did so, she was condemned to a loveless marriage with Luis. He had made it plain that the match was totally unacceptable, that he could never come to love her, nor even respect her. And then he had abandoned her in an act of abject cowardice.

She remembered the stoicism Captain Norwood had shown at his flogging. She was sure, without need of confirmation, that he had carried himself bravely in the engagements for the capture of the town. Hot colour travelled up her throat and dyed her cheeks as she thought how it might be to lie with him in the marriage bed. Last night he had kissed her and she had felt a response within her being, a response which she had ruthlessly denied.

Yet he, too, must hold her in contempt, his prize of war, of use to him only as long as he could expect a reward for her return to her kin untouched. For that reason only had he shown her any restraint.

If she were left to his tender mercies, how long would it be before he abandoned her in some dirty, seething sea-port of the Antilles, a haunt of cut-throats like himself, to a life of humiliation and debauchery?

No, though her traitorous heart told her it would be worth the later agony of regret to lie in his arms and know true passion, she realised she was being criminally foolish. Such a fate could result only in her early death and, more terrible still, the loss of her immortal soul.

Immodest thoughts reminded her that she was most unsuitably clad. The cabin boy would be here soon to clear away the remains of her breakfast. Reluctantly she put on the gaudy red gown after examining her riding dress and deciding that it would be almost impossible to repair.

Jem, the cabin boy, announced himself before entering and she gave breathless permission. She felt acutely uncomfortable before members of Norwood's crew.

She questioned him about the fate of the town. 'Are
hostilities at an end? Are the buildings badly gutted?'

'There's been some talk of fires, mistress, and I think
the damage is bad, but it'll soon be put right, I'm sure,
after Cap'n Drake has set sail again.'

'And have you any idea when that might be?'

'Cap'n Norwood's gone aboard the *Bonaventure* to
talk terms. When they've all decided, they'll go ashore,
likely, and we'll soon know if the town grandees are
willing to pay.'

'And if they don't?'

'That's not for me to say, mistress. I 'spect the town'll
be given over to sack.'

Maria had seen enough already of the English seamen's behaviour to know what the citizens' fate would
be. They'd already tasted the bitter draught of the corsairs' triumph. There would be impassioned pleas to the
Governor to find the necessary funds and send the dogs
of English on their way.

The boy cast her a pitying glance as if he read in her
questions an implied fear for her own fate. He backed
out with the tray, after bobbing her a clumsy, subservient nod.

Maria prowled the length and breadth of the cabin.
The stern window offered little to engage her attention.
From this distance she could not see the causeway or the
town to gauge the extent of the destruction. She had no
sewing implements or she would have made a determined assault on the damaged riding dress. She would
have borne any bodging if she could have changed from
the hated red gown, but no thorough search of the sea-
chests furnished her with what she needed; needles,
thread or scissors. The hours stretched before her, long
and lonely. If her ransom was set at a high figure, and
it was likely it would be, there would be many such
tedious hours to endure before she could be free of this
cabin.

Don Piero sat back in his chair in the ornate reception-
room of the Residency and regarded his captains and
town officials with an expression that was both frus-

trated and impatient. For the last two hours they had fretted and argued, frantically attempting to wriggle free of a situation which was impossible to avoid.

Finally he lost all patience and rapped the hilt of his dagger on the fine carved desk before him, one of the few treasures spared him by the despoilers.

'Gentlemen, you heard Bishop de Oribe. *El Draco* is obdurate. Yesterday's sack of the town gave us a sample of what we can expect if he orders its complete destruction. If we persist in our refusals to meet his demands he'll do it, make no mistake about that. I have the full responsibility for this colony and I tell you now we must pay. His original demand of six hundred thousand ducats has now been reduced to a hundred and ten thousand. There is the further matter of his threat to destroy the monastery and we must bribe him with gold to desist from that course. I command you to return to your homes, make an inventory of your immediate assets, report to my steward and make arrangements for the money's delivery to the Residency as soon as possible. You are dismissed.'

Wearily he waved off further expostulation and the company rose reluctantly, their chairs scraping disagreeably on the polished floor, as they moved, still argumentative, to the door. Don Piero waved Don Luis back to his seat as he made to go with the rest.

'Stay, Luis, I must talk with you.'

He waited until the doors were closed on his voluble officers and, taking a long pull from his wine cup, sat, regarding his aide, eyes narrowed.

'What's this I hear about your reluctance to ransom Maria?'

Don Luis scowled and moved restlessly in his chair. 'I haven't the means. The remainder of her dower allotted to me has not arrived. As you well know, my father has appropriated the greater part and——'

Don Piero said quietly, 'There are jewels in the dower chests she brought with her. We can thank the Virgin these English dogs did not sack the Residency. They've dug over practically every inch of promising ground in the town in search of hidden loot, as well as despoiling the church images. The rest of the sum must be found.'

'Twenty thousand ducats?' Don Luis's voice was shrill with outrage.

Deliberately Don Piero replaced his wine cup on the desk. 'Listen to me, Luis. Doña Maria must be returned to us. What could we say to her uncle, Don Felipe, if she is lost because we have failed to pay the sum demanded? The man is well respected at court, has the ear of His Majesty, is one of Santa Cruz's most trusted commanders. You will do as I commanded the others. Go to your chamber and collect up every trinket and gold piece in your possession. Get that duenna of hers to provide Maria's jewels. The rest must come from the treasury. The English captain, Norwood, has agreed to allow us to board his ship that we might reassure her that everything is being done to collect the ransom.'

Don Luis sighed. He knew better than to defy Don Piero, but the last thing he wanted was Maria's return to the Residency. Already he had found it difficult to answer the Governor's searching questions as to how the two of them had become separated in the attack. If Maria was to blurt out her account of his behaviour it would prove death to his hopes of preferment.

Don Piero continued, 'We'll go aboard after sunset. The Englishman requested that Maria's duenna should accompany us. She may be afraid, so see that you put her in a suitable frame of mind and make light of the dangers. Off with you, Luis. Were I your age, you dog, I'd be fretting every hour I was apart from my betrothed.'

Don Luis turned in the doorway, his body stiff with resentment. 'What if Maria,' he gave an embarrassed cough, 'should no longer be fit to become my wife?'

Don Piero smiled mirthlessly. 'You will show the restraint due from a gentleman and ignore the fact. Luis, Maria must become your bride. Your father is resolved on the match and we cannot afford to make an enemy of Don Felipe Santiago y Talavera.'

Don Luis bowed again and withdrew. He had no desire to encounter Consuelo again either. So far the woman had kept quiet regarding his cowardly behaviour, but he read the silent contempt in her eyes.

When Jem brought Maria's afternoon meal to the cabin, she laid aside her pride and openly quizzed the boy about his captain. He appeared to regard the questioning as natural female curiosity and was eager to oblige her.

'Cap'n Norwood, he joined Cap'n Drake early on in the voyage. We'd taken this prize, you see, and Cap'n Drake needed a reliable man to command the *Gloriana*.'

'You mean he came aboard this ship?'

'Oh, no. I was serving aboard the *Elizabeth Bonaventure*, Cap'n Drake's ship then. We attacked this Portuguese on course for the Low Countries.'

'Murdered all hands and commandeered the cargo, I suppose.'

'Aye, we took the spoils, but most of the survivors took to the boats. Cap'n Drake's not normally vindictive, like, only when he's in a foul temper, like this morning.'

'Oh?' Maria's eyebrows were raised, inviting him to continue.

'Well, it's being said they come across this letter from the King of Spain among the Governor's papers, calling him a corsair and pirate.'

'Well, isn't he?'

Jem scratched his head, his freckled face expressing puzzlement. 'I dunno, mistress. I only know as how the Dons has took all the spoils of the New World and tried to stop the likes of us from sharing. They treats the Indians awful bad, and the prisoners they take, sending them to the fires and others to the galleys—begging your pardon, like, forgetting you was one of them.'

She could hardly deny his accusation, for she had seen for herself the horrors below decks on the Cadiz galleass, and the general treatment of the Indians throughout the colony had not recommended itself to her.

'You say *El Draco* is very angry. Does that mean he will vent his fury on the town and its people?'

'Aye, if they don't pay what he's asking, I reckon.'

The boy backed, anxious now to be out of her presence, as if he realised he'd said more than his captain would approve.

She found the food appetising; both meat and fruit were fresh, showing the seamen were making full use of the town's provisions. When the boy came back to remove the tray he showed he dared not linger and said no more than common courtesies. He seemed suddenly in awe of her as he knuckled his brow in salute and drew to the door.

It could not be long now before Captain Norwood returned and revealed to her her fate: Had he already done so and did that account for the boy's new attitude towards her? It occurred to her that she had not heard the click of the key turning in the lock. Had the boy, in his haste to avoid more talk with her, forgotten to lock the cabin door?

She crossed the intervening space quickly and tried it, her fingers shaking. Her hopes were fulfilled—it wasn't locked. She was free to go on deck. She hesitated. Captain Norwood's orders had been explicit—and sensible. Clearly he had wished to remove all temptation from members of his crew. Dared she defy him and go above? From there she would be able to see the situation in the town more clearly. She had no intention of trying to escape. The boats would be guarded and, even if she were to achieve the impossible and reach the sanctuary of the Residency, her captors would demand her return.

There was no one in the dimly lit space leading to the companionway. Many members of the crew would be roistering and looting ashore, she surmised. If she was quick, she would manage to see what she needed to see and return to her cabin without being observed. And, later, Jem would come back and lock the door. He would be severely punished if his captain discovered his lapse.

The silk gown was over-long and hampered her climb up the ladder and she cautiously lifted her head above the stair top. This part of the deck appeared to be clear and she completed the climb and ran directly to the rail.

The devastation appalled her. Even from this distance, and some two miles of water separated her from the harbour, she could see how terrible the destruction was. Even as she watched, sections of the harbour fort fell to a charge of gunpowder and she could glimpse fires inshore still smouldering. The wind carried the acrid stink of smoke to her nostrils and she thought she could hear, though faintly, the yells of soldiers and seamen still pursuing their endless search for treasure and women, together with the cries of their victims. Sickened, she turned back towards her own cabin. Of what use would it have been to venture into that hell even if she could have managed to obtain a boat and rowed herself to shore?

Tears blurred her lashes as she blundered her way down the companionstair and along the between-decks corridor.

Suddenly her way was barred. Lifting her bowed head, she encountered a pair of predatory eyes and stifled a scream as she recognised the rat-like features of the man who had captured her in the stricken Cartagena.

Assuming a proud stance and arrogance of tone she was far from feeling, she demanded free passage, speaking clearly in English. 'Let me pass at once, *señor*.'

'So, our little Donnish woman talks the Queen's English, does she? And so proud, like. 'Cos the cap'n gives her the right to such airs. Well, he ain't got no right, neither. You woz my prize, and I didn't give him no claim, despite he paid me some.'

The man's red-rimmed eyes raked over her, noting the low corsage of her gown, now further dishevelled after her hasty flight from the deck.

'You've cleaned up a treat, as I'm sure he's told you, and showed you, 'aving 'ad you in 'is cabin all night. You won't be averse, like, to sharing your charms with me as 'as first claim?'

He put out a filthy paw to finger her exposed breast and she raked her nails down his face.

'Don't dare touch me, you piece of English filth.'

He gave a snarl of rage and seized her by the shoulders, pressing her back hard against the bulkhead.

'I sensed as 'ow you 'ad claws yesterday, and I promised to cut 'em, teach you some manners.'

He imprisoned both her hands in one huge, grimy fist and continued, unhindered, to fondle her breast, freed completely now from the low cut of the gown's neckline. His nails tore at the silk and Maria gave a sharp scream at his rough handling.

She kicked and fought, more furious than frightened, uttering Spanish oaths, culled from the stables, she hardly knew she had unconsciously stored in her memory.

The man seemed oblivious of his own danger. Surely he must know someone would be alerted by the commotion and rescue what must be accepted as the captain's prize. Yet no one appeared.

She tried reasoning, without success. 'Your captain is asking a large ransom for me, one he'll doubtless share with you and the rest of the crew. What do you think you'll get if I am despoiled? He'll have you hanged——'

'Will he now? I don't know 'as 'ow Cap'n Drake 'ud allow that.' He spat disgustedly. 'This Cap'n Norwood, who is he indeed? Comes out of the blue and Cap'n Drake gives 'im command over us loyal Englishmen as 'e's known for years. Who asked 'im to ransom you, eh? Whose prize are you, anyway?'

'I thought I had made that very clear, Evans.'

The captain's tone was ice-cold. Evans released his hold on Maria so suddenly she half collapsed inside the cabin doorway.

Catching at the door supports, she looked beyond her attacker to where Captain Norwood stood near the companionstair. Her bemused eyes took in his finery of black silk doublet and puffed trunk hose he had donned for the meeting with his fellow officers and subsequent appointment with the Cartagena officials.

Evans gave a snarl of rage and half drew his cutlass, but his captain had the advantage. He had already drawn his sword and, stepping lightly forward, and with a contemptuous flick of the wrist, he cut his blade deep into the wrist of the crewman and sent Evans's cutlass skimming across the well-scrubbed boards of the between-decks corridor.

'My prize, Evans, captain's privilege. I thought you had understood.'

Evans nursed his injured wrist with his good hand. Blood oozed wetly between his fingers as he stared down at the wound incredulously. Clearly he'd been taken as much by surprise by Norwood's appearance as Maria had been. He licked his lips nervously as he looked sullenly up to catch the merciless gleam in his captain's eyes.

'You were well paid. I gave orders that no one was to molest the prisoner. No one was to even so much as approach my cabin. Why did you dare to disobey me?' The words were spoken in so silky a tone that if the hardness of the captain's expression had not been so obvious, even here, viewed in the dimness of the corridor, Evans might have been led to believe that his misdemeanour might be excused.

The man swallowed, his eyes again looking at his blood-soaked hand. 'I didn't disobey no orders, Cap'n. The Don woman was out of the cabin, bin on deck.' The voice was submissive, but sulky, expressive of the cold feeling of fear welling up between his shoulder-blades.

'Oh?' Giles Norwood's eyebrows rose in interrogation.

Maria found herself unable to frame words of explanation.

Norwood barked out an order and two crewmen ran lightly down the companionstair. Maria was aware of a buzz of talk above and realised, to her shame, that there were men farther on deck whose heads now appeared above the stairway, staring avidly down at her. With trembling fingers she tried to draw together the torn portions of her gown in an effort to cover her now fully exposed breasts.

Evans made no protest as his hands were unceremoniously caught behind his back, secured with rope, and he was bundled off towards the stair.

'Put him in the brig until I have leisure to decide his fate.' The captain's voice was expressionless. Without turning he said quietly to the watching men on deck, 'Get about your duties. I want this vessel ship-shape within the hour. I'm expecting visitors. One of you bring a cloth and wipe away these bloodstains. *Muy doña?*' He gestured her into the cabin. Maria forced her recalcitrant limbs to obey her, for they felt unlike her own, and walked, as proudly as she could, inside.

She heard the door slam behind him and turned to find that her worst fears were realised and her rescuer had followed.

Before she could murmur a word in her own defence, he had flung aside the bloodstained weapon and pulled her roughly against him. For the second time in the last half-hour she found herself helpless in a man's grip. He shook her fiercely until her teeth rattled.

'Woman, are you totally without sense? Didn't I make it as clear to you as I did to Evans that you were not to leave this cabin or speak with any member of the crew, bar Jem?'

Her breath had left her and she was helpless to reply. His eyes blazed fury as he stared down at her.

'Perhaps you are not such an innocent. Will you play the wanton on my ship, mistress, as you did on the galleass? Was it your intention to flaunt yourself before my crew as you did before the slaves? What prompts you, mistress, a wish to taunt men into desiring you, or worse, did you believe that with me overside you might find yourself a true mate for the afternoon?'

His accusation brought back all her courage with her rising temper. She pummelled at his hard-muscled body with both fists, screaming at him in Castilian. 'How dare you, you dog of a pirate? Do you think I would demean myself so much as to look at one of that crew of scum you employ to pillage and rob my people?'

He ignored the blows as if they were fly-pricks. 'I think you asked for this,' he breathed hoarsely, as he tilted her head back so far she thought her neck would snap, and his lips came down bruisingly on hers. Her arms were held rigid against his body and she was totally helpless. Again she experienced that devastating weakness, almost a torpor, possessing her. Her lips parted of their own accord, as if willingly, to receive his, and she gave a little moan, whether of fear or of ecstasy she could not tell. Her heart was pounding within her breast and her limbs gave way beneath his. He gathered her up and carried her to the bed. She made no protest, although she uttered one little sob of despair. He bent close, and she saw his glazed eyes seek her exposed breasts. One hand reached down as if to fondle her, as Evans had done, then paused in the act. He sat up abruptly and pushed her roughly from him.

'This is your game, mistress. I'll be damned if I play it and succumb like that weak fool in the brig. Do you hope to persuade me to release you? God's teeth, I pity your betrothed. Has he any notion of the life you will lead him? Obviously not, for he's agreed to pay the ransom, or if he does know what you are, he's too besotted to leave you to your fate.'

She huddled as far from him as she could get, across the width of the bed, her eyes wide and dark with pain. Tears splashed on to her clenched hands and she turned away her face as she gave way to helpless sobbing.

'Is this an act, too?'

His contempt held as hard an edge as his tone to Evans. She conquered her distress and controlled the frantic trembling of her lips.

'What—what will you do with that man?'

'Why, have him flogged, *muy doña*, and then hanged. Isn't that what you like to see, a man humbled before you?'

'I will not dignify that with a reply,' she said quietly. 'It seems you have punished him enough. Will he ever use his right hand again?''

He shrugged. 'I doubt he'll draw blade with it again. Does that matter to you?'

She shook her head wearily. 'It seems it is useless to try to explain why I went on deck. Actually it was simply to view the town. I do have some concern for the fate of the inhabitants, who are, after all, compatriots of mine, or perhaps you think, in your disgust of me, that I have no feelings at all.'

'I think you've little regard for the well-being of others; still, I've noted that's a trait in those other compatriots of yours.'

'And you English are so kind, so generous,' she jibed back. 'What was the price you put upon me, *señor*? And what will you do with me if it isn't paid?'

His long lips stretched in a hard smile of derision. 'Use you as Evans tried to do? Would that be so hard for you to endure? You appear to invite men's notice, do you deny that?'

'Of course I deny it. Do you think I would have ventured on deck at all if I'd believed just one of your men would be near enough to see me, let alone place his dirty hands on me?'

'How did you get on deck?' His brows twitched together in a frown of suspicious anger. 'Sweet Virgin, did you play your game with Jem?'

'You are contemptible,' she snapped. 'Of course I did not. Jem is just a boy——'

'Man enough to disobey my orders and to suffer the consequences. With what did you bribe him?'

'I didn't bribe him. He would never allow himself to be bribed. Strangely, he appears to have some admiration for you. I imagine he just forgot to lock the door. Now, I suppose, you'll let your savagery loose on him.'

'You are right, *muy doña*, and I'm tempted to let you view the punishment of both men—though perhaps not, you seem to derive some enjoyment from such displays and I'm averse to pandering to your perverse desires.'

Fiercely, she controlled the tears which were beginning to prick again at her lashes. 'Please,' she begged, 'do not be too hard on Jem. As for that other creature, I think he could hardly be blamed. As you have pointed out to me, so forcibly, I am at fault. I was before, on the galleass, when I caused you harm.'

There was no softening of his expression as he continued to regard her.

Dear God, how beautiful she was, even in that tawdry and ruined gown, her blue eyes aswim with tears and the dark glory of her hair tumbled about her face. He could not, in truth, condemn Evans for what he longed to do to her himself, yet the man must be taught obedience due to his captain and publicly, or Giles would never wield authority successfully aboard the *Gloriana*. As for Jem, he, too, must learn that carelessness could not excuse disobedience. The great temptation had been to make her pay in full. Only by imposing the strictest restraint had he made himself forbear.

Drake had insisted that the Dons be allowed to ransom Doña Maria, and his reasons had been cogent enough. 'Come now, Giles, this girl is no common doxy. It's policy to allow the procedure. The Dons expect it and keep to the rules. Will you sail the high seas with such a woman aboard to be a constant reminder and temptation to the men that she's a prize for their captain only, one which they can never share? You know if one of them dared to bring a woman aboard, you'd deny him leave to keep her, for the selfsame reason I'm giving you. Very well, she is the woman who caused you pain and you'd like to be revenged on her. I'm telling you now, the twenty thousand ducats you'll get for her will prove a worthy salve for your wounded pride and, for that matter, for your hide.'

Norwood sighed, his hand on the door-latch. Doña Maria Santiago y Talavera had proved to be trouble in plenty, and Drake's rules must be kept for the good of all, but, by the sweet eyes of the Virgin, he would never find the twenty thousand ducats recompense enough for the prize he would be losing.

'I've given permission for your betrothed to come aboard with the Governor, so they can see for themselves you have not been harmed. I suggest you set about putting your appearance to rights in case they think, with due cause, that you might not now be worth the price we've set on you.'

'And your avaricious soul would be wounded by that.'

He shrugged. 'I think you might be the one who would find herself the loser. I might find it profitable for my own hurt feelings to take out the loss on your hide.'

He bowed in that mocking courtesy she found so exasperating and left.

She threw herself down on the bed and, beating the pillows in frustrated rage, sobbed out her fear and distress.

Jem appeared within minutes with a ewer of hot water and she hastily dried her eyes. He made very sure, this time, that he had secured the door, not that this was necessary, for he was soon followed by his captain. Maria clutched at the bed-covering, as she had now stripped off her torn gown.

He regarded it grimly and produced a small silver case and a pair of scissors. 'My seaman's hussif. You may be able to draw the neckline together for now and I've also brought you one of the peasant's drawstring blouses to wear beneath the gown. Later we'll arrange for some of your own baggage to be brought aboard.'

She nodded a curt acceptance and he glanced round the cabin, assured himself that she had what was needful and left her again.

She washed hurriedly and, seated on the bed, made hasty repairs to the gown. She would have much preferred to tackle her riding dress but there was no time. That required far more work, and, if she was honest, hands considerably more skilled with a needle than hers. In the captain's travelling-mirror she regarded herself critically and decided that she was, at least, presentable.

Her heart jumped into her throat when she heard the bosun's whistle proclaiming that the expected party from the Residency was coming aboard. She dreaded to set eyes again on Luis and feared the revulsion she felt for him would be too openly revealed on her face. When booted feet descended the companionstair, she rose, uncertainly, to receive her visitors.

Captain Norwood entered first and ushered in the Governor, Don Luis at his elbow. Maria gave a choking cry of relief and delight at sight of Consuelo behind them, clutching a large bundle which Maria presumed contained much needed gowns and underwear.

Don Piero stood back with jovial good humour for the duenna to enclose her charge in her arms.

'*Querida*, what have they done to you? I prayed and prayed the Virgin to keep you safe, and when they told me——' Consuelo's face worked. 'When they told me I would be allowed to come——'

'Consuelo, I have been so worried about you too. You managed to get to the Residency. I was so afraid I would never see you again.'

'When I rode into the town one of the guards escorted me back to the house. We tried to find you, but in the confusion——' Consuelo blew her nose noisily.

Maria smiled, though her own lashes were pricking with tears. 'I'm so glad you came, that you were brave enough to come.'

The older woman snorted. 'I'd like to see the man who could have kept me from coming. And now I am here, here I stay.' She placed herself squarely in front of Maria, and, arms folded, stared defiantly at the captain.

He grinned. 'It would seem a sensible idea, if the *señora* is prepared to share her charge's imprisonment over the next few days.'

Don Piero smiled his relief. 'That would reassure all parties, Captain. And now, would you do us the courtesy of allowing us speech with Doña Maria alone? I am sure her betrothed would be forever grateful for the opportunity.'

Again Captain Norwood shrugged. His gaze flickered from Maria to Don Luis and his body stiffened slightly. 'If that is Doña Maria's wish,' he said in faultless Castilian. 'Meanwhile, I'll show Señora Henriques what facilities there can be for the two ladies.'

Don Piero waited until the door had closed on him then gave Luis a slight push in Maria's direction, while he moved nearer to the cabin door and studiously occupied himself in the examination of a pair of fine silver candlesticks on one of the sea-chests.

Luis looked sullenly and insolently over Maria's tawdry silk gown. 'That is a most unsuitable garment for my betrothed to be wearing,' he said tartly, 'especially when she is so recently out of mourning.'

'Do you imagine I chose it?' Maria snapped at him. 'My riding dress was badly torn as I tried to get through the town after your cowardly desertion.'

'I had a duty to reach the Governor's side in case he had need of me,' Luis muttered, his eyes moving to Don Piero who stood with his back to them, but clearly within earshot.

Maria did not mince words. 'I wish to make it plain that, ransom or no, I will never consent to marry you.'

His eyes flashed dangerously as he moved closer and caught her arm in a pincer grip. 'You will do exactly as I say. Do I take it you've found consolation in the arms of that pirate dog?'

'You are even more contemptible than he is,' she said wearily. 'At least he does not pretend to be what he is not.'

'Pretence or not, you'll marry me, as the marriage contract sets out.'

'I'd rather starve in the gutter first.' The whisper was so fiercely uttered that Don Piero turned to ascertain the nature of her vehemence.

Don Luis smiled and made a reassuring gesture of his hand. 'You may find yourself starving in my household and suffering severe bodily discomforts, too, if you dare reveal the source of coldness between us,' he hissed close to Maria's ears. 'You know well enough I've no more desire for this marriage than you have, but my father commands it and Don Piero insisted we provide your ransom. But for that, I'd leave you to your fate, and an unpleasant one it would prove, unless you've a taste for rape. Some women have, I'm told.'

Her bright blue eyes caught and held his, but he did not lose countenance. She swallowed the lump suddenly rising in her throat and bowed her head that neither man should see her tears. What could she do to avoid this marriage? She was trapped. There was also Consuelo to be considered. If she angered Don Luis, he might well punish her by dismissing her duenna or life could be made a constant burden for her.

Don Piero sauntered over. 'Maria, I am relieved to see you well and unharmed?' The rising inflexion on the final word made it a question.

'Captain Norwood is very conscious of the need to protect my virtue since the amount of the ransom could be affected by the loss of it,' she commented bitterly.

Don Piero nodded. 'Now Consuelo is to stay with you, your honour will not be besmirched. I assure you, we shall make haste to obtain the remainder of the sum demanded. You will understand, Maria, that my first consideration must be the safety of the town and the colonists. These have first call on our resources.'

'Of course. Is Don Carlos well?'

'He is safe and sends his good wishes. He is most anxious about you.' Don Piero frowned. Clearly he was anxious about the report the Visita would eventually make to King Philip concerning the town's state of unreadiness to repel attack.

Captain Norwood appeared in the doorway, signifying that the permitted interview must now come to an end.

Maria was relieved to see the back of Luis. His sullen expression, even his carriage, revealed his deep resentment. Surely Don Piero must be aware of the hostility between him and Maria.

Finally alone with Consuelo, she gave vent to her distress and anger.

'Querida,' Consuelo consoled her, 'you must not be too distressed at Don Luis's departure. You will be together very soon now and able to put all this unpleasantness behind you.'

'Consuelo, how can you be so stupid? Do you think I want to be returned to Don Luis? I'd rather lie in my grave.'

The duenna's dark eyes were astonished and shocked. 'I know he is not one of the most attentive of lovers, but he is of good birth and attractive enough. If you refuse to marry him, your future could be very bleak.'

'I know that.' Through gritted teeth, Maria grated, 'I tell you I will not marry him. When the ransom is paid I shall insist that Don Piero escort me to the nearest convent.' She stood up and moved to look through the stern window. 'If only——'

'Querida?'

When Maria turned back to face her, Consuelo saw a shy, hesitant smile trembling on her slightly parted lips.

'If only Captain Norwood were not a piratical dog and an Englishman——'

Consuelo's bottom jaw fell in shocked bewilderment. 'Maria, you could not—could not be in love with the man?'

'Love? I—I don't know. I couldn't love him, could I? He is my enemy and he thinks only of the ransom, yet——'

'Has he—I mean, has he shown you that he might have some feeling for you?'

'He kissed me.' The word was a dreamy whisper. 'And this very afternoon, when he found me struggling in the arms of one of the crew, he showed a marked and unwarrantable fury. He blamed me, quite without justification.' Maria jutted her chin defiantly. 'Oh, Consuelo, he is handsome and strong and brave and——'

'A thieving pirate,' the duenna finished abruptly, 'and, most likely, a heretic.'

'Yes, a heretic.' Maria said the words so deliberately and coldly that Consuelo bowed her head from the deadly anger she read in her charge's eyes and her thoughts flew to Don Luis's unfortunate revelation on the hill above the harbour.

Maria smiled thinly. 'Well, we must pray that the ransom is acquired quickly or I might imperil my very soul with such improper thoughts. Now, let me see what you brought me. How I long to get out of this outrageous gown.'

CHAPTER EIGHT

THAT night Captain Norwood moved out of the master cabin and Consuelo took his place as trusted guardian. Maria's lips curled wryly as she considered the reason for his forbearance. The ransom would soon be paid and he would be rid of both women. Consuelo snored contentedly while Maria lay wakeful until dawn.

Consuelo had jumped so quickly to the idea that she was in love with the English captain. The notion was ridiculous, yet the thought of his mocking kisses brought the hot blood to her cheeks and set her heart pounding.

The captain had been a courteous but subdued host at supper. He had said very little and, once or twice, she had felt his brooding gaze upon her so that she had lowered her eyes from his hastily. Did he truly still hold her responsible for Evans's assault on her? He had said no more as to the fates of the two men he blamed, and she had not dared to refer to the matter again.

During the following day she saw little of him. Consuelo chattered endlessly as she set to work to repair Maria's damaged riding dress. Mostly she talked about the stupidity shown by the women at the Residency during the attack. No harm had come to any of them and they seemed more concerned for their jewels and fine clothes than their lives and virtue. None of them, apparently, had given a thought to the fates of less fortunate women in the town.

When Jem set food for them at noon he expressed the captain's regret that his duties kept him from attending on the ladies.

'Jem,' Maria queried, 'were you severely punished? I'm sorry I brought down Captain Norwood's anger on you. I had no intention of escaping. I thought my escapade would not be discovered.'

'Cap'n, he can be 'ard sometimes. He gives me a clout and warns me to mind me duties next time round. Don't give it no 'eed, mistress. I've suffered worse from me dad afore, aye, and from me mother when the drink was on 'er.'

'And the seaman?'

'Evans? He's still in the brig. Cap'n, he threatened to leave 'im ashore when we sail, to the mercy of the Dons, but I doubt if 'e'll do that when it comes to it. He knows well enough what 'ud 'appen to Evans. He'd go to the fire, most likely.'

Maria knew how true Jem's words were. Giles Norwood had first-hand experience of Spain's hospitality.

'Did you know your captain before he took over this ship?' she questioned idly, and Consuelo cast her a sharp glance.

'No, only these last months, mistress, but Cap'n Drake and Sir Giles knew one another at court, so it's said.'

'Sir Giles?'

'Yes, mistress. It's said in the fo'c'sle that his father died some years ago and left him heir to some manor in the North. He's not like most of the flotilla captains, who are mostly Devon men.'

'And you told me he joined the flotilla on the way out?'

'That's right, mistress. I 'eard he'd been making for home, then he changed his mind and joined Drake's expedition.'

The boy scuttled off, this time making very sure the door was securely locked.

Why had Captain Norwood changed his mind? Were those estates Jem spoke of impoverished? Had he joined the piratical venture for gain, or had he been drawn to Cartagena to find her? She thrust the thought aside as unworthy and foolish. He had said so, of course, to mock her, but he had come here purely for his own interests.

Sir Giles did deign to dine with them that evening and was less abstracted. Maria saw Consuelo becoming charmed by his easy manner. At the close of the meal he rose to his feet.

'Doña Maria, would you and Señora Henriques like to take a turn on deck?'

Maria stumbled to her feet almost too eagerly. They had been confined all day in the stuffy cabin and she longed to feel the cool night air on her face.

He stood back courteously to allow both women to precede him into the corridor. A sailor, clattering down the companionstair, gave them a curious stare, then hastily averted his gaze. Obviously the captain's averred intentions as to the punishment of Evans had been made known to all the crew, and this man had no wish to give offence.

The captain gestured to the stair. 'Can you manage?'

Maria nodded, though she made the climb clumsily under his gaze and heard Consuelo breathing heavily as she followed.

Stars shone clear from a velvet dark sky. He paced beside her gravely and with all the solicitude she might have found from some *hidalgo* at the Escorial palace. The poop deck was deserted and they stood together near the rail, Consuelo some paces off. Maria drank in the calm beauty of the night and shivered involuntarily as the night breeze stirred her hair. He stooped and placed his fashionable short velvet cloak round her shoulders.

She looked at him directly. 'Captain Norwood, how you must hate all Spaniards.'

He gazed out across the sea, towards the harbour, his grey eyes thoughtful. 'With reservations,' he said at last, turning back to her.

She felt tongue-tied, but pressed on determinedly. 'You must concede that we—that is, our Spanish officials— had every right to punish you, *señor*, to sentence you to the oar, terrible as it was, for the act of piracy is——'

'I was not taken in an act of piracy, *muy doña*,' he said mildly.

'You were not?' Her eyes widened in astonishment.

'I was merely travelling in Spain as I had in other countries and suddenly found myself arrested with other foreign seamen and travellers in a Cadiz tavern.'

'But why, if, as you say, you were committing no crime?'

'Perhaps, in the Spain of today, it is a crime in itself not to be Spanish.'

She was silenced, thinking, painfully, of her mother's fate.

'I am—sorry,' she said stiffly. 'I had not understood. Our officials are naturally suspicious of foreigners. There have been so many raids on our territories.'

'Indeed.' His eyes danced and she coloured hotly.

A seaman saluted as he passed them on his round of duty. Maria noted how badly the man dragged one leg.

'The result of the rack, *muy doña*, administered in the prison of the Holy Office in Cadiz,' Sir Giles whispered softly in Maria's ear. 'There are many others in my crew who've suffered yet more tortures. The monks of your Inquisition are both skilled and thorough. In this raid alone Drake has released literally hundreds of slaves and Indians who've felt the yoke of Spain on their hapless necks.'

She moved from him restlessly. He was reminding her that they were enemies, could never see each other's point of view. She sighed as she rejoined Consuelo and shivered again.

When the bosun, Tregarron, escorted the two ladies on deck next day, Maria saw further evidence of Captain Norwood's concern for the recently recruited men. From the fo'c'sle she heard the sounds of moans and a stifled cry and, on the deck itself, several men were having their wounds tended by the ship's carpenter. One man was leaning forward while his back was being treated with salve. Giles Norwood lifted his eyes to her horrified ones as he dried his hands on a towel. There were livid scars, marks of the overseer's whip, standing out starkly on the man's back and shoulders.

'Good day, *muy doña*.'

'It is a pleasant day, Captain, made so by this re-freshing breeze.'

She could not keep her gaze from the tortured man's stripes, and he grinned at her crookedly, catching at his forelock. Sir Giles murmured, 'One of the slaves freed from the captured galleass which was stationed in the harbour.'

'Will he sail with you now?'

The injured man grinned enthusiastically. 'Aye, that I will, mistress, when Cap'n Norwood 'ere says I can, but I 'opes as 'ow it'll be me last adventure. I wants to be putting my sea-chest down in Plymouth town soon, now, and there I'll be glad to stay.'

Sir Giles lifted one eyebrow and gripped the man's shoulder. Maria murmured some courtesy and moved on.

'The idea,' Consuelo remarked later, in the privacy of their cabin, 'stealing our oarsmen! There'll be scarce an Indian left to till the tobacco and sugar crops this year. Bad enough to sack our town, but disgraceful that these corsairs set our own servants against us. What Don Piero will do without...'

She grumbled on but Maria could only be pleased that the man was now free to sniff good air on deck after the fetid conditions in the slave quarters. Whatever he had done, he had paid for it and she, too, would pray that both he and his captain would go safely back to their homes when all this was over.

Why hadn't Captain Norwood continued his journey to England? She could not believe that the lust for spoils alone was all that induced him to adventure these waters. Why had he travelled to Spain in the first place and how was it that he spoke Castillian so purely? He had spoken to her in English on board the galleass. Was it possible that his captors were not aware that he spoke Spanish so fluently? Slowly a suspicion grew in her mind. Was Sir Giles Norwood an agent sent by the Queen's council to discover Spain's readiness for war? Her uncle's duties with the fleet had prevented him journeying with her to Cartagena. Could it be that King Philip was even now building and arming an Armada to attack England? His sister-in-law, Elizabeth, had long been a thorn in his flesh. It was Maria's duty to warn Don Piero about Captain Norwood, yet she could not risk the ships, which must come eventually to the rescue of the sorely stricken fort, following and engaging Drake's flotilla. Her heart contracted with fear and she knew clearly that her feelings for Giles Norwood ran deep. He was her enemy, yet never could she willingly bring him to harm.

Her thoughts were interrupted by his sudden appearance in the cabin. He bowed and she saw that his lips were held in the hard line which signified anger.

'News you've been waiting for, *muy doña*. Don Piero has signalled that the ransom is ready for collection. His officials will board within the hour to conclude arrangements.'

Her heart sank. 'Thank you, Captain Norwood. Consuelo and I will set about packing our chests at once.'

'You must be overjoyed that the amount has been assembled so quickly.'

'Naturally, *señor*.'

His lips parted in a sardonic smile. 'Such haste indicates the regard your betrothed undoubtedly feels for you.'

'It would seem so.'

'I regret we must part so soon, *muy doña*, but I know how much you long to return to the Residency.'

Did he know? Was he deliberately torturing her? She met his gaze squarely and bowed her head in acquiescence.

Consuelo was in a delighted dither. It was some time before she recognised Maria's silence as despair, and, stopping in her task of folding gowns for the small sea-chest Sir Giles had placed at their disposal, came hastily and gathered Maria into her arms.

'You must not fret, *querida*. All will be well once you are married. How could Don Luis fail to come under the spell of your beauty? He will come to love you, truly.'

Maria's lashes were wet with tears and she shook her head mutely.

The older woman looked hauntedly towards the cabin door. 'As for that spawn of the Devil, you must not even think of him.'

Half an hour later the bosun's whistle announced the arrival of the Spanish officials. Maria and Consuelo waited anxiously but no one came to inform them of what had been decided. Maria was left to bite her lip in suspense for at least two more hours before Captain Norwood again came to the cabin.

'All is arranged, *muy doña*. If you and your duenna will please follow me, a boat will row us ashore.' His tone was chillingly cold and his manner formal, as he stood aside to allow two sturdy seamen to enter and take charge of the baggage. As he assisted her to mount the companionstair, Maria felt a hysterical desire to refuse to move. But the moments of parting ticked on inexorably. She was helped into the longboat, Consuelo seated beside her, the baggage stowed. She looked up anxiously, for one moment panicked into thinking Giles Norwood would not accompany them ashore. It was foolish of her to expect it, or to take comfort from the thought that there might yet be some time before she was bereft of all sight of him. He slipped nimbly down the ship's ladder and took his place in the boat. She breathed a great sigh of relief. Though she tried to read his feelings in his expression, he seemed to be studiously avoiding her gaze but sat forward, in the bows, his eyes fixed steadfastly on the land steadily drawing closer.

Now she could see the Governor's carriage drawn up ready on the causeway, its curtains drawn against the sun for her comfort. Three Indian slaves held umbrellas above the heads of the Governor, Don Luis, and the Visita, Don Carlos, who had come to oversee the safe handing over of the woman he'd guarded on the voyage to Cartagena.

Maria thought, wryly, that Don Luis would be forced to make a show of concern for her under the hard gaze of His Majesty's representative, who would undoubtedly report back to both her uncle and Don Luis's father.

The boat grounded in the shallows and Sir Giles lifted her clear of the water, after crisply ordering one of the seamen to do a like courtesy for Señora Henriques. For precious moments Maria felt his heart beat close to her own. She made no effort to struggle free and thanked him quietly when he set her on her feet.

Don Piero opened the final negotiations. 'Well, now, Captain Norwood, everything is as you demanded. The lady's dower chests and the extra sum required are here spread out for your inspection.'

Maria was aware of a well-built stranger with a small forked beard who headed the English party. He smiled at Norwood.

'And here, Don Piero, is the lady, quite unharmed and delighted, I'm sure, to be returned to your care.'

He came forward and, taking Maria's hand, lifted it gallantly to his lips.

Sir Giles made no move to approach the ransom chests. He nodded to his bosun, at Drake's prompting, and the man went and examined the treasure.

Maria stood by Norwood's side, unwilling to make the slightest move in Luis's direction.

As if from a great distance, she could hear the English commander addressing Sir Giles.

'All is well. We can order the men to load the chests into the boat and the ladies can enter the carriage.'

Maria's limbs felt leaden. At any moment she would be forced to take Luis's hand and enter the Governor's carriage. The very thought of his fingers on hers revolted her. She turned away, sickened, and found Giles Norwood's hard grey eyes assessing her. She longed to plead with him, beg him to save her from the horrifying fate which awaited her as Luis's wife, the chilling certainty of hours, days, months, years—an eternity of loveless emptiness stretching ahead of her, a purgatory, without hope of salvation, until death mercifully claimed her.

Yet she was as much Norwood's chattel as Luis's. Both men saw her as a valuable commodity. This English pirate could never be persuaded to forgo the golden prize waiting here for him to claim so simply. If she were to fall on her knees before him and confess her love, her longing to be his, he would only laugh at her contemptuously. She was a prize of war, fit only to be exchanged for gold and gems.

She could hear the talk of the English crewmen near the longboat. So far her own baggage had not been brought ashore. She gave a little desperate sob and turned to face the Spanish party, their faces blurred through the curtain of her unshed tears.

'Giles?' Drake's voice held just a trace of impatience.

Don Luis stepped forward then and offered Maria his arm to escort her to the carriage. She shrank from his touch.

'Thank you,' she said coldly, 'I will proceed only when Captain Norwood has expressed himself satisfied.'

Luis came closer. His eyes bore that unnatural glitter she had learned to fear. Before she could move back from him he had taken her arm and pulled her towards him. His fingers bit so hard into her flesh that she could not forbear a hastily suppressed cry of pain.

Don Carlos said, sternly, 'Don Luis, I think you are hurting Doña Maria.'

Luis released his hold, but his mouth hardened. She knew he was finding it hard to suppress his temper. 'Doña Maria would be better out of this fierce heat within the shade of the carriage,' he replied suavely and she knew it was not concern for her which prompted the comment.

Her eyes appealed silently to Don Carlos, who gave her a puzzled frown. 'My dear, Don Luis is right. All is concluded now. You must be anxious to be out of sight of your captors. Allow me to escort you.' He offered her his arm.

Her hands fluttered uncertainly. Don Carlos had nothing but her welfare at heart, yet he seemed now to be acting as her gaoler carrying her to a place of permanent confinement.

She turned back to Giles Norwood. Out of the corner of her eye she glimpsed Luis's face, chalk-white with anger at her temerity. 'You have been very considerate, Señor Captain,' she said hesitantly, 'I have been a trial to you at times—and you have been very—forbearing. Will you not bid me farewell?'

He stared down at her, his fair brows meeting above that straight, arrogant nose. The sight of that beloved face she would never see again was so unbelievably dear. She gazed and gazed, longing to imprint it deep on her mind, that it might never leave her.

Things happened then so startlingly fast that, for long afterwards, she was totally bemused. Sir Giles moved to her side and lifted her high into his arms.

'Back to the boats,' he ordered. 'Tregarron, you bring Señora Henriques.'

Already his long legs were covering the short distance between the waiting longboat and the astonished group of Spaniards on the mole. Maria felt herself dumped unceremoniously into the boat. Her head bumped the thwarts and she was hampered by her voluminous skirts as she tried to struggle up to a sitting position. There was a babble of confused sound. Men were shouting. Bare feet slapped across the smooth sand and shallow water. There was a cry of protest, probably from Consuelo, then the boat shuddered as it was pushed into deeper water. Any attempt to rise to her feet was forestalled by Sir Giles, who held her down with an iron hand.

'Why?' she shouted at him across the noise of creaking oars and the rush of water. 'Why? I don't understand!'

His face was set, lips drawn into a grimace of concentration. He looked like the vicious stranger who had forced her back into her chamber in her uncle's house in Cadiz. She was completely unable to see what was happening on shore nor could she tell whether Consuelo was with her in the boat.

Sir Giles was shouting orders. He slung her across his shoulder when the boat grounded against the *Gloriana*'s side, and he carried her up the ship's ladder as if she were a side of beef. Before she could be aware of what was happening, she was back in the master cabin,

Consuelo was thrust in beside her and the door was slammed and locked after them.

Consuelo faced her, open-mouthed. Her hair had torn free from its pins and was streaming down her back. She was panting, unable to get out so much as a squeak of indignation.

At last she managed to croak, 'They are mad. All Englishmen are quite mad. He got the ransom, what is he doing abducting you?'

'Consuelo, be silent,' Maria snapped.

Her ears strained to hear sounds from on deck. There were commands, the slapping of feet on the boards, a trumpet call. The ship was being made ready to sail. But could Giles get clear of the harbour? The currents were treacherous, she knew. What of the other captains? Drake would be furious, as much so as the betrayed Spaniards.

She must look even more a sight than Consuelo did, and her head ached where it had banged the boat thwarts. She stumbled to the bed and sank down before her unsteady legs gave way beneath her.

He was running away with her and she could not guess his reason. Everyone's hand would be against him now. Even his own crew would be in mutinous mood, if not driven to action, for, surely, they had all stood to gain by her ransom, which had been left on the causeway.

She gave a little choked sob, her hand moving to her trembling lips, for she couldn't tell whether to laugh or cry, yet, despite all doubts as to her future, her heart was singing a paean of pure joy. If he took her and later discarded her, it would be worth the pain and suffering of loss. She was still in Giles Norwood's hands while the hated Luis was left, bemused and humiliated on the quay, and the ship was steadily putting miles of ocean between them.

It was over an hour before Giles came to them. He stood, glowering, in the cabin doorway. Consuelo opened her mouth to protest and he made a single decisive movement of one hand. 'Woman, get out.'

'*Señor*——'

'I said, get out.'

Maria caught her eye and she nodded imperceptibly. Consuelo scuttled by him into the corridor.

He closed the heavy door with a slam and stood with his back to it. Those eyes of his, changeable as water and sometimes as steely as slate, were glittering oddly, as if he had been drinking.

Maria seated herself and faced him calmly. 'Captain Norwood, I am sure you must have some logical reason for your behaviour, but I am at a loss to understand it.'

He said, brusquely, 'Are you telling me you wanted to be handed over to that coxcomb? The man's a poltroon and, clearly, has no deep feelings for you.'

'And you have such concern for me that you think it is in my interest to be discovered sailing across oceans with an English pirate? You believe that will better my situation?'

'Who said I was anxious to better your circumstances? All that interests me is pandering to my own needs.'

'Which are?' Deliberately she taunted him into putting his intentions into words. If he was to rape her, hurt her, he must be made aware of what he was doing, not act in some blind rage, or drunken state of insensibility.

He had been drinking heavily, she was sure of that, but the reason for this strange mood lay much deeper. It had been festering all day and erupted at sight of Don Luis Ortego waiting on the quay for his bride. Maria dared not hope that the wild surge of emotion Giles Norwood had experienced this afternoon was the dawning of his love for her. He had been at sea for months. He needed a woman, attractive or otherwise, but her desperate hope was that his feelings were more fully involved than a mere lust to assuage desire.

He came close to the bed and swept her into his arms. 'You dare to ask what my needs are?' One hand traced the swell of her breast and she forced herself to remain passive. 'I believe you are the most desirable woman it has ever been my misfortune to meet,' he said thickly.

His hands moved to the heavy mass of her disordered hair, for she had still not replaced the combs which formerly held it in place.

'Perhaps you have been unfortunate in your choice of women, Captain, but, then, I imagine you have also been indiscriminate.'

He laughed. 'I'll say one thing for you, *muy doña*, you have spirit, but then, pride—arrogance, I'd sooner deem it—is considered a virtue in your damned country. Am I being indiscriminate now? You are trembling, *muy doña*, and I do not believe it is with fear.'

She made an ineffectual movement to free one hand and strike at him. 'You insult me, *señor*, and without reason.'

'Because I suggest that, like all women, you are a slut at heart? You've no desire to go to the bed of that cold-hearted devil in Cartagena without first tasting the delights a true man can give you, and who could accuse you now of having invited such unwelcome attentions as mine?'

'You are drunk, *señor*,' she told him quietly. 'If you give rein to your baser instincts now, in the morning, when you have slept this off, you will be sorry.'

'But will you, *muy doña*?' His grey eyes mocked at her.

'I——' She drew a deep breath. 'I shall think very much less of you than I have done erstwhile.'

He checked, staring at her a little owlishly, as if her words had begun to pierce the wine haze and found their mark. 'Then you have some tender feeling for me, *muy doña*?' he said wonderingly.

'I believe you to be a gentleman, even if——'

'I am a dog of a pirate,' he finished, laughing, 'but then, you have told me that before.'

'But we know one another a little better now, have taken each other's measure.'

'Sometimes I even begin to believe that I might trust what you say.'

She forced herself to breathe steadily, evenly, though her heart was thudding close to his and she longed to fling caution to the winds and throw her arms about his neck, tell him of her love, of her wish that he might sail the oceans with her forever. But that would only confirm his notion that she was wanton and her more careful nature warned against such conduct.

'Captain, you will regret this action. Your commander——'

'Sweetheart, do you think I care a fig for what Drake thinks of my conduct?'

'He will censure you, try to stop you leaving the flotilla.'

He shrugged. The wild, strange, drunken passion was giving way to a more normal reaction and she gave thanks for it. 'I am right? You do despise your betrothed?'

'It is an arranged marriage,' she said slowly.

'I saw you look at him, there, on the quay. The man disgusts you.'

She turned her head away. 'The Virgin knows I would be free of Don Luis Ortego y Castuero, but it is my uncle's wish that I marry him, and if I do not, what will become of me?'

'Who knows, sweetheart? Something better than a loveless marriage——'

'Captain?' Tregarron, the sailing officer, scratched urgently on the cabin door.

Norwood cursed beneath his breath and stood up. 'Well, what is it?'

'We've received a signal from the *Elizabeth Bonaventure* to heave to, sir. Are we to obey?'

Norwood turned back to Maria, his eyebrow raised in amusement. 'It seems you were right, *muy doña*. Drake is more than a little annoyed by the loss of your ransom. I must go on deck immediately.'

'What will you do?' she breathed, fearfully. 'Will the ship be endangered——'

'Nay, Drake'll not fire on the *Gloriana*, never fear.' He stooped and kissed her hand, the gallant English gentleman once more. He called to Tregarron and then quickly left the cabin.

She sat back tearfully upon the bed. This should not be happening now. He had calmed, was beginning to see her as a woman to be respected, not a prize of war to be taken in sport and as quickly abandoned. Now he was at war again, and with his own brothers-in-arms, and she was the cause of it.

CHAPTER NINE

THE women waited anxiously for news of the ship's progress through the harbour waters. Maria tried to peer through the cabin window but it was impossible to determine what was happening on deck. She heard no sound of firing and, at last, judged that the galleon had made open sea safely.

When Jem appeared with food for the passengers he explained that the captain sent his excuses but was, for the moment, unable to leave the poop deck.

'He asked me to tell you, mistress, that there is nothing to fear. We signalled our intentions to the *Elizabeth Bonaventure* and Cap'n Drake has allowed us to proceed.'

'But, Jem, where are we going?'

The boy looked embarrassed and shook his tousled head. 'That's Cap'n's business, mistress. I can't tell you anything more.'

Consuelo frowned at the boy's retreating back. 'I just can't make out what can be in the man's mind. I thought it was your ransom he wanted, but now...'

Maria drew a deep breath. She could not think how to answer her duenna. She had no idea, either, what was in Giles Norwood's mind. When Consuelo had questioned her about what had taken place in the cabin she had been evasive. How could she tell Consuelo that, in spite of all her forebodings, she was relieved that the exchange of her person for the ransom had not taken place? Though she had no appetite for the food she settled down at table and forced herself to eat. While she and Consuelo did so it gave her time to think. Grumbling beneath her breath, the duenna joined her and made a hearty meal.

Since Captain Norwood did not appear in the cabin that evening Maria spent a restless night. Jem brought breakfast as usual the following morning but Maria was forced to swallow her impatience for sight of Giles. When Tregarron, the sailing master, called to ask if she wished to go on deck she accepted eagerly.

The ship was sailing well before the wind and they were far out to sea. Seamen cast the two women curious glances, but there was no sign of hostility displayed by any of them. Either their captain had compensated them for the loss of loot or he had threatened reprisals for any insults which might be offered to his prisoners.

Pacing beside the sailing officer, she was surprised to see Sir Giles busied beside a palliasse which had been placed in a sheltered corner of the deck, protected from wind or rain by a canvas awning. He rose as they approached and smiled at Maria. He looked much calmer this morning. The frenzied glitter she had noted the previous day had disappeared and, though he was frowning in concentration, she knew he was not angry with her.

'Good morning, ladies. I'm sorry I have not been to the cabin to ask after you both but yesterday I was busied with sailing matters and this morning I was summoned to one of the crew taken ill.'

Maria glanced at the sick man and recognised the former galley slave who had talked so bravely of wanting to be home. The man was breathing heavily and she noted the bluish tinge to the lips which reminded her of her father's suffering.

Bending, she smiled down at the patient, whose eyes flickered open as her shadow crossed his face. He grinned at her and struggled up on the palliasse.

'Why, it's the lass with bonny brown hair like my Joan's.'

'Yes, and you are the man from Plymouth.'

'Aye, lass, and glad to know we're on our way to England.'

Maria glanced sharply at Sir Giles, who inclined his head. 'I hear you are still not well,' she said to the sufferer.

'Pains in me chest, like, but I've had 'em before. They'll pass. I wants to pull me weight with the rest of the crew, pay me passage.'

Sir Giles said quietly, 'I've told you not to worry about that, Cope. You rest as long as needful. You've earned it.'

He moved away from the palliasse and Maria followed. Tregarron saluted his captain and looked at him as if for orders.

'You can return to your duties, man,' Sir Giles said evenly. 'I will see to it that the ladies are escorted back to their cabin after their walk on deck.'

The sailing master put a hand to his forelock and quickly left them. Consuelo glanced uneasily at Maria but, seeing her determined expression, stepped back and allowed her charge and the captain to proceed to the rail.

Maria looked back towards the sick man. 'Is he worse? It is his heart, I think. My father suffered so.'

Sir Giles lifted his shoulders and let them fall in a regretful little shrug. 'He was too long at the oar. It is often so. The strain of the pull affects the heart in the end. I saw too many good men thrown overside not to recognise the signs.'

Maria looked horrified. 'You think he will die, after all he has gone through, and when he had hopes of seeing his wife again?'

Sir Giles sighed. 'We have no physician aboard. There is very little we can do for him. Fortunately, there was a medicine chest with syrup of poppy to ease the pain, but there's precious little of that, so I hope matters will resolve themselves soon.'

Maria shook her head. 'I am so sorry. Men should not be treated so cruelly.' She looked up to find him staring at her intently.

'You really are concerned for him, aren't you?'

'Certainly I am, as you are.'

'You are a strange woman, Doña Maria Santiago. You watch men being flogged without a tremor then sigh for some English seaman who is nothing to you.'

'You wrong me, sir, if you believe I watched your pain without being affected by the sight of it. It was necessary to behave so, before my uncle. He would not have understood any show of weakness.'

He smiled thinly. 'I can believe that.'

'It is true what the man said, that we are sailing to England?'

He nodded.

She made to question him further but thought better of it. He was staring beyond her across the creamy waters made in the wake of the stern, his brows drawn tightly together again, then he turned abruptly.

'Doña Maria, I must ask your pardon for my disgraceful conduct yesterday. I had been drinking and was not myself.'

She drew a hard breath. 'Yes, sir, I realise that.'

'It will not happen again, I assure you. You will be subjected to no further insults aboard my ship. Now, allow me to escort you both below. The wind is freshening and you will take cold.'

Once left to themselves in the cabin, Consuelo, tight-lipped, set about her sewing. Maria watched her ruefully and then said gently, 'You are alarmed for me, Consuelo. I do not think there is need. Captain Norwood has assured me that my welfare will not be threatened and I believe him.'

'But what is to become of us? Did he say?'

'No, and I did not press him.'

'But——'

'I do not think it wise to do so, yet. He will tell us in his own good time. The ship is on course for England.'

'England?' Consuelo mouthed, dumbfoundedly. 'But how can we fare in England? I had hoped he would carry us to Spain and there press your uncle for the ransom, but what he will say I cannot think——'

'No, I do not think my uncle will be approached,' Maria said turning from her. 'In all events, I will not marry Don Luis. I told you that on the hill above the harbour. I have not changed my mind.'

Consuelo was silent and Maria turned back to her. Then Consuelo spoke.

'You are angry with me, *querida*, for not telling you about your mother. Your father forbade it. Had I spoken of it, ever, he would have sent me away from you. I thought, like him, it were better you should not know.'

'I still cannot understand. My mother was not a heretic. Of what was she accused?'

Consuelo plucked awkwardly at the silk of her gown. 'She was a sweet lady. I could see no signs of heresy. She attended mass with the family, made confession. There was a search of her rooms. It was whispered books were found, English books, heretical writings.'

'Did she—did she go to the fire?' Maria whispered the words, dry-mouthed.

'No, no, *querida*. She died in the prison of the Holy Office in Malaga, soon after she was arrested. It was said she was not strong——'

'Then they tortured her?'

Consuelo avoided the terrible, bleak expression in Maria's eyes.

'I do not think they would find that necessary, *querida*. Your mother would not prove stubborn. I think it was just that she was weak. She took a long time to recover after your birth.' She drew a long, hard breath and crossed herself. 'God give her gentle soul rest. Who knows what happens in the prison of the Holy Office? Once immured there, no one can help. Your father tried. He made so many appeals. They would not let him see her.'

Maria bit her lips until they bled. She could picture the terrible suffering of her father, helpless to do anything for the woman he loved more than life itself. No wonder, after her death, he had refused to speak of it, or allow any of the *estancia* servants to refer to it.

'Who could have betrayed her?' she said, at last.

Consuelo's eyes opened wide as if such a thought had not occurred to her before. 'I do not know, *querida*. Everyone on the *estancia* loved her dearly. She was a truly gentle mistress.'

'Yet someone must have reported some suspicion of her heresy to the Holy Office.' Maria tasted the salt blood on her mouth again. Who among her father's friends or his relatives could have dealt him so deadly a blow? A sudden thought struck her and she blinked as if to clear such a terrible suspicion from her mind. Who could have profited from her father's disgrace, for he had been forced to retire from court? Her father's friends had continued to visit him and associate with him. Only Don Felipe Santiago y Talavera had kept from the *estancia*. It was an unpleasant thought, yet it refused to leave her. Her uncle would have had freedom of the house, would have had opportunity to see the proscribed books. Yet what could he have gained by destroying his brother's wife? She knew well enough that younger brothers often felt resentful that their elders inherited the greater part of their parents' fortune. Don Felipe was well thought of at court. Had he ingratiated himself with the pious-minded King Philip by proving his own loyalty to the faith in so dastardly a fashion? Don Luis had made no bones about the contention that any suspicion of heresy would doom his own prospects. Don Felipe might well have thought that true of his brother's dubious alliance with an Englishwoman.

Maria murmured a swift prayer to keep her thoughts pure from the taint of unproven suspicion of her uncle's motives. More and more she was beginning to question her own loyalties. She had told Giles Norwood that they would always be to Spain, but she had seen so much inhumanity over the last months that she was now doubting her own feelings. Could it be that her love for him was clouding her senses to all but her need to stay with him? If she was honest, she could not see evidence of any more kindly dispositions in the English who had sacked and looted Cartagena.

When the captain joined them for supper she was very quiet and he looked at her thoughtfully. 'You are not feeling unwell, Doña Maria?'

'No, no, Captain. It is just that events have been so horrifying over the last days, I am, perhaps, feeling the reaction to the calm, at last.'

He nodded. 'It will be some time before we reach the Canaries, where I intend to take in fresh food and water. It will give you both time to recover. Incidentally, if there is anything you may need, which we can get you there, please let me know.' His lips twisted in that wry little smile which had become so familiar to her. 'I am aware that we left Cartagena so hastily, that you must be short of many articles of clothing and toiletries which ladies find essential.'

Consuelo glared in agreement but, on finding Maria's warning gaze on her, made no comment.

Next morning Jem tapped very early on the cabin door and requested that they join the captain on deck.

Sir Giles was waiting at the head of the companion-stair. He took one of Maria's hands in his own.

'It's Cope. I'm afraid he's dying. He's asking for his wife, Joan.'

Maria looked hurriedly to the palliasse where the sick man lay. 'I am so deeply sorry, but what can I do?'

He hesitated for a moment. 'You could take his hand, comfort him.'

'You think he will take me for her?'

'He has talked of your bonny dark hair, like hers.'

'But my speech cannot be like hers.' Maria was distressed at the intended deception. 'He knows I am Spanish, he cannot be deceived——'

'My dear, Cope is far gone. I doubt if he can see or hear clearly. You are a woman, the only young one aboard. He will believe what he wants to believe.' He bent forward and looked intently into her eyes. 'You do not have to do this, if the thought of it upsets you.'

Her troubled blue eyes met his grey ones and she read there his very real concern to grant this galley slave who had suffered so terribly, as he had, this last request.

'Of course I am ready to do what I can,' she said.

'You are sure? Yesterday, you spoke of your father dying so.'

She swallowed and nodded. 'He did, but he had me by him to love him at the last. Let us see if we can give a like comfort to your crewman.'

She knelt by the palliasse and gathered the dying man's head and shoulders on to her lap. As Sir Giles had said, he was far gone. His breathing was laboured but she praised the Saints he did not appear to be in great pain. His hand reached out for, and grasped hers.

'Joany, my Joan, are you there, my sweet lass?' The voice was hoarse and so low that she had to bend close to hear him.

She glanced up questioningly at Sir Giles and he whispered, 'His name is Tom.'

'I'm here, Tom,' she said softly. 'I've been waiting so long for you. It's good to have you home at last.'

'Aye, lass, home, and I never thought to see it. Thought as how the *Gloriana* 'ud take too long, but the wind was fair and God good to me. I thought of you so much, my lass, in that hell-hole, and the house we was going to build when I come home with good coin in my purse.' He coughed and tried to struggle up in her arms.

'Lie quiet, Tom,' she said, 'all is well now.'

The heavy breathing quietened as he sank back. 'What time is it, lass?' he whispered, fretfully. 'It's getting dark so soon.'

Maria closed her eyes and caught back a sob of pity. 'It's all right, Tom,' she soothed. 'It's evening. You'll be stronger tomorrow.'

'I tells meself so, but——' He blinked and tried, ineffectually, to sit up again. 'Kiss me, my lass.'

Maria looked up at Sir Giles and he frowned and shook his head. She bent down and kissed the man gently upon the forehead, then the cheek and, finally, on the blue-tinged lips. His wind-chafened skin was wet with her tears and he grinned. 'Nay, don't cry, Joany, my lass, you'll spoil good homespun.'

He made one last effort to lift his head, possibly to return that kiss, and the hand grasping hers slackened, there was a curious rattle in his straining throat and his head sank back against her breast.

She sat there, cradling him, her tears wetting his cheek and throat till, gently, Sir Giles bent and lifted the slack form from her lap. 'It's over, Doña Maria,' he said gently, 'and thanks to you, he went easy. Let me help you up now. Come away, the men will do everything necessary.'

Consuelo had shown every intention of preventing her charge from going near the seaman but one of the crew, at a signal from his captain, had taken her arm and gently, but forcibly, led her further along the deck where she could not hear what was taking place. Now, shocked beyond measure at the sight of Maria being lifted and drawn away from the palliasse, she tried to struggle free from her captor. To her further horror she saw her charge burst into unrestrained sobs against the captain's chest. Over Maria's bent head the seaman saw Sir Giles's second signal to him, and continued to hold fast to the older woman.

Maria could not check the desperate weeping, and buried her head against the leather of Sir Giles's doublet and cried as if her heart would break. He made no effort to stop her, but stood, grimly silent, one arm gently patting her heaving shoulder.

At last the storm passed and she lifted a swollen and blotched face to his. 'Oh, oh, I am so sorry,' she gulped. 'I could not prevent that happening. Please, please, release me.' She was conscious of their nearness and shocked by the depth of her feelings.

He released her and drew her to the rail where she took in several gulps of air.

'I knew he was—going, that it had to be, you told me yesterday how ill he was, and I did not know him but——' She gave a convulsive shudder. 'After all he had suffered it seemed dreadful that he should not have been granted his heart's desire, that little house he wanted to build for her.'

'I will see that she gets it,' he said quietly. 'You were not just weeping for Cope, though his death will touch all of us, but for your own lost innocence. You have seen so much recently of death and ugliness that it released all that has been pent in you these last months. I suspect it all started even before I saw you on the galleass, with the death of your own father.'

She nodded tearfully. 'I could not cry then, not properly. I have always been taught that I must appear——'

'The true-born daughter of a Spanish *hidalgo*,' he finished sternly. 'Yes, I know, all too well, all that that entails. There is nothing to be ashamed of in such a display of sorrow. The very last time I wept so, I remember, was for my old brachet bitch in the stables at home. The stable boys stood round and gaped at me, yet I couldn't stop. After that, breeding took over and I have never given way again, not even when I had news of my father's death.'

'You were very fond of your dog? You like dogs?'

'Doesn't everyone?'

'Oh, no,' she said simply. 'Many people just use their animals. My father loved his horses. He would have wept for them, I know.'

'He bred them?'

'Arab stock with Andalusian strain. They were beautiful. It was a wrench to leave them on the *estancia*, though I know they will be well cared for, and I have missed my little pet dog such a lot.'

'An Italian greyhound?'

'No, a little one, I do not know what you English call them. She has a curly black coat and long ears. She was my father's last gift to me.'

He smiled. 'I know the breed. They are just coming into England. The Queen has one, and a monkey one of her sea captains brought her.'

She knew he was talking to allow her time to recover her self-control and was grateful. Already seamen had carried the body of their dead comrade away.

'Will you bury him soon, overside?' she asked diffidently.

'As soon as possible in this heat. This afternoon we'll hold the service on deck. He'll go overside as he would have done if he'd died on the galleass, but after Protestant prayers and from beneath the flag of St George with his comrades to give him a send-off.'

She knew he was remembering other comrades flung overside like so much rubbish. He must have seen many during his life on the rowing-bench.

'I would like to attend, if you think I would not intrude,' she said shyly.

'Certainly, I'll escort you on deck when it is time.' He looked to where the embarrassed seaman was endeavouring to keep Consuelo in talk, but since his Spanish was poor and her English almost non-existent, it had proved a hard task. 'I think we should return you to the care of your duenna, now, Doña Maria.'

She gave a shuddering breath. 'Poor Consuelo, she must be shocked to the marrow by my conduct. I'm afraid I have led her quite a dance these last months.'

At a nod from Sir Giles the seaman brought Consuelo over. One glance at Maria's tear-stained face told the duenna she must utter no word of condemnation. She nodded grimly at Sir Giles and he escorted them below.

Consuelo was further scandalised by Maria's avowed intention to attend a heretical service but, in the end, she accompanied her charge without argument. It was a simple ceremony and soon over. Maria and Consuelo stood some way apart but had a clear view of the proceedings. Maria found her cheeks wet once more and knew Sir Giles had been right; she was not only weeping for the dead galley slave but for all those unfortunates who had suffered and died during these last eventful weeks. The tears cleansed her from bitterness and she felt better when she retired to the cabin afterwards.

Sir Giles sat with them for supper. He saw that she was still subdued and, at the close of the meal, elected to stay with them for the remainder of the evening.

'Will you really try to find Cope's Joan?' Maria asked.

'Oh, yes. It shouldn't be too difficult. He was a Devon man and some of Drake's men will know where to look when the flotilla returns. I will see to it that she does not lose by his death. Had he served aboard this ship he would have gone home a relatively wealthy man.'

'I am glad of that.' Maria sighed. Though Cope had meant to achieve his wealth by piratical means, he had sorely suffered for his wicked intentions and she knew how poor men were assailed by such temptation.

Sir Giles rose and searched in one of the chests. He came back to them with a beribboned lute. 'Do you play, Doña Maria?'

She lowered her head in confusion as Consuelo nodded encouragingly. Consuelo and her father had assured her she played and sang well but she had no wish to assert herself before Sir Giles.

'No?' He touched the strings softly. 'It is long since I played but my father, who served at one time in King Philip's service at Westminster, was very fond of Spanish love-songs and had me taught.'

He seated himself and experimentally tuned the instrument then sang in a fine tenor two of the songs of Andalusia. Maria was touched by the beauty of the music. It brought back her memories of warm, flower-scented evenings on the *estancia* seated by her father's chair. When he handed the lute to her with a little bow, she played for them willingly. She had a rich contralto voice and he sat back in the chair, his eyes half closed, his lean body, for once, at rest.

'I do not have to tell you that you sing very well, Doña Maria. Our Queen, Elizabeth, is an accomplished musician but she could not better you on the lute, nor does her voice match yours in mellow beauty.'

She blushed. 'Thank you, sir.' She played again, an English song, this time, her father had taught her, one her mother had sung for him in the palace of Nonesuch. 'Alas, my love, you do me wrong, to cast me off discourteously, for I have loved you well and long, rejoicing in your company.'

He joined in lustily, 'Greensleeves was all my joy, Greensleeves was my delight, Greensleeves was my heart of gold, and who but Lady Greensleeves?'

'You know the song?'

'Indeed, I do. My father says it was rumoured that the Queen's father, King Harry, wrote it of her mother, the ill-fated Anne Boleyn.'

'Poor lady. She was executed. Do you think she was guilty of the sin of adultery, Sir Giles?'

He shrugged. 'I doubt it, but Henry needed a son and statecraft demands many sacrifices.'

'Is the Queen beautiful?'

He hesitated, pursing his mouth. 'Gloriana is beyond man's conception of beauty. She is past her first youth, but no man who sees her fails to fall beneath her spell.'

She was silent for a moment, recognising in his declaration of loyalty to his Queen one of the barriers which must always stand between them.

'When we arrive in England, what will you do with us, sir?'

He did not answer immediately, his grey eyes staring directly into hers. 'You told me something of your mother, that she died at the hands of the monks of the Inquisition, that she was an English lady.'

'Yes.' It was the softest of whispers. 'Mistress Mary Gascoine.'

'Had she sisters, relatives that you know of?'

Maria looked appealingly towards Consuelo, who shook her head helplessly.

'I know very little about her parentage or even where her home was. My father was too unhappy to talk of her much, only sometimes, when he would talk of his wooing at the court of Queen Mary. I do not think she came of a noble family but she must have been well born, for she was one of the Queen's ladies.'

'Possibly from the North,' he mused, 'if she served the Queen from the beginning; one of the loyal Catholic families, like my father's.'

'Then your family clung to the Old Faith?' she asked eagerly.

'It did,' he said grimly, then, bringing her back to the subject, 'It should not be too difficult to trace any relatives you have once we arrive in England.'

'Then you will return me to them, if and when my ransom is paid?'

His lips twisted sardonically. 'Ah, the ransom. You think they would be willing to pay for your return, Doña Maria?'

Her face fell. 'I would doubt it. Why should they? If I were they, I would not be pleased to have some half-Spanish relative foisted upon me.'

'Yet I take it you have no wish to be returned to Spain?'

There was a second's hesitation before her answer and she knew Consuelo was waiting anxiously on it. 'No, sir, I have no wish to be returned to my uncle, Don Felipe.'

'Then you must trust me to do the best I can for you.' He came to her chair and, stooping, lifted her hand to his lips. 'I bid you goodnight, Doña Maria, you should sleep well. You performed a truly compassionate act this morning, one which revealed your character to me in a totally different light.'

Her cheeks flushed with genuine pleasure at his praise. She stared after him, wonderingly, as he closed the door of the cabin.

Life on the *Gloriana* was more pleasant for Maria after the incident of the dying seaman. Members of the crew treated her with more warmth as well as the marked respect they had afforded her on the orders of their captain. Sir Giles spent as much time as he could in her company. When his duties allowed it, he walked with her on deck or ate with the ladies in the cabin, often spending the evenings talking with them or playing and singing to the lute. Consuelo appeared to accept the situation. She remained in the background, always watchful, but not exhibiting the air of disapproval she had shown earlier for their captor. After Maria's declaration about not wishing to return to Spain, Consuelo had decided that life in England with her charge would be infinitely preferable to life without her, and there were no more oblique references to Sir Giles's heretical leanings or his thieving ways.

On their walks, Maria discovered a little more about her captor. He told her enthusiastically about his home in Yorkshire and the old nurse who acted now as house-keeper for him and would be eagerly waiting for the return of her nursling. He related various humorous stories of his life at court, some which involved Captain Drake, and she gained some insight into his need for ready gold to refurbish the home which had been im-poverished after the rebellion in which his grandfather had lost their fortunes and so nearly forfeited his life.

On her part she told him something of the quiet, un-eventful life she had spent on the *estancia* and he gained some knowledge of the sheltered, cherished existence which had been so rudely shattered by her father's death.

Neither of them made further reference to the attack on Cartagena. It seemed there was a tacit understanding between them to avoid the subject and not once did he attempt to do more than kiss her hand in greeting or farewell.

As had happened on the galleass, Maria appeared to be living these days of the voyage in a kind of limbo. She had put from her mind her old life and was not yet ready to face the new and frightening one which could face her when the *Gloriana* docked in England. He had said he would see her settled, but she dared not look so far ahead. Her whole soul revolted against the day when they would be parted.

Matters came to a head when she was summoned on deck and Sir Giles drew her to the rail.

'See that grey haze in the distance? That's the Lizard, your first view of England. We shall be in London within a few days now.'

Maria's fingers gripped tight to the rail so that the knuckles gleamed white with strain. So soon? The feeling of panic brought a tightness to her chest so that she feared she would be unable to breathe.

'Do we sail into Plymouth?' she asked in as normal a voice as she could muster. 'That is in Devon, Jem says, where many of the men live?'

'No, I dock in Southampton. The journey from there is shorter.'

'You will take me ashore?'

He turned his head to face her, his lips parting in surprise. 'Certainly. I shall lodge you with friends until your relatives can be traced. You will be perfectly safe under my protection.'

'Yes,' she murmured. 'I trust you, Captain, I just wondered if I should have to remain aboard until you had arranged for my future.'

He made an impatient tut-tutting sound with his tongue. 'Your future is in my hands. There is not the slightest cause for concern.'

Consuelo pursed her lips at the news they were so near now to their destination. Like Maria, she had tried to put aside her doubts and fears, but they appeared to her now greatly magnified. She had no liking for Don Luis Ortego but, at this moment, she would have been considerably more satisfied if her charge had been married to him and settled into the life of the New Spain colony. The unknown terrified her, and with good cause.

In spite of that she ate and drank well that evening, perhaps too well, for she was nodding in her chair long before the hour when they usually retired. Sir Giles had taken supper with them, but instead of his usual custom had tonight excused himself directly after the meal, to deal with duties claiming his attention on deck.

Maria watched Consuelo in exasperation. She prowled the length of the cabin and shivered. Now that they had left the Canaries behind, the weather had worsened and it was very chilly on deck. Her silk gowns had been replaced by heavier velvet ones Sir Giles had obtained in the islands, and she was glad of the extra warmth. Her forebodings deepened. England would be cold and damp in the spring, he had warned her. Was this a sign of the welcome which might await her there?

Snatching up a cloak, she moved impulsively to the door, giving one thoughtful glance at the slumbering Consuelo. She bit down on her lower lip. She had done this before, moved deliberately out of her duenna's sight, and it had brought her into deep disgrace. It had also brought her into contact with her heart's love. She needed to be alone with Giles tonight for what might be the last time. She drew a hard breath at the foolhardiness of her intentions, whispered a hasty prayer to the Virgin, and left the cabin, drawing the door to very quietly.

Jem was in the corridor as she emerged. He looked up startled.

'Where is the captain?' she asked, avoiding his eyes, then, 'There was something about which I need to consult him before we dock tomorrow.'

'Aye, mistress. He's on deck near the wheel, giving the steersman last instructions.'

'Thank you,' she said, a little breathlessly. 'No, I don't need you. I'll find him.'

She climbed the companionstair at a stumbling run which left her further breathless as she reached the quarter-deck. She smoothed down her skirts self-consciously and drew the heavy freize cloak around her, pulling up the hood. It was clammy and damp up here, a sea mist dewing her face and hands.

Sir Giles saw her as she approached and spoke hurriedly to the steersman. He came towards her and drew her to a part of the deck half sheltered by one of the longboats and out of the wind.

'Doña Maria, there is nothing wrong in the cabin? It is too cold for you up here. Where is Señora Henriques? She isn't ill?'

'No.' Maria fidgeted awkwardly with the front of her hood, pushing stray tendrils of hair beneath it. 'There is nothing wrong. I just felt—stifled down there.'

He looked surprised. Despite the chill he was dressed in leathern doublet and stout woollen hose, but no cloak. 'We are making good speed. You will be glad to be ashore again tomorrow.'

'Will I?'

He looked at her sharply and put a hand on her arm. 'What is troubling you, Doña Maria? England will not prove dangerous for you. I can assure you of that.'

She gave a little gulp and tears came splashing on to her hand. 'Yet, I am afraid.'

'Why?' He sounded incredulous.

'You will leave me with strangers. They will not want me. What if they reject me utterly?'

'Then I shall make other arrangements.'

Her heart beat faster. What arrangements? Would he take her to his Yorkshire home? That was more than she could hope for.

'I have been a trouble to you, from the first time you saw me and now—you will lose financially if my kin are not prepared to pay——'

'Doña Maria, there is no question of ransom. I thought you understood that I was teasing you when we talked in the cabin.'

'But why should you burden yourself with care of me?'

He gave a little shrug. 'Fate brought us together...'

She caught at his arm. 'You must believe I am genuinely sorry about that flogging. I begged the captain to stop it. I pleaded with my uncle to ask for your life. I meant you no harm.'

'Doña Maria, I know all that.' He turned her to face him and took both of her cold little hands in his. 'It will be an honour to serve you. When I am free to do so, I will come to you again.'

She stared beseechingly into those light grey eyes of his. 'You are in the service of your Queen?'

He hesitated. 'I have important duties in London. I hope to complete them soon. If I have managed to place you in the keeping of your own kinsmen, I will come to you then. If we cannot trace them, you must stay with my friends. It will not be for long.'

'I know no one in this strange, cold land——'

'I understand how you feel but, again, I ask you to trust me.' He lifted her chin and smoothed back another stray tendril of hair.

How lovely she was, and completely in his hands. At this moment she believed that she cared for him. He recognised that instinctively and was tempted to take advantage of the situation. If he declared himself now, made her truly his, extorted a promise, she would have no way of retreat later. In honour he must give her a choice. Once settled among her own people, she would look upon this voyage with her piratical captor as an incident in a nightmare. It was not unusual for prisoners to look upon their gaolers with false reliance. She needed him desperately to assure her welfare. When that need was no longer there, she might look upon him with loathing as she once had. There was, too, the question of his service to Walsingham. Maria knew nothing of his real purpose in Spain. He dreaded to see that expression of contempt for his calling he had half glimpsed on Drake's face. No, he must see to her comfort first, then pray that she would come to him willingly, accept his heart as he had already given his into her keeping. He had known on the mole at Cartagena that he could not give her into Ortego's keeping, had thought, selfishly, that he would keep her himself, force her into compliance, but her courage that first night had reminded him that he was an English gentleman.

He drew a hard breath and bent to kiss her fingers.

'Allow me to escort you back to your cabin, Doña Maria. You must try to sleep now. The journey from Southampton may not be pleasant. It will be much colder in England this time of year than you are accustomed to.'

His formality chilled her. She had hoped to make him love her, had deliberately offered herself, but she could not humble herself further. He would take responsibility for her as his duty, but he could never love her. That wild passion which had come to flame immediately after he had brought her from the mole in Cartagena had been due to drinking too well. She had feared that was all it was then, now she was convinced of it. Always, to him, she would remain a daughter of Spain, the race which had imprisoned and tortured him. She choked back the words of love she longed to say and went with him meekly back to the security of her own cabin and the restricting presence of her duenna.

CHAPTER TEN

THE *Gloriana* anchored off Southampton on a typically wet spring day. Maria sat in the cabin and watched raindrops cascade down the stern window. Her father had told her how wet and dreary England could be in winter, but he had spoken enthusiastically of the balmy spring and summer days when he had ridden joyously through the verdant countryside.

'That is its particular charm, Maria, its wonderful greenness and the palace gardens heavy with the scent of roses and honeysuckle. English flowers are beautiful and your mother was the loveliest flower of all.'

Its greenness, Maria thought with grim amusement, came from this drenching rain. She shivered petulantly. Consuelo hurried up with a shawl. She too was wrapped to the eyes for warmth, and her expression told all too plainly what she thought of the miserable prospect viewed from the window.

A clatter of feet on the companionstair brought Sir Giles into the cabin, shaking raindrops from his cloak and hat. 'We can go ashore now, if you are ready, ladies? Good, I see you are wrapped up well. You'll need to put the hoods of your cloaks up. It's very cold, even for an English spring.'

As she sat beside him in the longboat, Maria asked, 'Do we stay here for the night?'

'No, we'll take coach immediately for London and stay at some inn on the way. If the weather had not been so foul we might have made London by nightfall, but I'll not press you too hard. You'll need to get your land legs.'

Their sea-chests had already been loaded into the carriage waiting on the quay. Its curtains of Cordoban leather were drawn tightly against the driving rain. Maria

171

had dressed for the journey in a dark blue velvet gown trimmed with grey fur with a patterned brocade undergown of grey and silver. Her partlet of grey silk at her throat was untrimmed, as was her close-fitting ruff. The gown was dignified if not ostentatious, one of the many warmer garments Sir Giles had provided for her and for Consuelo during their brief stay in the Canaries. Maria expected Sir Giles to take his seat opposite them in the carriage, but he had chosen to ride beside the vehicle.

Spanish protocol had always decreed that she never stayed in public places other than nunneries on her one or two journeys from the *estancia*, and she was avidly curious to see the public rooms of the wayside inn where they drew up in the early evening, but Sir Giles hurried her above stairs to the private chamber he had bespoken for her.

It was small, but the bed-linen seemed clean enough and Consuelo, after inspection, pronounced it well aired. There was a fire in the hearth which cheered her spirits though, since Sir Giles had taken himself off to inspect the welfare of their horses, she felt very strange and lost. Their supper was brought up to them by a buxom chambermaid whose English was so accented that Maria could scarce understand one word of what she said. Sir Giles did not join them for the meal. He tapped on their door before they retired to assure himself all was well with them and she judged that he spent the night in one of the inn's common-rooms.

In the morning he again tapped upon the door and requested courteously that they both dress without delay and take a hasty breakfast. 'I would like to be on the road as soon as possible.'

Maria assumed he had already breakfasted and that he was anxious to occupy himself with preparations for their departure, for he did not join them for their meal and, again, she felt a sense of neglect and loss.

The rain had stopped and cold sunlight poured through the horn windows. She moved closer and undid the casement. The grass and trees glistened and she gave a little gasp at the sudden sense of bright colour which assailed her eyes after the grey curtain of mist and rain which had enfolded them the previous day. Behind the inn, chickens squawked on the dirt road. To her right was the open stable door where, already, their horses were being harnessed to the carriage. Behind the outbuildings was a small garden containing primroses and the bright green of herbs. The earth smelt fresh after the overnight rain. The sky was the soft, light blue of a Madonna's robe and Maria thought the little fluffy, hurrying clouds very lovely after the unadorned bright blue of the Caribbean. So this was England. Despite its strangeness, she felt a curious kinship with the land her mother had known and loved and a feeling of guilt, almost as if she had thought something treasonable, swept over her.

Sir Giles greeted her cheerily. 'Well, Doña Maria, what do you think of England today?'

She laughed. 'Oh, very much better. Everywhere seems so fresh and green.'

'There is no place more beautiful in the world than England in May, but there, I confess I'm prejudiced. Wrap up well again. Though the sun shines it is still cold. I've provided foot muffs for you both this morning.'

Now the carriage curtains could be drawn back apace and Maria was able to revel in the cool, fresh air, though Consuelo soon grumbled at the draught and Maria had to give way and pull the curtains over the window apertures again, so losing her sight of Sir Giles riding beside them. Food had been provided by the inn servants for the noon meal and they made good time. Consuelo soon slumped into slumber against the leather cushions and Maria too began to feel drowsy wrapped up warmly and lulled by the swaying of the carriage.

It was late afternoon before their vehicle jolted over the first cobblestones of the capital. Consuelo woke with her usual snort and stared open-mouthed with Maria as they crossed the great bridge across the Thames river. Maria was now determined to get her first views of the city and had thrust aside the curtains again. Tall buildings loomed on either side of their way across the length of the bridge and, for once, the heavy city traffic had lessened and they were not delayed, much to their driver's relief. Sir Giles rode close now and smiled grimly at Maria's shudders when she glimpsed the mouldering heads on pikes which decorated the parapets. She shrank back within the carriage's shaded interior, recognising her own sense of loyalties within this alien city.

Once on the city's northern bank, Sir Giles continued to ride close beside them as if for added protection. He pointed out the tall spires of the great church of St Paul's rising above the tall-fronted shops and houses, their upper storeys jutting above the lower ones and almost shutting out the light in the narrow streets. Maria had never been to Madrid and had been hastily drawn through Cadiz in her uncle's closed carriage. She watched with fascination the noise and bustle of this large city and wrinkled her nose against the insidious stinks from the open kennels.

Soon they were driving under a wide archway and into a flagged yard. Ostlers ran to take the horses' heads and servants erupted from doorways to challenge the visitors and, if acceptable, to issue instructions for their comfort. Maria sat uncomfortably still now, feeling vulnerable, waiting for Sir Giles to return to her side. For the moment he had left her and she looked anxiously to Consuelo, who shrugged helplessly. Apparently they had arrived at their destination. Sir Giles had promised she would stay with friends of his until he could make arrangements for her, but how would they greet this stranger from Spain? Would they be as prepared to accept her into their home as he appeared to expect?

Then he was back again; the carriage door opened and the steps were let down. Sir Giles offered her his arm to help her descend.

Now she saw that he was not alone. A tall, soberly dressed, dark-complexioned, thin-faced man, older than Sir Giles by at least ten to fifteen years, was stooping to kiss her hand. He bade her welcome in faultless Castilian.

'You are very welcome to my house, *muy doña*. You must be wearied after so long a journey and chilled to the bone. Giles tells me you came from Southampton yesterday. A chamber shall be placed immediately at your disposal.'

Sir Giles nodded encouragingly at Maria's bewildered face. 'Allow me to present the Queen's Secretary of State, Sir Francis Walsingham.'

She curtsyed low and allowed herself to be led towards the doorway. She continued to look anxiously for Sir Giles, but he gave her into the keeping of a soberly dressed, plump individual who clanked the keys of the household from her belt as she escorted Maria upstairs to the chamber set aside for her.

Norwood sat with Walsingham in his study after the ladies had retired following supper. As he had expected, the Secretary of State and his lady had greeted Maria warmly and tried to set her at her ease, but he noticed she had picked at her food and her eyes, huge with anxious doubts, had rarely left his face. He would have liked to have private talk with her, but his superior had hustled him off to make his report.

He had only information about Drake's raid on Cartagena. All his more urgent information had preceded him long ago and he was relieved to hear it had done so safely and in good time. From below came the muted sounds from the still busy streets. This would have been his time of day to be moving across the bridge to sample the many and varied pleasures the South Bank had to offer. He stirred lazily before the fire. There would be time for such sports. Tonight, when Walsingham dismissed him, he'd seek his bed.

Walsingham questioned him carefully about his encounter with Drake's flotilla, which had led to his joining the Cartagena expedition. He sat now, silent, his shrewd dark eyes veiled by those familiar drooping lids. It was always impossible for Giles to guess at the Secretary of State's thoughts.

Giles frowned, considering. What were Walsingham's secret motives? He had been cursedly civil during supper, wooing Doña Maria's confidence with courteous enquiries about her former life on the *estancia*. He never did anything or befriended anyone without good reason.

At last he said, thoughtfully. 'She is very beautiful.'

Norwood crimsoned. Walsingham had this trick of making him feel and behave like some awkward schoolboy. He found his superior's eyes watching him closely.

'What are your plans for her, Giles?'

'As I explained during supper, I hope to find Doña Maria's kinsmen.'

'And afterwards?'

'I wish to ask for her hand.'

'Ah. I take it she is still a virgin?' Walsingham lifted one hand to stem Norwood's angry protest. 'It is imperative I know the truth of it.'

'She is still a virgin. I would lay my oath on it.'

'Good,' Walsingham observed, silkily, 'then it is possible I could place her among the Queen's ladies.'

Norwood was dumbfounded. His grey eyes opened very wide. He was aware that Walsingham was fanatically opposed to allowing any Catholic to approach the Queen and knew that the man's deliberate avoidance of questions regarding Norwood's own faith carried its own reason.

Walsingham continued. 'As you well know, I was not in England when the Queen's sister was reigning. I know nothing about the girl's mother. I can find out, of course, and I will do, speedily. If Mistress Gascoine was acquainted with our Queen, as well she might have been, for they must have been much of an age, Elizabeth may feel well disposed towards Doña Maria, a young girl alone and unprotected in a strange land, especially when she is informed of the manner of Mary Gascoine's death. There does happen to be a vacancy among the ladies in attendance. Only yesterday Mistress Maltravers was packed off to her home following some minor misdemeanour of the usual amorous kind.'

Norwood could readily imagine how the Queen would be incensed against Mistress Maltravers. She had scant patience with lovesick girls. Courtiers were present at court to attend on Her Majesty and to proffer to her all their devotion.

He was silent, considering, and Walsingham shot him a brooding glance. 'It would suit my purpose to have Doña Maria at court. You have no objections?'

Norwood did not take his eyes from his superior's direct scrutiny. 'I would not have her in danger, even to further your schemes, Sir Francis.'

'Very direct. I see no real danger. Yet, even if there were, I would ask—no, demand—your compliance.'

'You hinted earlier of your fears for the Queen's personal safety. This situation is not new. Her Grace is well guarded——'

'True, yet who is to know if those she depends on most can be trusted?'

'We who love the Queen would gladly die for her.'

'There are those who proffer devotion to another queen.'

'Mary of Scotland?'

Walsingham drained his wine goblet. 'Aye, the Stuart slut. Until that lady lies in her grave, Elizabeth cannot rest easy in her bed nor can the realm be secure.'

'The Queen will never accept the need for her execution.'

'She'd sign a warrant speedily enough if I could lay before her irrefutable proof of the Scottish queen's complicity in a plot against her life.'

'Mary has been a prisoner too long to be unwary.'

Walsingham rose and walked to the window, his back to Norwood. 'It may be that, this time, I have baited a trap with sweet enough inducements. The lady, as you say, is wearied of imprisonment. She would do anything to secure her release.' He shrugged. 'Who could blame her? All you need to know at present is that I am aware of a conspiracy for just that purpose. I know the leaders, could draw them tight within the net whenever I choose, but I need to know all the rebels.'

Norwood's mouth was suddenly dry. 'You'd not draw Maria into such an entanglement?'

'She is Spanish, of the Old Faith. It is possible, even likely, that she would be befriended by such people around the Queen.'

'Doña Maria would prove a stout enemy, a brave one, I've seen evidence of that, but, Spanish or no, she would never willingly become an accomplice to assassination. That sense of treachery does not exist in her nature.'

'I agree. Even on such a short acquaintance with the lady I can see she is as true as tried gold.' He added, his lips twisting wryly, 'Your love for her tells me all I need to know. You are no youthful, lovesick fool. If you have come to love Doña Maria then she is, undoubtedly, worthy of that love. Yet, such a hawk among the Queen's doves might allow me opportunity to gauge the reactions of those around her. You understand?'

'If it was thought she was your tool—sweet Virgin, she'd not be safe for one moment after——'

'An unwitting tool.' Walsingham smiled, meaningly. 'Have you declared yourself to the lady?'

Norwood lowered his gaze. 'I have not told her directly that I love her—I believed it necessary first to complete my service to you, but——'

'It would be best if you delayed your ardent declaration. You could remain, of course, very close to her to watch over her and—for me.'

'You suspect someone within the royal household?'

Walsingham shook his head regretfully. 'I suspect everyone, you included, my dear young friend. Do you believe Doña Maria would be willing to accept such a position at court?'

Norwood nodded slowly. 'She is in need of some reassurance. She has no wish to return to Spain. I believe she is questioning both her heritage and her loyalty, but she would never do a dishonourable act. She is a skilled musician. She sings well and plays the lute. That would please the Queen.'

'On board the ship, was she attended at all times?'

'Most of the time,' Norwood conceded uneasily.

'We will simply never refer to any time when she was not.'

Norwood realised that the matter was now settled to Walsingham's satisfaction and that he was being dismissed. He rose unwillingly to his feet.

'Sir Francis, it is only fair to warn you that should my loyalty to either you or to Doña Maria be tested, it is to—— '

'We'll not consider that contingency until it presents itself. Yet I remind you now that your loyalty is primarily to your Queen. Doña Maria will need one or two days to recover from her ordeal and the journey. She will be made very welcome and comfortable within my household. Meanwhile, you and I, Giles, will present ourselves at court.'

Maria self-consciously smoothed down the pristine softness of her white velvet gown and gave a hasty sidelong glance at Sir Giles Norwood at her left. To her right, and very slightly ahead of them, stood Sir Francis Walsingham, sombre and elegant as ever in black and silver. How like a Spanish grandee he was, and Maria already knew him as Spain's most implacable enemy. Sir Giles had no such inhibitions concerning the colours of his attire. Today he was finely decked out in scarlet velvet slashed with white silk, his sunburnt skin dark against the pale, lace-edged splendour of his starched ruff. Maria wondered about the source of wealth which had enabled him to equip himself so fittingly. The same gold, dubiously obtained from some merchant ship or from the household of some prosperous plantation owner in Cartagena, had probably been used to dress her so finely.

Sir Francis had insisted on overseeing every step of the gown's fashioning. The velvet was embroidered with tiny sprigs of golden broom flowers, her lace ruff was gold-edged and the high comb which held in place her gold and white lace mantilla was also of gold.

She was to see the English Queen, the great Elizabeth, and though part of her mind whispered 'traitoress', she could not resist the sheer excitement and delight of the occasion. Sir Giles had been summoned to present himself at court and Sir Francis had decreed that she must be at his side.

The Great Presence Chamber was crowded and noisy. Gaudily dressed courtiers predominated, but there were one or two ladies present and several sombrely clad clerics and clerks in evidence. As yet the throne chair was empty and the noise and laughter grew shrill.

The clamour was instantly stilled as the Queen was announced and all turned to the doors at the far end of the chamber. The Queen's halberdiers preceded her, then came Elizabeth herself, followed by a bevy of ladies, all of them, like Maria, clad in white. Maria saw the reason why immediately. Against that simple backcloth the Queen's splendour shone out like the sun on a misty morning. Maria craned her neck to see more clearly.

Elizabeth was clad in an overgown of yellow velvet and, beneath, an undergown of white satin so patterned with gold thread and pearl embroidery that the original colour was hardly discernible. The great sleeves glittered and shone with the same adornments in the sunlight from the oriel-window, as did the Queen's enormous gilded lace collar. She was not tall, but she moved with stately grace to the throne chair while all before her bowed and curtsyed low and the silence was broken only by the frou-frou of velvet and brocaded skirts on the polished floor. Maria found herself staring in fascination at the dyed red hair, topped with the tall, bejewelled head-dress from which descended one single great pearl falling on to the Queen's forehead. But the Queen appeared old, tired and drawn, and raddled with paint and white fards. All Maria had previously heard concerning this woman had convinced her she was a sorceress who wove spells to attract all her male attendants into a state of slavish devotion. Maria had noted how Sir Giles's grey eyes had softened at mention of the Queen's name. That he adored his sovereign was patent. Yet now, to Maria, the Queen appeared overdressed and jewelled, an ageing woman, certainly no goddess to be so worshipped.

The Queen seated herself, her ladies dutifully grouping themselves behind her. The court chamberlain, bearing his white wand of office, began to present the waiting petitioners.

Covertly Maria watched Sir Giles, but he stood rock-still, patiently waiting his turn, as did Sir Francis Walsingham.

At last the chamberlain called their names. 'Sir Francis Walsingham, Sir Giles Norwood, Doña Maria Santiago y Talavera.'

Maria advanced nervously as Sir Francis presented her. She curtsyed low and found the Queen's sharp dark eyes regarding her curiously as she rose.

'You are welcome to our court, Doña Maria.'

Instantly then she gave her attention to Sir Giles, who dropped gracefully upon one knee to kiss the white, slim hand his sovereign graciously extended to him.

'We are very pleased to have you back, Sir Giles. You have been far too long absent from our side.'

Sir Giles's curly fair head was bent very low. 'Only work most necessary to Your Grace's well-being would keep me from your presence.'

Maria saw the raddled red mouth relax in a smile. Visibly, the ageing Queen became almost radiant under the spell of Sir Giles's sincere admiration. And it was sincere, Maria was sure of that, and a small stab of jealousy shot through her.

The Queen waved her hand almost testily, though her eyes continued to smile. 'Away with you. You are a graceless dog, always cozening your sovereign. Bring him to my chamber later, Sir Francis, and also bring me the girl.'

Sir Francis conducted them from the Presence Chamber and proceeded to show Maria some of the glories of the palace of Whitehall; its three galleries, including the magnificent stone gallery from which guests could look down upon the River Thames, the fine ceiling of the long gallery, painted by Holbein. Maria's eyes were dazzled, but her mind was bemused. What was she doing here? Why had she been honoured by presentation to the Queen? She was an enemy of England, but the Queen's gaze, though coldly scrutinising, had revealed no trace of animosity. She trailed obediently after her two escorts into the beautiful gardens her father had spoken of; surveyed the bowling green, the cockpit and the enormous tiltyard where the Queen enjoyed the spectacle of royal tournaments arranged in her honour. It was all very interesting but wearying, and Maria was relieved when the three of them withdrew to a small room used by Sir Francis as an office, where they were served a simple repast of cold meats and wine.

They had scarcely concluded the meal when they were summoned to the Queen's privy chamber. This time Elizabeth was attended by only one lady-in-waiting. Elizabeth had divested herself of her ornate state gown and was dressed in a more simple one of heavy silk.

She waved the three to their feet after they had made their obeisances. Maria noted that her voice was harsh, a little mannish, but her tone conciliatory.

'You have eaten?'

'We have, thank you, Your Grace.' Sir Francis nodded.

'Then to business.' The Queen tapped Sir Giles's hand smartly with the handle of her fan as he stooped once more to kiss her fingers. 'I hear you brought back enough plunder to reimburse you for your misfortunes.'

Sir Giles grinned, now more obviously at ease in the Queen's apartment and granted this private audience. 'Sufficient to compensate me, Your Grace, and plenty to offer the royal coffers.'

The Queen's dark eyes narrowed. 'Good. The sum will be put to good use. We have read your reports and are fully cognisant of the dangers you foresee.'

Sir Giles's expression became more sober. 'Your Grace must take advice from your officers concerning your personal safety. Even the crises which afflict the realm pale into insignificance beside the very real threat to Your Grace's life, for you are England. Philip knows that and will take any steps, however ruthless, to deprive us of our Queen.'

'I know it,' she said irritably. 'If I did not, my Moor here would constantly remind me.'

Sir Francis refused to be drawn at her use of the nickname she herself had given him.

The Queen turned her attention to Maria. 'So, this is the Spanish prize you brought home with you, Sir Giles.'

Maria blushed to the roots of her hair and the Queen chuckled.

'I see you understand English, Doña Maria. Don't take offence, girl. I have been informed by Sir Francis how carefully you were kept aboard Sir Giles's ship, chaperoned well by your duenna. I would not be willing to accept you among my ladies if I had any doubts regarding your virgin state.'

'A position among Your Grace's ladies?' Maria blurted out the words before remembering the need for caution in her mode of address to the sovereign. 'Your pardon, Your Grace,' she whispered, curtsying once more and very low, 'I had no expectation of such an honour.'

'I knew your mother, mistress.' The Queen's harsh tone softened. 'I was sorry to hear the circumstances of her untimely death.'

Maria's lips parted soundlessly. So the Queen remembered her mother among the other ladies at her sister's court. Possibly Mistress Gascoine had been kind to the unfortunate girl suffering under Queen Mary's displeasure, as Maria knew Elizabeth had done then. She dared not ask more.

The Queen beckoned to her single attendant, a youthful, brown-haired girl about Maria's own age who came instantly and sank into a deep curtsy before the Queen's chair.

'Ursula, Doña Maria is to join your company. Befriend this Spanish lady who must be feeling very lost and homesick. Acquaint her with her duties. Inform the mistress of the wardrobe of my commands and see to it that Doña Maria is provided with everything needful for her comfort.'

'Your Grace, it is my pleasure to provide Doña Maria with a suitable wardrobe and all monies necessary to her welfare until she is reunited with her kinsmen.' Sir Giles came close and brushed the tips of Maria's fingers formally with his lips. 'Until we meet again, Doña Maria.

I will send your duenna, Señora Henriques, to attend you.'

Maria stared at him in utter astonishment but, already, the English girl was beckoning to her to leave the chamber. She was to be parted from Sir Giles now, this instant, without time for adequate expressions of gratitude or farewell? Panic bubbled up within her. She clung, distractedly, to his hand, her eyes brimming with salt tears. It had happened so suddenly. All the uncertainty about her fate she had determinedly thrust aside over these long weeks of their friendly association. She had come to regard him as her defender, her mentor. Now she was being torn, summarily, from his side, and the pain was unbearable.

Noting her distress, he stooped to reassure her. 'I shall see you often at court. There is nothing to fear.' He spoke urgently in Castilian. 'The honour the Queen does you is great. You will remain under her protection while I do everything I can to find your kinfolk. God guard you, Maria.'

The Queen was plainly impatient for Mistress Ursula to hasten Maria to her assigned chamber. Maria curtsyed stiffly to Sir Giles and then to Sir Francis Walsingham. With Mistress Ursula she sank deeply into a low curtsy to the Queen and, reluctantly, allowed herself to be led away, not daring to turn her head for a last sight of Sir Giles.

CHAPTER ELEVEN

THE next few days were to remain in Maria's memory as a blur of constant pain. She and Consuelo were allotted a small room within the Queen's private apartments. Later she was to discover this was a signal honour indeed, for most of the ladies were accommodated in large dormitories under the watchful eye of the mistress of the wardrobe.

Her duties were not arduous; to attend upon the Queen in public, and, occasionally, to help her dress and, if chosen, to sleep within call near to the privy bedchamber, but it was far more usual for the ladies of higher rank to fulfil these tasks and she was left to her own devices most of the time—which hung heavily indeed. The more senior ladies were neither welcoming nor kind and Maria thought they distrusted the foreign woman suddenly thrust into their company.

In the quiet hours of the night she found herself weeping unaccountably and knew she was missing Sir Giles Norwood even more than she could have believed possible. Since those terrible last hours in Cartagena and the horrifying moments in the longboat when she had feared ravishment or worse, he had been constantly near her. She had come to rely on his protection. She longed to see that familiar mocking smile, his tall, elegant figure in its brave finery, to feel the strength of his muscled body as he moved beside her on deck.

She saw him only twice at court. They had exchanged formal pleasantries; indeed, under the curious gaze of her companion ladies he could have said nothing else to her. He had been solicitous on her behalf, had expressed himself delighted that the Queen had extended her favour to Maria. She began to believe that he was glad to be rid of his onerous responsibilities. So far he had been unable to give her any news concerning her own kin.

She had been playing the lute for the Queen's private pleasure one evening when she heard the sounds of desperate weeping as she moved along the corridor in the direction of her own small chamber. She stopped by one of the oriel-windows, the space between the corridor and the casement behind divided by a tapestry depicting the goddess Diana. Maria hesitated. Whoever was in such distress would perhaps not welcome the notice of anyone else, but she had been so unhappy herself of late that she felt she must try to offer comfort. The sufferer was undoubtedly one of the Queen's ladies and Maria knew, after only a short time at court, that Elizabeth could be cruel to any of the women who displeased her.

She put her hand on the tapestry and said quietly, 'Please, nothing can be worth such pain. Can I help?'

The weeping stopped and was replaced by a little gasp, then there was silence.

Maria tried again. 'It is I, Doña Maria. I am very lonely myself sometimes.' Her voice trembled a little. 'I tell myself I shall get used to life at court—in time.'

The tapestry was thrust aside and, in the flaring light from one of the corridor sconces, Maria recognised the tearful, swollen features of the young attendant lady who had first conducted her to her own chamber.

'Mistress Lester, can I be of service? Whatever can be wrong?'

Ursula Lester gulped back another sob. 'I'm sorry. I thought—everyone had gone to their beds—that no one would hear me.'

'I was summoned to play for the Queen. She could not sleep. I am on my way to my own chamber. Are you ill, Mistress Lester, in pain? If so, I could summon the mistress of the wardrobe.'

'No, no, please don't do that. I—I am not ill—just so very unhappy here.' She broke into crying again, turning from Maria towards the leaded casement.

'Are you homesick?' Maria enquired gently and the weeping girl's shoulders shook convulsively. 'I can understand that, only too well. I, too, am very far from home and though my duenna is very kind, like my own mother, I miss my home very much. Where is yours?'

'In Northamptonshire. My—my brother, William, asked the Queen to accept me at court and I thought nothing could be more wonderful. I have been here for three months now and—and——'

'You miss your sisters and brothers, your mother and father? Is that it?'

Mistress Lester shook her head. 'No, no, my father and mother are dead. There was only William and I——'

'Did he force this appointment on you?'

'No, it was as I said, I was very proud to become one of the Queen's ladies. We are not of the old nobility, you understand, and I had no hopes—and then—when William told me I hugged and kissed him but I did not know...'

'What didn't you know, Mistress Lester? Is the Queen unkind to you because you do not come from noble stock?'

'No, the Queen is kind enough.' Mistress Lester smiled wanly. 'At least as kind as she is to everyone when she is in a good mood. The other ladies are not friendly—they,' she gulped again despairingly, 'they despise me—oh, not because of my family—well, yes, in a way, because I am a recusant. I had not understood how it would set me apart and it is not something I could explain to the mistress of the wardrobe.'

Maria sat down beside Ursula on the window-seat. 'I do not think I know that word.'

'No, of course, you would not. Yet, I suppose, being Spanish, you must be of the Old Faith, too?'

Maria's blue eyes opened wide. 'You mean you are Catholic, a true daughter of the Roman Church?'

'Yes, William and I are Catholics.'

'I had thought it forbidden to hear mass——'

'It is. We are not persecuted but we are fined for our non-attendance at church so we do not talk openly of our faith. I would not be so foolish but the others know and are unkind. They say Catholics are all traitors, that I should not be in attendance on Her Grace, that I am not welcome among them, and then, tonight, someone spoilt my embroidery. I had been working on a hand-kerchief to give to Her Grace to celebrate the day of her accession. I am not good at embroidery and the work has been hard, then—then tonight, I found it torn, shredded to pieces. It was almost finished. When I dis-covered it, Mistress Wainwright laughed and the others sniggered. I just ran out of the dormitory and came to hide here away from them all.'

Maria put her hand on the distressed girl's sleeve. 'You must not let them see how they have upset you.'

'I won't go back,' she uttered passionately. 'I can't. I shall ask William to take me home. He must petition the Queen—— '

'But, Mistress Lester, that would play into their hands, and it would not suit your brother's ambitions to do such a thing.'

Ursula considered. 'No, I had not thought. William is kind but he would not be pleased.'

'There is no need for you to return to the dormitory tonight. You can share my bed. The Queen has granted me a little room on my own, I suppose because she understands that my foreignness would place me apart from the other ladies. It is very cramped but there is room for you. Would you care to come with me?'

Ursula lifted her tear-stained face to Maria's. 'That would be so kind. You are sure that——'

'Yes, I'm sure.' Maria nodded encouragingly. 'We—recusants—must stay together. In the morning I will ask the mistress of the wardrobe if you can move in with me. I do not see why she should object. My duenna would chaperon us both.'

So it was that Maria's friendship with Ursula Lester made her stay at court bearable. The brown-haired English girl with the timid smile and large, myopic brown eyes proved an affectionate companion. They were of an age, Ursula being only three months younger than Maria. She had been the latest of the Queen's ladies to

be appointed before Maria. Her father had been only a
lesser baron, now deceased, and her brother, of whom
she never ceased to talk, had recently inherited the manor
just before the previous Christmas.

'William came to court in the New Year and it appears that the Queen is very taken with him,' she told
Maria proudly. 'Of course, that does not surprise me.
William is very handsome and self-possessed. I know
you will agree with me when you see him. We have always
been close and he wished me near to him at court. That
is why he petitioned the Queen for a place for me in the
royal household. But I see him so seldom now and I
have been so lonely here till you came.'

The mistress of the wardrobe had placed no obstacle
in the way of Ursula joining Maria in her own small
chamber and the girls settled down contentedly together.

Perhaps it was because she was so lonely for sight of
Sir Giles Norwood that Maria found herself delighted
by the attentions William Lester lavished on her. He was
every bit as handsome as his sister had described him,
slightly built, compared to Norwood's massive form, but
comely enough. He had brown hair, curling on to his
shoulders, soft brown eyes like his sister's, set candidly
wide apart, and Ursula's fresh complexion. His court
clothes were well cut but less ostentatious than those of
other gallants who crowded Whitehall's galleries and the
Presence Chamber. His manner to Maria was gravely
courteous.

'Doña Maria, I cannot tell you how grateful I am to
you for your kindness to my sister. She has told me how
you have befriended her and agreed to share your
chamber. I know she has been unhappy at court and I
was uncertain what to do about it. Now it appears she
is radiant again.'

Maria smiled. 'I was only too happy to find a companion. I, too, am homesick, Sir William, and, like
Ursula, my faith has not won me popularity among the
ladies.'

He shot her an anxious glance but the brown eyes grew
warm and she knew he was aware that she longed for

the consolation of her faith as much as he and his sister did.

It was natural enough that she found herself often in his company, for now he came frequently to court, since she and Ursula had become such close friends.

He squired the three of them, Consuelo often in attendance, into the town whenever freedom from their duties allowed him to do so. Maria discovered herself blushing furiously when, at court functions, she looked up to find his gaze fixed longingly on her. His extravagant compliments she found flattering and gratifying, since her foreign beauty must have proved somewhat disturbing to the other courtiers who tended to avoid her company. She was not unaware that her fellow ladies found her sudden appointment so close to the Queen surprising and, though they dared not show open hostility, she knew they mistrusted her motives. Little wonder then that she valued the friendship of the Lesters so highly.

She was surprised and a little alarmed when William at last broached the subject of their shared religion. They were sitting together briefly in the garden. Ursula had been with them but had been summoned to the Queen's side and had rushed to obey. William caught at Maria's hand as she half rose from her seat in the pleached arbour to follow.

'You must find the constant intrigues of court very disturbing, Doña Maria. Ursula tells me that you lived a very sheltered life on the *estancia*.'

'Yes, that is true.' Maria grimaced. 'I would not be averse to living away from court. I had not expected such a life, certainly not in England.'

'And you are without the consolation of your religion.'

Though he spoke very low and no one else was near, Maria felt suddenly chilled and looked hurriedly round as if she feared they would be overheard.

'I understood that to hear mass is forbidden.'

'It could be arranged for you to speak with a priest, if you wish to do so.'

'But that would be dangerous, most of all for the priest.'

'There are those who take no heed of danger when their consciences and duties bid them act.'

'Does the Queen know that Ursula——?'

'Elizabeth is tolerant so long as her Catholic families pay their fines and abstain from treasonable activities. Yes, I am sure she is aware of the sympathies of both of us. You must not forget that she herself had instruction in the Old Faith, though she chooses now to set that aside.'

Maria swallowed hard. It had been long since she had been confessed and she had great need of it. 'I would not put you in any danger, Sir William, yet I would speak with a priest if it could be managed safely.'

He bent his brown head over her hand. 'Trust me, Doña Maria. You know I am anxious to serve you in all things.'

'As Doña Maria's present guardian in London, I am delighted to hear you say it.'

Maria glanced up sharply to find Sir Giles Norwood looking genially down at them. Her face flamed. Her hand was still within Sir William Lester's grasp and she pulled it quickly free.

Sir William rose and bowed. 'Doña Maria honours my sister with her friendship, Sir Giles. I am always most anxious to assist her in any way she may desire.'

Sir Giles favoured him with the mocking smile Maria found so heartrendingly familiar and infuriating.

'As I said, I am delighted to hear it, Sir William. If you will excuse us, I will escort my ward into the Queen's presence. She has requested that you sing for us, Maria.'

Lester bowed stiffly and Maria surrendered her fingers into Sir Giles's hold. She was embarrassed at being found alone with Sir William and yet her heart sang at the sight of Sir Giles after two weeks' absence from court.

'So, you have made a friend.'

'You mean Sir William?'

His grey eyes danced. 'I was referring to Mistress Ursula.'

'Oh, yes,' Maria stammered. 'We have much in common——'

'The Lesters are Catholics.'

'That disturbs you?' she said defensively. 'As you know well, I——'

'I would counsel you not to sit apart with young Lester,' he said mildly. 'The Queen disapproves of any flirtatious behaviour in her ladies and will make you suffer for it.' He grinned again broadly. 'Young Lester is very personable and the Queen favours him at present.'

'Ursula had only recently left us——'

His grey eyes were regarding her keenly. 'I see. Do you find him personable, Maria?'

'Both he and his sister have been very kind to me. There has been no impropriety. Always before, Consuelo has been in attendance.'

'Good,' he said softly as he steered her towards the Queen's side.

Two days later Ursula hurried her outside the palace where they could not be overheard and whispered, 'To-morrow afternoon, at my brother's lodgings. There will be little time, since we must go and buy some trinket to explain our absence from the palace. Consuelo can accompany us.'

Maria was both excited and alarmed. 'Suppose the Queen demands our attendance on her?'

'That is unlikely. Her jeweller is summoned for that time and the choosing of gems will occupy her for hours, but, if so, then we must give up our plan to visit William until another occasion.'

Maria had longed to unburden herself to a priest of all her grief and doubt. In Cartagena she had not dared to speak to any other person but Consuelo of her horror at the discovery of the fate of her mother, yet she was sure that if she could speak of such soul-searching to an English priest he must surely understand, suffering dangers and persecution as he did. It would be hard, but perhaps some of this great trouble would pass from her and she would find consolation and acceptance of her faith again.

Consuelo was as alarmed as Maria. '*Querida*, are you sure we shall be safe?'

'Ursula assures me that Sir William has made the arrangements with great caution, as much for the priest's safety as our own.'

'But to go to a man's lodging—even in this country where girls live such wayward lives, such conduct is surely very reprehensible. What would Sir Giles say if he knew?'

'I do not see that it is any business of Sir Giles Norwood. He has abandoned us here and——'

'*Querida*, you are hardly abandoned, granted a position at court, honoured with the Queen's favour, for she does so love to listen to your music. I think you should do nothing which might earn you her anger.'

'Consuelo, do you not wish to confess yourself?'

Consuelo looked uncomfortable. 'Certainly I would like to do so, but if it is dangerous——'

'There will be no danger if we place ourselves unreservedly in Sir William's hands.'

Consuelo looked at her doubtfully but made no further objection.

It was as Ursula had said. The Queen summoned her favourite ladies and closeted herself with her jeweller next day. It proved a simple matter for the three women to leave the palace. Sir William Lester's lodgings were off the Strand and it was not far for them to walk. They were admitted by Sir William's saturnine servant and taken instantly to the parlour. He rose at once to greet them and Maria saw that seated at the table with him was a fresh-faced young man who also stood and bowed courteously as they were introduced. Most likely he was some companion of Sir William who accompanied him nightly to the theatre or the bear pit across the river in the South Wark. Maria felt deeply disappointed that the unexpected arrival of this young man would force them all to cancel their proposed meeting with the proscribed priest. Sir William clearly read her doubts in her regretful expression, for he smiled reassuringly.

'Father John will hear your confession in private while the rest of us repair to my bedchamber.'

Maria stared wonderingly into the merry eyes of the priest, who was nodding in agreement.

'My daughter, I hear you have great need of my comfort.'

When they were alone he insisted that first she should sit down beside him and take wine. Her hand trembled when she lifted the goblet. Even here, in the privacy of Sir William's lodgings, she felt afraid for him as much as for herself.

He was very gentle with her, as she had hoped and prayed he would be. He understood her distress and even her anger directed at those clerics who had doomed her mother and granted her absolution for her feelings of alienation from the Church. Afterwards, he celebrated mass for the household, Consuelo, the Lesters and the manservant attending.

Soon Ursula hurried them out into the Strand again, for they must account for their absence by some purchase and could not be long gone from the palace. At the door of the parlour Maria whispered her profound gratitude to their host. His kiss on her palm was warmer and more ardent than a customary courtesy required.

'I will soon see you at court, Doña Maria. May the Virgin guard you until then.' She could not mistake the throb of true longing in his voce and was faintly disturbed by it.

Pondering on this as well as other problems, Maria was startled to be accosted by Sir Giles Norwood in the Strand. He looked very fine in a new doublet of murrey velvet and she could not forbear to compare his massive masculinity with the slighter, youthful form of Sir William Lester, the subject of her concern. Sir Giles smiled at them genially.

'I give you good day, Doña Maria, and you, Mistress Lester.' He nodded kindly, acknowledging Consuelo's presence. He doffed his feather-trimmed hat and bowed extravagantly. 'And a fine day it is to be sure.' He looked thoughtfully behind them at the door from which they had emerged and it was clear that he knew exactly to whom they had gone visiting. 'Do I find you ladies in search of shops?'

Maria felt, uncomfortably, that those narrowed grey eyes of his had missed nothing of her agitation. 'Yes,' she said, a little breathlessly, her own eyes appealing to Ursula for guidance, 'I have need of some fine woven cambric.' At Ursula's faint nod of acquiescence, she added, 'We were first visiting Mistress Lester's brother.'

Sir Giles's eyes twinkled at her overt reference to the need for materials for shifts. Always she felt he was mocking her, even when he seemed at his most courteous, then his eyes narrowed at her reference to Sir William.

Ursula appeared equally at a loss and Maria found it necessary to take the initiative and chat about inconsequential matters. He attached himself to them for the rest of the expedition and insisted on making them both presents of some bright ribbons at one of the booths nearby.

On the pretext of matching Maria's ribbons to her gown, he drew her slightly apart. 'I am pleased we met. I have news for you of your aunt.'

'You have found her?' Maria gave a glad cry. 'Is she pleased to have news of me or is she . . .?' Her voice trailed off uncertainly. It was more than likely that her remaining kin might prefer to have no truck with their Spanish relative.

'Sir Francis Walsingham dispatched one of his men north in search of her. We discovered that you have one relative only, as far as we could determine, your mother's elder sister, Mistress Anne Winterton, who married Sir Thomas Winterton of Morpeth in Northumberland. She married and travelled north before your mother's marriage to Don Diego and has not been south since. She is delighted to have news of her niece, though saddened to hear of the death of her only sister. She has sent you a letter which Sir Francis's men delivered to me this morning. I had not expected to meet you and will bring it with me to court tonight.'

'Do you think I can see her soon?' Maria's tone was eager. Her pleasure in the discovery that she was not completely alone in England had, for the moment, blotted out her embarrassment at meeting Sir Giles immediately following her illicit meeting with Father John at the Lester lodging.

Sir Giles shook his head doubtfully. 'Northumberland is very far north and your duties in the Queen's household make that quite impossible at present. Later, if you have leave, it might be possible for me to escort you north.' He glanced back at where Mistress Ursula and Consuelo were attempting to haggle with one of the apprentices. Since Consuelo's English was still almost non-existent, they were making little progress.

'Was it imperative that you accompany Mistress Lester to her brother's house?' His tone was sharp and Maria's heart jumped within her breast. Was he merely concerned for her reputation or angered by her meeting with Sir William Lester so soon after his warning?

'Ursula wished to see her brother on family business,' she explained awkwardly. 'Since I had agreed to go shopping with her, it seemed natural I should accompany her. Sir William behaved with true courtesy.'

'I am sure that he did,' Sir Giles said waspishly, and she glanced at him sharply once more.

'Have you some reason to dislike Sir William?'

'I? No, I scarcely know the man.' There was a strange gleam in those grey eyes and, as he turned back to her, she thought them unfathomable, as water in a deep, rain-drenched lake. 'He is new to court, a young coxcomb with his fortune to make. As I said, it is unwise to antagonise the Queen by allowing him too much dalliance with you.'

She was about to retort that no such purpose existed in her mind, to blurt out the true reason for her visit to Sir William's lodging, but was forced to bite back the words. The secret must be kept for the safety of all of them. She lowered her eyes from Sir Giles's searching gaze and reached out for some deep blue ribbon which had taken her fancy. It was the first time in their acquaintanceship that she had kept anything from him and the thought gave her deep pain.

Sir Giles escorted them back to Whitehall and took his leave.

As they hurried through the corridors towards the Queen's apartments, Maria said nervously, 'Do you think Sir Giles suspected our reason for visiting your brother's lodging?'

Ursula chewed her underlip reflectively. 'I don't know. He is a friend of Walsingham. Even so, it was natural that I should visit my brother and take you with me.'

'Ursula, are you always afraid on these occasions?'

'It is for the priest we fear. Sometimes I think William is too trusting.'

'He assured me there is no real danger.'

Ursula shook her head. 'I doubt the trustworthiness of some of his friends.'

'You think them wild, that they lead him astray?'

'What young man does not mix in bad company when he cuts the leading reins?'

At court that evening Sir William Lester signalled Maria out for more attention, which she found increasingly embarrassing under the sardonic eye of Sir Giles. She was aware of Norwood's brooding gaze as she passed him in the dance. Though he passed no further comment and was assiduous in choosing the finest morsels of food for her when they were seated next to each other at the table, she knew he was still angered by Lester's interest. Some perverse desire to further nettle him led her to agreeing to accompany Ursula and her brother once more into the rose garden. Ursula found some excuse to slip away and Maria, suddenly awkward in Sir William's presence, caught her gown on a thorn. In freeing it she pricked her finger, drawing blood. Without hesitation Sir William tore free a portion of the silken cloth which slashed his doublet sleeve and stanched it, preventing it from marring the whiteness of her gown.

'I am sorry sir,' she said. 'You have spoiled your fine new doublet. I know how costly such garments are.'

He shrugged, keeping his hold on her fingers. 'I count such as little cost, when it is of help to you, Doña Maria.'

His voice was faintly slurred with desire and she moved from him somewhat, alarmed by her own foolishness in coming apart with him.

He recognised the instinctive withdrawal. 'Please, do not be angry with me. Have I offended? I swear I had no intention of causing you distress.'

'No, Sir William, I am grateful for your kindness and, most of all, for risking yourself and your household to serve me. You cannot know what this afternoon's visit has done for me.'

'Your time with Father John was a comfort to you?'

'A great comfort.'

'Then I am more than repaid.'

He looked up as a shadow darkened his path, and she saw that he was visibly angered. 'It seems that you are concerned for Doña Maria when she is out of your sight, Sir Giles,' he said stiffly. 'My sister has only this moment left us. As you see, Doña Maria has hurt herself and I was endeavouring to be of assistance.'

Norwood was not to be nettled. He smiled blandly. 'I came in search of Doña Maria before I leave the palace. I have the letter I promised.'

She rose agitatedly and took the proffered package. 'Thank you, sir. We should all return to the banqueting hall.' Her expression warned both men that she wished to see no disturbance between them. She walked between her two escorts back into the crowded chamber and Sir William bowed stiffly to them both and left her side.

'How did you come to injure yourself?' Sir Giles questioned abruptly.

'It is nothing. I caught my skirt on a rose thorn.'

'See the wound is cleansed thoroughly. I have known of grave danger from thorns.'

She was conscious that he was not referring to the one which had torn her gown but hinting of more serious complications. She coloured hotly. 'Thank you for bringing my aunt's letter.'

'I had promised to do so.' He put a detaining hand on her sleeve. 'Maria, I do not speak out of pique. Watch yourself at court.'

Her blue eyes opened very wide. His tone had been so intense that he alarmed her. She looked after Sir William's retreating figure. 'Again, sir, I have to say he has treated me with nothing but the greatest courtesy.'

'That is well, but remember, the court harbours many men, aye, and women too, who have but one burning ambition: to further their own advancement. See to it that you do not become involved in any dangerous schemes.'

She watched his departure thoughtfully. Could it be that he was aware of her purpose in going to the house in the Strand and was warning her of the dangers in consorting with members of the Catholic faction? If so, that did not bode well for her friendship with the Lesters.

Her small chamber was deserted, Consuelo and Ursula still within the banqueting hall. Maria read her aunt's letter eagerly. The tone of writing was warm and Maria was relieved that, apparently, her aunt bore her dead father no rancour because of his marriage with her mother, nor did she appear to blame him for Mary Gascoine's death.

'You will ever be welcome at Morpeth, if Sir Giles Norwood can bring you to us,' she wrote. 'I have not been blessed with children and will be glad to see my niece after this long time. I am proud to hear you are one of the Queen's ladies, and realise that until she releases you from service or you marry we are unlikely to meet. The Virgin guard you, my sweet niece, and bring you soon to Northumberland.'

Maria was touched and cried a little. The letter reminded her of the loss of her parents and emphasised her longing to be with her own kin. While the Queen was kind, Maria was beginning to feel the court a cold place indeed, and set about with many snares.

Ursula returned to find her friend drying her eyes. 'What is it, Maria? Was Sir Giles angry? I saw him escort

you back into the hall. Surely William said nothing to
offend you?'

'No, nothing. I have received a letter from my aunt
and was overcome by the warmth of her sentiments.'

'Then Sir Giles does not suspect?'

'I do not believe so, though he warned me not to in-
volve myself in any intrigues.'

'He warned you against William?'

Maria coloured. 'Not directly. I think he fears any
possible dalliance would anger the Queen.'

Ursula sat silent for a moment, then she said abruptly,
'Maria, William loves you.'

Maria turned, startled. She had been flattered by
William Lester's attentions but had not expected this
direct declaration. 'No, he must not——'

Ursula sighed. 'Ah, then I am right. Poor William,
there is no hope for him. He had hoped that since there
is no dowry... Forgive me, Maria, for mentioning that,
and the knowledge that your reputation renders you
perhaps ineligible for other suitors. He had hoped that
the Queen might be brought to give her consent to his
suit. But you love Giles Norwood, don't you?'

'He hates me, considers me his enemy. He was held
in a Spanish prison, chained to a galley oar. He took
me as a prize of war, that is all. Sometimes I am even
afraid of him.' The last words were whispered. 'Can you
believe what it was like to be his prisoner—to wait for—
to dread——?'

'Yet he did not claim his prize in full?' Ursula probed.
It was the first time she had put into words what Maria
knew the other women had thought and gossiped about.

'There was nothing between Sir Giles and me aboard
his ship,' she said deliberately. 'I know you find that
hard to believe but——'

'Neither William nor I would hear a word against your
virtue, you know that.' Ursula's voice took on a pleading
note. 'Then there could be no barrier between you and
William should you—— There could be many advan-
tages to a match with William. He has no great estates,
yet he is no pauper, and he has hopes——' She stood

up suddenly as if she had started to say something her brother would not have wished her to divulge. 'I talk too much. I have no right to plead my brother's cause. He would chide me for my foolish tongue.' As she moved to shake up her pillow, she said curiously, 'If Sir Giles did not harm you, why are you afraid of him, Maria?'

Maria shook her head. 'I don't know. There is so much enmity between us that I feel—that, one day, he will wish to take vengeance.'

'That is a frightening word.'

'Once I did him a great personal injury.'

Ursula shook her head, bewildered. 'Had he meant to, surely he would not have brought you safely to England and given you into the Queen's keeping?'

Later, restless, after Ursula and Consuelo had fallen asleep, Maria pondered over her friend's words.

What were Sir Giles's intentions? Why had he brought her to court? Most of all, if he had no love for her, why was he so anxious that she should not associate with Sir William Lester?

CHAPTER TWELVE

ONE morning several weeks later Maria was summoned to the Queen's apartment very early. She was somewhat alarmed, for the Queen rarely sent for her younger ladies at this time of the morning unless some urgent matter needed to be discussed. Very often such matters were of an unpleasant nature and meant that the Queen was extremely angry with the lady in question.

Maria had been circumspect, as Sir Giles had warned her, but she was determined not to break her friendship with the Lesters and, though she had not encouraged Sir William, she had not completely avoided him either. Only yesterday when riding in attendance on the Queen her horse had gone lame and Sir William had immediately dismounted to render her assistance. It had been unfortunate that Sir Giles had ridden up only moments later to find them alone together. He had not troubled to hide his disapproval and had remained by her side for the remainder of the excursion. Had the Queen been informed of her reprehensible behaviour and summoned her now to either castigate her or worse?

Elizabeth was seated at the virginals and quite alone. She greeted Maria warmly, which resolved her fears. She was instructed to seat herself on a low stool at the Queen's feet.

'Maria, you look very well and so fresh, more so than many of my ladies, who, I fear, do not always sleep the night through, as they should do when their duties require them to attend on me next day.'

'Your Grace?'

Elizabeth gave a grim little chuckle. 'My child, I am fully aware of what goes on in the corridors of the palace, even after I have retired. Sometimes it suits me to cast a blind eye on the proceedings and sometimes I send the offenders home to their estates to bethink them of their sins. However, I have no such problems with you. I'm sure you remain as virginal as the traditional white of your gown.'

Maria flushed hotly. She had always wondered just what the Queen privately thought of her relationship with Sir Giles Norwood.

Her doubts were hastily set at rest. 'I have just had Giles Norwood in here. He begged me to allow him to pay court to you. It would seem an eminently suitable match. After all, you have a predicament, Maria—no dowry. Norwood is a rascal, but a handsome devil, and, I believe, would treat you well. What do you think of the match?'

'Your Grace, I have not thought——'

'Really?' the Queen's eyebrows rose as if she doubted the truth of that statement. 'Well, think now, chit. You're unlikely to receive a better offer, that is unless your heart is already engaged elsewhere. If so, we should know at once and decide how best to advise you.'

'No, Your Grace, there is no one. At least——'

'Young Will Lester has eyes for you, that much I've noticed. Has he made pretty speeches?'

'Yes, Your Grace,' Maria whispered uncertainly. 'But nothing improper has happened between us.'

'No, I should hope not,' the Queen said tartly. 'And it doesn't bother Lester that half the court thinks Norwood has prior claim?'

'I do not know, Your Grace.'

The Queen stilled Maria's attempted explanation with a raised hand. 'I believe what Giles Norwood tells me, that you are untouched and perfectly suitable to attend on me. It is not what others think and I do not doubt that you have been chillingly received because of it, except for the kindness of young Ursula Lester.'

'She has been like a sister to me.'

'And Will Lester like a brother?' The Queen gave a bray of coarse laughter then, just as quickly, sobered again. 'Do you care for the man?'

'I like him, Your Grace.'

'And Norwood? Do you like him? Speak up, child. You cannot deny you had ample opportunity to get to know him.' Maria was silent and the Queen tapped her arm impatiently with her fan. 'Do you dislike Norwood?'

'No, Your Grace.' Still the answer was hesitant.

'You would not oppose the match if I give it my approval?'

Maria's eyes were hidden from the Queen's piercing gaze as she kept her head studiously lowered. 'I would not dare go counter to Your Grace's wishes.'

'Hmm.' The Queen tapped her fan on her knee while she considered. 'This proposal seems to have come as a shock to you. Norwood gave you no indication that he would ask for your hand?'

'No, Your Grace.'

The Queen made no further comment, but Maria was aware that the answer surprised her. At last she said, 'I have told Sir Giles that I have no objection to his courtship provided that he behaves within the bounds of propriety. He is waiting in the antechamber and I have sent for your duenna. I will send him to you. Consider well what he has to say. He may have his faults, but he is a true man, Maria. Were I younger, I might envy you.' She smiled indulgently, rose and left Maria, who sank into a deep curtsy as the Queen passed.

She had no opportunity to come to terms with the suddenness of Sir Giles's declaration for, on rising from her curtsy, she found he was already within the chamber and coming close to her. He was dressed faultlessly if less flamboyantly today in doublet and hose of blue trimmed with silver braid. He bowed low and she found herself trembling so much that he was forced to put out a hand to steady her.

'You are unwell?' He spoke in Castilian and she was grateful for that. Concern showed in his tone.

'No, no. I just—sat cramped on the stool at Her Grace's feet. I am well.'

She felt so confused and was glad when Consuelo tapped and came to seat herself on the window-seat just out of earshot.

'The Queen has told you?' Still he spoke in Spanish and she answered in the same language.

'She told me that you have asked for my hand.'

'Surely you must have been aware of my intentions. I wished you to be placed at court so that, later, there would be no harmful gossip concerning us. The Queen's approval would put an end to any of that. You understand?'

'I understand that, always, there will be unkind gossip.'

'I assure you no one will dare——'

'If the Queen wishes this match, indeed no one will dare.' She looked up at him directly. 'Why do you wish to marry me, Sir Giles?'

He leaned forward and took her hand, imperiously waving back Consuelo who had half risen from the window-seat. 'You know why I wish to wed you. You belong to me, you've always belonged to me. Even from the first, you came to me of your own free will in that hell-hole of the galley slave deck. I paid the price for your—curiosity.'

It was long since he had reminded her of that terrible flogging he had endured because of her foolishness, and she went deadly cold. His grip on her hands was punishing, crushing the slender bones, the glitter of those grey eyes frightening.

Her will was deserting her, her bones melting, so that she felt breathless and unable to stand without support. Blindly she reached behind her for a chair and sank down into it. All these weeks at court she had longed for him to declare himself, yet now she was filled with panic at the thought of belonging utterly to him. In those strong brown hands would lie her fate. She recalled her deadly terror as he had lain by her side that night in Cadiz and the long hours of dry-mouthed fear she had endured in the cabin that first night aboard the *Gloriana*. She could not envisage life without him and yet, once she was his, he had power to make or destroy her. During the later weeks aboard his ship she had thought she was beginning to know Giles Norwood, the man, as opposed to Captain Norwood her corsair enemy. But lately she had seen him look across the crowded court at her with a grim intensity in which she had read nothing but hostility. Wherever she had been he had been close, yet there had seemed a barrier between them which she had felt it impossible to pull down. He had shown solicitude for her yet behaved like a coldly courteous stranger. She had been utterly bewildered by his frequent changes of mood. Now, out of the blue, he had requested her hand in marriage and, just when she should have been ready to surrender to him, she was unaccountably afraid.

As if he read her doubt and was angered by it, he ignored Consuelo and suddenly stooped and kissed her full on the mouth. It was not the bruising, frighteningly violent kiss he had bestowed on her in Cadiz. Decorum placed boundaries upon his conduct here, within the palace, where, at any moment, someone might enter this room, but it was no courteous kiss of greeting. It seared her soul and she gave a little gasp of fear as he released her.

He felt her tremble and scowled. 'What is wrong? Is it that young dog, Will Lester? He is not for you. I know he has been making you flattering speeches and you have been too much in his company. Several times you have visited him in his lodgings, which was ill-advised. On one occasion his sister was not with you.'

Stung to anger she retorted, 'Why have you been spying on me? Always I was accompanied by Consuelo. There could be no harm in my visiting the lodgings of my friend's brother.' How could she explain that those visits had been to see Father John, not Sir William Lester?

'I would keep you safe,' he muttered grimly. 'I warned you. The Lesters are known Catholics and some of their friends are not well disposed to the Queen or her advisers.'

'Do you accuse William Lester of treason?' She stared at him open-mouthed.

'I did not go so far as to say that. His associations have not always been wise.'

'You are jealous of Will Lester,' she said contemptuously.

'Very well, I will admit it. I command you to avoid his company.' He had gripped her wrists again and she made a little grimace of pain.

'I am not your slave, sir, do not belong to you yet, cannot be commanded by you. I will go where I please, keep company with whom I please.'

'You are my betrothed and will behave with discretion.'

'I have not given my consent,' she jibed back at him. 'Until I do, do not attempt to order my life.'

'It is the Queen's wish that you become my wife.' His eyes had become hard, opaque. Her heart fluttered again. One part of her longed to be his, another warned her that life with him would not be easy.

She pulled her wrists free. 'You—must give me time, Sir Giles.' The words were coldly formal and he made an impatient gesture of his hand as if he would force her to surrender, then, recollecting his court manners, he rose and bowed very low.

'Forgive me, I am impatient to announce to the whole court how fortunate I am in my choice. I have startled you, alarmed you. I had no intention of so doing. You look decidedly pale. Send Consuelo to the wardrobe mistress to beg leave of absence for the rest of the day from all duties. The Queen will understand. Plead a headache.'

She swallowed and nodded.

'When may I call on you again?'

'At your convenience, Sir Giles. As you are at pains to assure me, the Queen approves your courtship.'

If he was angered by the coldness of her answer, he did not show it, merely bowed and took his departure.

Consuelo came anxiously to her side. '*Querida*, is it as I thought? Has Sir Giles asked for you?'

Maria avoided her duenna's eye. 'Yes, the Queen informed me of his request and commanded me to listen to his courtship. I am——' She turned back to Consuelo, her eyes swimming with tears. 'I—I do not know what to do.'

'But you love him, *querida*.'

'Yes, yes,' the words were softly muffled, 'I love him, but—I am afraid of him.'

Consuelo opened her mouth to say something, then catching her charge's eye swallowed back the words and silently accompanied Maria to her own chamber, which fortunately was deserted.

After she had dispatched Consuelo to the mistress of the wardrobe, Maria lay on her bed, thoughts jangling in her head. The assumed headache had become a fact. She had wanted Giles to hold her, possess her. The hot blood raced in her veins whenever he drew near her, yet she feared her life as his wife. He could well dismiss her to his estates in the North while he ruffled it at court. She knew she would probably be far more content wed to William Lester. He would cherish her, truly devote his life to her. Giles Norwood would constantly be off on some escapade he hoped would enrich his estates and she would spend her days praying that he would return to her safely. Yet the Queen favoured the match and she could not defy Elizabeth. But why had he asked for her? She had no dowry, no hopes of inheritance. Her aunt in Northumberland had expressed herself anxious to see her, but there had been no suggestion that she would take responsibility for her niece. Giles Norwood was behaving in an utterly bewildering manner. He had abandoned her at court, now he wished to hasten her away from it by a quickly arranged marriage. Try as she might, she could make no sense of his motives.

Consuelo returned with the expected permission which freed her from court duties and the information that Ursula had left the palace.

'Mistress Rhodes believes she has gone to her brother's lodging in the Strand. A groom rode with her.'

Both Ursula and William must be informed of the way events had shaped. Maria bit her lip thoughtfully. She knew the Queen's avowed wish for this marriage would be a blow to his hopes. Ursula would be devastated by the likelihood of Maria's withdrawal from court service.

She sat up on the bed. 'We will go in search of Mistress Lester,' she said determinedly, to stifle any argument from Consuelo. There was a hope, too, that Father John would be present to add his advice and the consolation that only he could give.

The obsequious servant who admitted her to Sir William Lester's lodgings looked surprised to see her, but, when she asked for Sir William, he showed her into the parlour.

'I regret, mistress, that Sir William is engaged. The moment his guests leave I will inform him you are here.'

'Actually I am in search of Mistress Ursula. Is she here?'

'No, Mistress, but I heard Sir William say he expects her later today. If you will wait——'

'Thank you, I will.'

She seated herself on the cushioned bench near the window while Consuelo sat on a stool by the door. Through the leaded panes Maria could see the busy thoroughfare of the Strand. This panorama of teeming life and commerce of London never ceased to fascinate her. She could never have enough of her new freedom to walk abroad with her duenna, to hear the merchants and apprentices calling their wares, the constant noise and bustle of it all, a procession of colour side by side with the squalor and fetid corruption of the London streets.

The servant provided them with wine. On leaving, he left the door slightly ajar and she could hear the murmur of talk in the study close by. The English voices droned on and she took little heed until one name arrested her attention.

'Be very cautious, Will, the Spanish woman was brought here by Norwood and I've every reason to believe he's Walsingham's creature.'

Maria's head jerked up as she heard Will Lester's confident laugh. 'She has assured Ursula that there was nothing between them. You and I find that hard to believe, but it was so, I'm sure.'

'You are besotted, my friend. I pray she has never clapped eyes on Father John Ballard.'

Consuelo rose to close the door, but Maria gestured her to leave it ajar. Very softly she moved to take Consuelo's stool and waved her to the window-bench.

Another voice, familiar, though she could not place it, continued. 'Will knows his own business. He is fully aware of what is at stake. I have everything in hand now. The Queen has been informed of Parma's willingness to send troops. He needs only a safe harbour at which to land them. Gifford has visited Morgan in the Bastille and carries letters directly to the Queen. Despite Paulet's close watch on her, she has received them and will answer me personally. I have insisted on that.'

Maria's brows contracted in bewilderment. Parma's name she knew well. He was the Spanish governor of the Low Countries. Yet the reference to the Queen was strange. Why should Elizabeth contact one who might prove to be a deadly enemy and why should Parma wish to land troops in England? She thought she recognised the voice now as that of Anthony Babington, one of the most handsome of the Queen's dilettante courtiers. Elizabeth had been amused by him, flattered, perhaps, by his obsequious attendance, but Maria could not believe she would ever be guided by his opinions. Nor was the man in any position to insist that she correspond with him.

The talk went on, more quietly now, as if the men had moved closer together, further from the study door. True, Sir Giles was a friend of Walsingham. Why should Will Lester be concerned by that?

Maria jumped slightly in her seat. Giles's hostility towards Lester had been obvious. She herself had taxed him with charging Lester with treason, which he had not fully denied. Walsingham's main concern was the Queen's safety and he was a fanatical enemy of the captive Queen of Scots. She, then, must be the Queen referred to. And Lester and his associates were in treasonable correspondence with her? Maria was appalled. Did Will fully understand the consequences both to him and to Ursula, should his actions be discovered?

Will's voice, louder now, as if he'd changed his position, possibly risen to address the company. 'Then it is settled. Smeaton's brat must die, and soon. It is an affront to God that she continues to sit on England's throne. Is there a man at court who does not know how Harry of England was cuckolded by the Boleyn whore, even before he took her to wife?'

Maria's face drained of all colour. The words were uttered with such vituperative hatred she could hardly believe it was her friend's brother who uttered them.

She hardly understood the import of it. She had known that Queen Mary of England had never fully accepted Elizabeth as her sister. Maria understood her feelings. Elizabeth's birth had brought Queen Mary's mother the terrible suffering many believed had brought about her early death. Could what Lester said be true? Did some people in England suspect that their Queen was not a Tudor, not Harry's daughter, but some bastard got on Anne Boleyn by some man called Smeaton? The Queen's mother had been executed for the dire sin of adultery. Maria crossed herself as she thought of the young Queen's sad death on Tower Green, yet all acknowledged Elizabeth as King Harry's heir, England's rightful sovereign. And Will had spoken, sneeringly, of a plot to murder her.

A chair scraped across the floor in the study, as if the party was preparing to split up.

Babington sounded cheerful about the progress of their deliberations. 'Then we meet once more at St Giles's Fields. By then I should have my answer from Queen Mary. I will summon John Charnock and Savage. I leave Tichbourne to you, Lester, and you, Barnwell, will be in touch with Jones. You do assure me your sister knows nothing of this, Will?'

'Nothing, I swear it.'

'Good. If we choose a day when she is in attendance, she will admit you to the Queen's presence without surprise or alarm.'

Will called for his servant to see out his guests. Maria stumbled from her stool in sudden panic.

She had heard too much. Her face would betray her and the horror of what she had overheard had her in an icy grip. She must escape, contact Sir Giles. He would take her to Walsingham. The Queen must be immediately informed of her peril.

Consuelo was watching, puzzled. She had insufficient English to understand, but she knew by Maria's expression that she was frightened and rose hastily to her feet.

'Go into the hall and find if the way to the outside door is clear.'

Consuelo nodded, wasting no time in pointless questions. She slipped out of the parlour and, returning quickly, beckoned that all was well.

Maria steadied the stool which her unwary foot had threatened to send spinning, then hurried from the room through the hall, in an agony of fear that they would be seen and prevented from leaving. She rushed thankfully into the clamour of the Strand. Without even waiting for Consuelo, she broke into a stumbling run as if she feared that the plotters would come racing after her. Her foot caught in her skirt and she fell sprawling, half in the stinking filth of the open kennel which ran the length of the street, now dry but choked with the refuse of the town.

She gave one sharp cry of fear as a strong arm reached to lift her to her feet and looked into the cool grey eyes of Giles Norwood. They were no longer mocking, but narrowed in steely concern. He caught her close, not caring if they were observed.

'Steady now, *querida*. Whatever it was that made you run from that house as if the devils in hell were at your heels cannot hurt you now. I am here to protect you.'

She gave a great sob of relief and laid her head on his shoulder. 'Thank God, oh, thank God. I was coming to find you. Will Lester and his friends—they plot—they intend——'

'Hush, *querida*, not out here. Gently, all is well.'

She stared up at him, amazed. 'How can you know. It is only just now that I heard——' She shuddered. 'But you do know. That is why you—followed me?' She was beginning to understand, but was numbed by the discovery.

He placed his cloak round her shoulders to hide the ruin of her gown. 'Come, we'll go to Walsingham's town house. It is closer than the palace.'

Calling to Consuelo to attend Maria, he put a supporting arm round her waist. 'Did you hurt yourself? Can you walk?'

She shook her head. She was shocked and trembling, but, leaning heavily against him, she was able to go where he wished.

They were admitted to the Secretary of State's house without being challenged and Sir Giles called for a maidservant to take Maria above stairs where any hurt she had sustained could be tended and her soiled gown either cleaned or changed.

Consuelo divested Maria of the gown and one of Walsingham's serving maids provided a wrapper from her mistress's wardrobe. She brought wine and Maria drank thankfully, knowing she must gain control of herself quickly. Consuelo regarded her grimly and Maria reached out and gave her duenna an affectionate, reassuring hug. Sir Giles and Walsingham would need her to remember as much as she could of what she had overheard and it was essential she be accurate.

'Norwood...he's Walsingham's creature,' they had said. Yes, she understood now, and thanked God for it. Her blue eyes smouldered with contempt for those vain and foolish creatures of the King of Spain, for they were all pawns, Lester, Babington, and the others. She had been a subject of Philip, but she knew her loyalty now. She could not stand by and allow an act so foul as they proposed to be perpetrated. The Queen had been good to her, never once questioned her allegiance, though she had been brought captive to England. Neither had she judged Maria wanton, though there had been evidence enough to support the charge.

Giles had called her *'querida'*, had looked alarmed for her. Did he truly care for her, or was he simply intent on discovering quickly all she knew? She suspected now that she had been deliberately placed at court knowing that, since she was Catholic, she would be befriended by members of that faction. Several times she had come across Sir Giles outside the Lester lodging. How simple it had been for him to spy upon the Lesters when all at court knew his interest in Maria. How natural that he should keep his eye upon the woman who had come to England under his protection. The idea struck her as from a physical blow and she was still reeling from it when Walsingham entered the chamber, Sir Giles at his heels.

'Are you hurt, Doña Maria?'

She shook her head.

'Well enough to talk?'

This time she nodded, though tears started to her eyes.

Walsingham dismissed the maid then seated himself on a chair by the bed where Maria was resting, her hand still gripping Consuelo's.

'Take your time. Be as exact as you can. The Queen's safety may well depend on it.'

'Sir Francis, did you suspect Sir William Lester and his friends were plotting against the Queen?'

He nodded, one hand stroking his dark, pointed beard.

Maria said furiously, 'Her Grace is in peril of her life yet you let those men walk free!'

'Doña Maria, we do not know all of them. If we take those we suspect, bigger fish may escape the net and the Queen's danger would then be greater. We assemble fact by fact, piecemeal. Tell me all you know.'

She told her story slowly, deliberately, pausing afterwards to stare up into Sir Giles's face.

'You think you recognised the voice of one of them as Anthony Babington's?'

'Yes. It is rather high-pitched, distinctive.'

'And the names mentioned. Tell me as many as you can recall.'

She bit her lip. 'I'm not sure how many were present; Will Lester, certainly, and Babington, oh, yes, and Babington spoke directly to someone called Barnwell, ordered him to contact a man called Jones and someone named Savage. That is truly an English name?'

Sir Giles smiled grimly. 'Aye, *querida*, and, in this case, tells us truly the nature of the man. Any other names? Be very sure.'

She frowned, concentrating. Those names had all been strange to her, as all English names were. 'Wait, Babington spoke of the meeting at St Giles's Fields, and said he would summon——' she racked her brains '—someone like Fish—Fishborne?'

'Tichbourne?'

'Yes, I think that was it.'

The two men exchanged knowledgeable glances.

Maria shook her head doubtfully. 'I'm sure there was one other name, something "knock", I could not be sure—and yes——' She broke off awkwardly.

'A priest was named. Was that it, Doña Maria? I can understand your reluctance to betray the man.' Walsingham's tone was dry. 'Ballard, was it, John Ballard?'

She coloured and bowed her head.

'And nothing was said of the method of the actual attempt?'

Maria lowered her eyes again and plucked restlessly at the bedcover. Ursula Lester was innocent. Her brother had declared it, and Maria believed him, but she was involved, and, if she was taken, questioned in the Tower—Maria's blood ran cold at the thought. At last she said, hesitantly, 'Mistress Ursula was, all unknowingly, to usher Sir William into the Queen's presence on some pretext or other. He swore she knew nothing of his intentions——'

'And the day?' Walsingham's grim expression revealed nothing of his feelings for the doomed girl.

Maria shook her head helplessly. 'The meeting began to break up then and I was anxious not to be found there.'

'Naturally.'

'No harm must come to Ursula. I'm sure she does not know anything of the plot.'

Walsingham turned abruptly and moved to stare out of the window. His hands, clasped behind his back, were twitching spasmodically. Sir Giles gestured Maria to silence as she made to plead Ursula's cause more vehemently.

Walsingham turned back to her at last. 'Lester did not see you, has no idea you heard?'

Sir Giles snapped, 'I won't allow her to imperil herself further.'

Maria felt numbed now that her suspicions were confirmed. They had used her to get close to Ursula Lester. Sir Giles had no need for her other than to further his work for his superior. So anxious was he for preferment that he was prepared to marry a dowerless captive.

And she had given him her heart. She loved him so deeply that she thought she would die slowly, bit by bit, if she were to be parted from him. Yet how could she allow him to sacrifice himself? He had suffered so terribly at the hands of the Spaniards that he must hold nothing for her but revulsion. He had brought her here, worked with her, deceived her with talk of genuine concern for her interests, so that she had dared to believe he would come to love her. It had been necessary, as much so as his business of spying in Cadiz. Gentleman though he was, he would use her, if it furthered the cause of his beloved sovereign, and pay the price, pretend to love Maria Santiago y Talavera, marry her and devote his life to her, though his heart was not in it.

The two men were plainly at odds. She brought her thoughts back to concentrate on their words.

'Doña Maria will be in no real danger. We shall have Lester watched every moment.'

'But he must have been told by his servant that she was there and might have overheard.'

'He's besotted with Doña Maria. He will wish to think well of her.'

Sir Giles made an impatient gesture. 'The man's a fanatic. If he thinks she betrayed him, he'll kill her without mercy. The love of his sacred cause will come first.'

Yes, thought Maria bitterly, the love of the cause would always come first for these men.

Walsingham was regarding her with that chilling black stare. 'Doña Maria, these plotters are dangerous, as you realise only too well. If you refuse to help there can be no way open to us but to arrest Mistress Lester. She may know something of her brother's plans, however unwittingly.'

'What do you wish me to do?' Maria asked quietly.

'No!' Sir Giles exploded into defiant fury.

Walsingham ignored him. 'Return to the palace. Find Ursula. Convince her that you felt ill while waiting at her brother's lodging, so that you left hurriedly, without seeing the servant to explain your decision to leave quickly. She will be likely to believe you. After all, you say you excused yourself from duties on the grounds of ill health. It is a risk.' He shrugged.

'I understand.' Maria rose to her feet, deliberately avoiding Sir Giles's eyes. 'And now, if you please, if a clean gown could be provided, I will go straight back to Whitehall. I take it you will expect me to report anything I feel is suspicious to Sir Giles?'

Walsingham bowed and nodded. 'I'll order a carriage. Giles will escort you.' It was a direct order.

Sir Giles barred her way to the door after he had left. 'Why were you visiting Lester?'

'I was in search of Ursula.'

'You wished to discuss my proposal with her?'

'I thought she and Sir William had a right to be informed of it.'

'You felt such a need to escape my influence that you fled the palace?'

'It was natural enough for me to seek counsel of Ursula. She has been dear as a sister to me.'

'The sister of a traitor.'

'I had no knowledge of that,' she flashed at him, 'though you appeared to do so.'

He sighed. 'We will speak of this further when the immediate peril is over.'

His words jarred her from her resentment. 'You think the Queen's danger is so great?'

'Certainly, and yours. Why were you so foolish as to agree to work with Walsingham? He could not have forced you to it, had you resisted, as I wished.'

She turned from him angrily. 'I had no wish to have Ursula tortured.'

He did not deny her allegation.

'Leave me now,' she said curtly. 'I need to dress for the journey.'

A clean gown was duly provided by someone in the Walsingham household and Maria was informed that a coach stood ready at the door. She took her place at Sir Giles's side, thankful there could be no more intimate talk while Consuelo sat facing them.

At the entrance to the Queen's apartments Sir Giles gestured for Consuelo to go inside. 'I shall be in touch with you constantly. No one can be surprised at my nearness to you now. Keep watch on all who speak to the Lesters, but take no unnecessary risks.'

Ursula was not in their chamber and Maria was relieved that she would not have to explain her change of gown or the circumstances of her meeting with Sir Giles. Hastily she told Consuelo what she felt was needful without going into details. Naturally, Consuelo must be warned not to mention either her accident or her visit to Walsingham's town house.

CHAPTER THIRTEEN

IT WAS easier than Maria had feared. When Ursula joined her that evening, she readily accepted Maria's tale, startled though she was to hear of Sir Giles Norwood's sudden proposal.

'You cannot refuse him, if the Queen commands, yet William will be distraught.'

Maria lowered her gaze from Ursula's brown eyes. The mention of the man's name brought sharp bile to her throat. 'I have not yet accepted him.'

'And you love him, Maria, don't you?'

'I don't know what I feel for Sir Giles. I only know I am afraid.'

Ursula shook her head vehemently. 'Obey the Queen. Receive him graciously and play for time.' She kissed Maria affectionately and turned to her bed.

Maria was left wondering what she meant. Play for what time? For Elizabeth to be succeeded by another who would be more tolerant of William Lester's desires? She dismissed the thought as an unworthy suspicion. Ursula simply could not be aware of such a dastardly plot.

Next day Sir William was all concern for her health. Ursula had told him of her reason for leaving his lodging so urgently.

'Ursula told me the reason for your distress. The Queen's wishes are all-powerful. Norwood is deep in her favour and his ill-gotten gains make him a more worthy suitor than a man of my poor means.'

The warm summer days passed in a flurry of courtly pleasures. It was as if no one about the Queen was aware of her peril, yet it seemed to Maria that those of the council made knowledgeable by Walsingham waited in a kind of breathless hush like the quietness which often presaged a storm. Always she felt as she rode by the Queen on hawking parties, watched the men at tennis, or danced in the heavy-scented cloying air of the palace that she dared not take her eyes from the bejewelled forms of the plotters. Babington appeared gayer than ever, his high-pitched, almost effeminate voice raised in some extravagant flattery. If the Queen had been informed of his or any of the others' perfidy she gave no sign, accepting their honeyed compliments and, coy as a young girl, playing one against the other in the glittering play and counterplay of court intrigue.

Sir Giles was always close to Maria's side. She longed to believe that he truly wished to be in her company, and was not simply playing his part dutifully in the dangerous game of espionage ordered by his sardonic master, Walsingham. He had not, as yet, demanded an answer to his proposal, nor had she referred to it.

It was four more days before she had anything she thought significant to report to Giles.

She and Ursula were summoned by the mistress of the wardrobe. That austere dame's cold eyes assessed the pair and appeared to find both wanting.

'The Queen has graciously requested that you two should be in attendance in her bedchamber tonight.' She sniffed, an outward acknowledgement of their unworthiness of so singular a mark of favour. 'You, Ursula, will sleep within the royal chamber. Doña Maria, you will be in the ante-room, should there be a need to summon a page or officer of the court, since the Queen must never be left unattended.'

A tingle of excitement shot through Maria. Had Walsingham arranged this as a trap in which to ensnare William Lester? She found it hard to concentrate while Ursula chattered of her delight.

'I thought the Queen had never noticed me. It could be a forerunner of some special interest, even an arranged match. She has already been busy on your account.'

'That is what you want, to be sold off in marriage?'

Ursula wrinkled her nose. 'It would depend on the proposed bridegroom.' She blushed. 'There have been one or two gentlemen who have been very attentive recently.'

'Master Christopher Ruddington, for example, one whom you would not be averse to accepting?'

It was a shrewd guess and Ursula wriggled in delighted embarrassment. 'He is wealthy and handsome, but I doubt if his mother would approve. She is a grand lady, yet if the Queen were to remark on the suitability of the match, that would not come amiss.' She laughed again and hastened off to inform her brother of her good fortune. Maria noted he had just entered the Stone Gallery.

She watched them, their heads close together. Maria thought she detected a start of surprise from Sir William and a distinct stiffening of the spine, as if the knowledge of his sister's closeness to the Queen and its sinister opportunity for him was not lost on him. She continued to watch him closely throughout the day and was able to inform Sir Giles later that evening of a conversation Lester had had with Babington. They were strolling together in the rose garden. She was aware that many of the ladies now accepted the notion that they were already betrothed.

'If you are right, and Sir William will use her in the plot, they will not turn down this opportunity.' He took her chilled fingers in his firm clasp. 'You will be very close to the Queen. This frightens you?'

'You think Sir Francis has arranged this?'

'It seems likely. He has not informed me, but it is ever his way never to allow his left hand to know what his right hand is doing. Be sure I shall be on hand should you need me.'

'But how? The Queen's apartments are close-guarded. Neither you nor Sir William could be allowed in.'

He smiled grimly. 'There are ways. Trust me.'

She knew she could and let out a relieved breath, but after he had left her she found herself realising that he, too, would be in danger, and the fear of that left her weak at the knees.

The Queen announced her intention of retiring early that night. 'My head pains me. The heat and stink of musk in the Presence Chamber has quite overpowered me. No,' she snapped, as the mistress of the wardrobe prepared to divest her of her ornate overgown. 'Doña Maria and that minx, Ursula Lester, are perfectly capable; give them something to do, allow Doña Maria to consider how much better off she would be ordering her own household than waiting upon her sovereign.'

'Your Grace knows it is a great pleasure to me——'

Before Ursula could add her protestation of loyalty to Maria's, the Queen, irritably, began removing her jewels and handing them to Maria.

'Mistress Lester, the jewel box. Hurry, girl, am I to wait all night? Do you think I retired ill to be served by chits with their minds on other things—gallants, for instance?'

She was at her most fractious, rejecting all proffered nightrobes and demanding others less heavy, cuffing Ursula when she dropped the smaller of the jewel boxes and fanning herself vigorously while she berated courtiers who had forced their attentions upon her during the evening.

Maria began to wonder if Walsingham had informed the Queen of his intentions and, if so, she was likely to be feeling as apprehensive about the outcome as Maria. Like Ursula, her hands were clumsy and shook as she carried the bowl of scented water the Queen had used to refresh herself away from the bedside. Ursula shot her a sympathetic glance and dropped her voice to a whisper.

'Honour or no, I shall be glad when this night's work is at an end.'

Maria shuddered. The words could well be prophetic. She avoided her companion's eyes and hastened off on her errand.

At last the Queen was settled and the curtains round the royal bed pulled. The truckle-bed had been pulled out for Ursula's use and Maria prepared to retire to the ante-room. Consuelo helped the two girls to undress in the ante-room where their whispers could not disturb the Queen, then she was dismissed and Ursula returned to her watch.

Maria glimpsed the solid, reassuring figure of the halberdier on guard as Consuelo left. Finally the noise of court revelry ceased and the only sound she heard in the corridor was the repeated tramp of the guard's feet as he approached the door and moved from it again on his beat. How could it be possible for any of the plotters to reach the Queen, or, if they managed to do so, how could Walsingham's men or Giles come to her assistance should she need them? She prayed fervently that the security of the palace guard system was as the Queen expected and required it to be and that the night would pass without incident.

Tonight it was suffocatingly hot and airless, even for Maria, who was used to the heat. This cloying humidity was typical of this land of uncertain weather. There had been a thunderstorm two days ago and Maria thought the pressure was building up to another. If so, it might bring welcome relief and refresh the air.

She lay down and tried to rest, but her breathing appeared over-loud in her own ears and the darkness when the heavy velvet curtains were pulled seemed to be pressing down on her like a weight. She flinched at some sound outside and struggled up in the bed. Her eyes moved to the thin bar of light from the slightly opened door of the Queen's bedchamber where candles still burned. She waited, anxiously, lest Ursula summon her, though the sound she thought she had heard had undoubtedly come from the corridor. She was about to reach for the rush-holder on the stand by the bedside with its tinder and flint when her wrist was caught in a punishing grip. Her scream was cut off by a firm hand over her mouth.

'*Querida*, do you not remember when this happened before and I dared not then let you cry out, as I dare not now?'

The hand was withdrawn and Maria was drawn protectively close to the perfumed velvet pile of Sir Giles Norwood's doublet.

'Giles, I thought——'

'Of course you did, but I told you I would keep watch on you.'

'The guard?'

He chuckled. 'The fellow was amused by my desire to be with my sweetheart. Don't be afraid, *querida*, it will ill behove him to talk of tonight's adventures and I've made sure he's well aware of it.'

'Don't you trust him?'

'I trust no one, and especially not tonight.' His tone was grim. 'And now, *querida*, we will share this narrow cot of yours for a while and lie as close as once we did in that fine house of your uncle's in Cadiz.'

She lay close to his heart, could feel it beating against her own breast. They were close confined in the narrow bed and their limbs entwined. Now she felt no fear, not even for her own maiden state. She had needed him and he was here. Whatever occurred now, they were together and the enveloping darkness no longer held menace. His breath, not unpleasantly wine-fumed, fanned her cheek and she felt a thrill of delight at the rasp of silky beard against her soft flesh.

There was movement outside in the corridor once more, the murmur of voices. Sir Giles's voice was very soft in her ear.

'Can you be very brave and lie perfectly still? I must leave you for a while, yet I will be very near.'

He slipped away so silently she could hardly believe his presence beside her had not been a fantasy of her own weaving. Her body shook as she drew the disturbed covering back over her shoulders and waited, in an agony of doubt.

Though, in obedience to Giles's instructions, she kept her eyes tight closed and feigned sleep, she was aware of someone entering the ante-room. There was a muffled oath as an unwary foot caught a stool while in progress towards the Queen's chamber. Maria's fearful body froze into complete immobility.

A voice unknown to her whispered harshly, 'Does your sister sleep in here?'

'Ursula told me she was to be in attendance within the Queen's chamber. I told her I needed a private audience to beg the Queen to consider a special suit.' William Lester's tone was low and brusque.

'Then who is this?'

'The Spanish lady, Doña Maria.'

'If she should wake——'

'She's unlikely to wake if you keep quiet.'

'If she does, she must be instantly silenced.'

'That will not be necessary.'

'Who says what will or will not be necessary? Undo the shutter from the lantern. Check she really is sleeping.' The first man's tone was breathless, conveying acute fear.

Maria actually felt the faint warmth from the light glow which fell upon her closed eyelids as the cover was partially withdrawn from the dark lantern and held close to her bed.

Sweet Virgin, where was Giles? If these men were to discover that she was indeed awake, her throat could be cut as cleanly and expertly as dispatching a slaughtered lamb and before he could come to her.

The first man spoke peevishly. 'It seems that she did drink from the same wine jug supplied to your sister for the Queen. Pray God Elizabeth was thirsty and drank deep.'

Sir William Lester's voice betrayed impatience. 'I told you Ursula has no suspicions, neither has she any idea the Queen's wine was drugged. She was expecting me to come to the chamber door, but it's likely she will be asleep herself by now. Elizabeth will have insisted that her attendant drink first. She has not survived so long without due caution. If they both slept, better so.' There was a slight catch to his voice. 'If anything should go wrong, Ursula cannot be blamed.'

His companion gave a faintly contemptuous snort. 'Do you think Walsingham would allow her to escape? We cannot afford to fail. Charnock and Tichbourne should be here by now after dealing with the guards. Admit them and let us finish this business.'

Again Maria heard the door-latch click and held her breath as further movement close to the bed alerted her to fresh peril.

Sir William's voice, now grimly determined. 'Tichbourne, stay here and watch the Spanish woman. She must not interrupt us. Despite my fondness for her, if she makes the slightest movement...' He left the threat unspoken but a thrill of horror shot through Maria.

She felt breath hot on her face as her guard leaned over her; not fresh wine scent now, but the stark stink of soured vomit. The man had sickened already in his deadly terror.

She swallowed the bile which rose in her own throat, dreading the action would betray her and mean her death.

By the blessed saints, what could she do to warn the Queen? If Ursula slept, the men could do their deadly work and be gone before dawn. Her thoughts teemed in her brain. What of the guard? Had he been cut down at his post? Had Giles entered the Queen's chamber? If so, Maria had not so much as heard the click of the latch. This room was so small he could surely not still be with her, hidden in the shadows. The lantern, faint as it was, would have revealed his presence. She prayed silently and desperately for help; that Walsingham was aware of the impending attack and had allowed these men to walk into the trap. It would be like that saturnine, black-clad spider—but, dear God, let them come now, before she died of sheer terror! Yet, if they did so, she was surely doomed, for her guard would kill her before being overpowered——

Suddenly it seemed all hell was let loose. There was a shrill scream from someone within the Queen's chamber. Ursula? Then the Queen's voice, harsh, mannish, commanding silence over a cacophony of noise, the click of men's boots on the polished floor, the barked orders of the guard officer, a rasp of weapon on weapon, a sharp gasp of pain, then a despairing cry.

'Tichbourne, finish it, man, get out. We are betrayed——'

Sir William Lester had survived, then.

Maria was conscious in that split second of her captor's relaxation of his guard. She half saw, half felt him lift his head in shocked bemusement. She acted instinctively, knocking his hand up and dislodging the dagger from his grasp.

He gave a grunt of fury, instantly alerted, and returned to the attack. She was kneeling upon the bed now and fought him viciously. He beat at her in desperation, but she did not flinch under the terrible rain of hard blows.

He had one chance of escape now and one only, she knew that. If he took her prisoner, it was possible he might be allowed to back down the length of the corridor and flee while the guards hesitated, reluctant to see one of the Queen's ladies butchered before their eyes.

She was hardly aware of the confusion within the royal bedchamber, only of her own grim struggle with this conspirator. Behind her the door was wrenched open at the very moment Tichbourne was able to overpower her and force her away from the bed to stand, barefoot, her back hard against his heaving chest.

'Let her go, man. She can't help you now.' Giles Norwood's voice was steady. He sounded hardly winded and without the least trace of fear or anxiety.

'Damn you, Norwood. I'll cut her throat now if you don't all stand back and let me move.'

'You are surrounded, man.' Giles's tone was almost wearied. 'Where could you go? We've known, from the moment the Queen commanded Mistress Lester to attend her tonight, just when and where you would strike. The others are already taken. You do yourself no good by threatening Doña Maria.'

'God's curse on you, Norwood. I can take her with me.'

Maria felt the slow trickle of blood on her throat and the icy feel of the blade where he nicked her flesh. She dared not move a muscle, nor could she command her own vocal cords.

The harsh rasp of the Queen's voice silenced all the clamour. 'Stand back as he says, all of you. If Doña Maria is harmed, I'll have the head of the man who disobeys.'

There was a sudden murmur of submission. Maria swallowed painfully. She was positioned so she could see the Queen, regal, as always, in her furred bedgown, despite the straggling grey hairs revealed so cruelly by the removal of her familiar red wig. It was an ageing woman who stood there, devoid of state gown, massive lace ruff, jewels and panoply of monarchy, but a Queen for all that. There was sovereignty in the rigidity of her slight form, in the decisive note of her voice, in the uplifted hand, which forbade the slightest infringement of her orders.

Maria saw Giles clearly at the Queen's right hand, his unsheathed sword menacing Tichbourne. He moved back apace in deference to the Queen's command and Tichbourne blew a gusty sigh of relief in Maria's ear, then she was hurled around to face the door into the corridor.

The Queen's voice rang out again. 'You men in the corridor, let him pass. Do it, I say.'

Maria was trundled roughly forward to the door. Her bare feet slipped on the waxy surface of the floor and she half stumbled. There came a concerted gasp from the watchers as the knife trembled in Tichbourne's hand and he cursed roundly. His hands were slippery with sweat and he eased the weapon momentarily away from her flesh as he forced her to her feet. Maria's terrified gaze took in a long expanse of corridor. Ahead of them armed guards slid aside as they passed, mindful of the Queen's instructions. Behind her, Maria felt the watchers close in again, their weapons at the ready, anxious for the shouted order to pounce, should there be an opportunity to do so with impunity.

Walsingham had laid his trap well. There were more than a dozen more within the chamber, possibly another detachment in the courtyard. Had he not held her as hostage, Tichbourne could have had no chance of escape at all.

And when he was clear of the palace precincts, if he managed to win free to the Great Gate, what of her? Could she be sure he would abandon his hold, or would he force her further, only to dispatch her when she became of no further use to him?

Maria gritted her teeth, concentrated only on the peril of the moment. There must be no more stumbles. She had been very close to the knife-edge severing her jugular vein. The Queen apparently thought her of sufficient worth that she gave this traitor his chance to escape. The notion comforted her and she held on to every grain of solace. Wordlessly she uttered a prayer to the Virgin and a swift act of contrition. Her thin shift clung to her body shamelessly, as, wet with the sweat of fear, she was moved relentlessly onward.

When her release came, it was so sudden and unexpected that she fell face down on the ground and lay whimpering, believing the dagger had done its work, despite the lack of pain she felt at her throat. There had been no sound, no warning. She half clambered to her feet to see Tichbourne engaged in a life and death struggle with Sir Giles Norwood. The dagger had slipped from his nerveless fingers and, stupefied, Maria crawled towards it, her bemused mind attempting to take in the truth of how Giles had come to her rescue. She secured the weapon and a guardsman hastened to her and wrapped her in his cloak, though she protested weakly in her effort to see what was happening to the combatants.

Already Tichbourne was down, Norwood's fingers tightening around his throat, and the man gave gurgling half-screams, his hands sawing the air in frustrated impotence. Maria recognised that animal fury in Sir Giles's expression. It had shone from his slate-grey eyes in the half-lit dimness of the slave deck off Cadiz harbour. He meant to kill and he was enjoying the suffering of his victim.

The Queen's voice halted him as she impatiently shouldered aside the men who had drawn closer to the struggling pair.

'Giles Norwood, I'd have that traitor in the Tower, and, after, at Tyburn. Would you deprive me of my rightful vengeance?'

For one moment Maria thought Giles would defy her, then he relaxed his hold and Tichbourne fell to the ground writhing and retching. He was pounced upon instantly by two guards and wrenched to his feet, then carted off, his legs trailing and scraping the ground wretchedly.

The murderous light faded from Giles Norwood's eyes and he opened his arms. Maria, sobbing her relief for his safety, moved instinctively into them.

'*Querida*, forgive me,' he murmured softly, as his hand gently soothed back the sweat-soaked tendrils of her hair, 'I hastened to the Queen, never thinking the craven wretches would turn on you. I was close, very close all the time, yet not close enough to protect you.'

'You did save me,' she choked, and then the recent terror took its full effect. She could no longer control the terrible trembling of her limbs and fell against him, so that he lifted her high into his arms, and, at the Queen's command, carried her into the royal bedchamber.

CHAPTER FOURTEEN

MARIA woke in her own chamber to find Consuelo seated by the bedside. Ursula's bed was empty and unruffled, and tears sprang to Maria's eyes as she turned her face into the pillow and sobbed despairingly. Consuelo brought her warm water and towels and begged her not to distress herself.

'It will do you no good, *querida*,' she whispered dolefully. 'The Queen's physician has been to attend you, sent by Her Majesty. He will blame me if he finds you in such a state and Sir Giles——'

Maria sat up at once, her eyes wide with concern. 'What of Sir Giles? He was not badly hurt?'

'No, no, *querida*. He carried you to the Queen's chamber and the ladies tended your hurts and dressed you in clean night-rail till the physician came, a fierce, tall man. He frightens me——'

'Consuelo, please, tell me of Sir Giles.'

'He would not leave the antechamber till he was sure you were not seriously hurt. There was blood on your throat. He carried you here afterwards, would let no one else touch you. The physician had given you a sleeping draught. You do not remember that?'

Maria shook her head impatiently. 'How long have I slept? What of Mistress Lester?'

Consuelo shook her head. 'I do not know. There has been talk. I haven't understood all they say but—I think soldiers took her away to the Tower.'

'Sweet Virgin, no, not there. I must get to the Queen.'

'*Querida*, no one can get to the Queen but her most favoured ladies. You've slept many hours. It is long past noon. There has been much happening. Some men have been arrested and the guard has been doubled. No one

231

is allowed in or out of the palace without being checked. Some of the ladies are hysterical.'

'I can imagine,' Maria said drily. 'Do you know where Sir Giles is?'

'He told me he would be back to see you later. He seemed very preoccupied. I think he went into the city.'

'I must see him as soon as possible, but, please, Consuelo, not like this. Fetch my gown and help me dress. If anything is to be done for Ursula it must be done at once.'

'The physician said you were to remain in bed all day.'

Maria's eyes snapped with anger. 'Consuelo, much as I love you, I swear I shall slap you if you keep trying to prevent me from going to the Queen.'

She thrust aside the bed-covering and made to get up. Once on her feet, she realised her mistake. The room swam dizzily before her eyes and she sank down again on to the bed hastily. The sleeping draught had had its effect and it would take longer than she thought to thrust aside her weakness.

Consuelo tutted her concern but brought Maria a clean undershift and gown. The scratches and bruises Maria had received in the struggles with the traitor, Tichbourne, were now beginning to make themselves felt and she was thankful to hide the worst ravages the man had inflicted on her throat beneath the starched ruff.

If the Queen would not receive her, what could be done for her friend? Her soul quailed at the thought of Ursula immured within the grim fortress of the Tower she had seen from the ferry journey she had made with Sir William and his sister. Walsingham and his minions would be merciless. All conspirators would be put to the question and Maria could not be certain if she herself would not be suspect, sleeping as she had done in the antechamber and seen often in the company of the Lesters. Yet Walsingham would surely save her, and the Queen had shown genuine concern for Maria's safety by risking the traitor's escape in order to save Maria's life, then she had sent her own physician to tend her.

Consuelo's head jerked up nervously as the imperious knock sounded on the door. Maria's hand tightened on her duenna's arm so that she winced with pain.

'Find out who it is.'

Such was the state of tension within the palace that Consuelo was white-faced as she hurried to obey.

'It is Sir Giles, Maria. He asks if you are well enough to receive him.'

'Yes, of course. Please bring him in, Consuelo.'

Sir Giles Norwood showed no sign of injury, but his mouth was set in a grim line and dark shadows beneath his eyes told of more than one sleepless night.

He bent to kiss Maria's hand. 'You are better?'

'Yes, I thank you; I am dizzy still after the drug the physician gave me, but I shall soon be completely recovered. Sir Giles, what of the conspirators? Were they all taken?'

'All but Babington. He has fled, probably to the North. His estates are in Derbyshire. The priest, Ballard, has been arrested also.'

She nodded, her eyes lowered in anguish for the man who had listened so gently to her problems and tried to give her comfort. Even now she could not believe that a Jesuit, a man of God, could have lent himself to such a plot, to murder his Queen.

'I am most concerned for Ursula Lester. I am convinced she was totally innocent, yet Consuelo tells me it is rumoured she is imprisoned in the Tower.'

'She is.'

'Then I must plead with the Queen——'

'I don't recommend such a course. Elizabeth has been well frightened, a condition which does not put her in a merciful mood. There's no real cause for alarm. The girl will be questioned closely, must be so. Unwittingly she may have overheard some of her brother's plans and be able to reveal some part of the conspiracy as yet we do not know.'

'But if she is innocent——'

'She will know of other men who visited her brother. Walsingham will be able to construe any shreds of evidence to make the whole case he needs. The Queen of Scots has also fallen into his trap.'

'She was mentioned at that meeting, at least; I thought at first it was our Queen they spoke of.'

'Walsingham is determined to bring about her death. This time he will be successful.'

Maria was appalled. 'Yet she is kin to the Queen.'

'Aye, she is, but that did not prevent her plotting her cousin's murder. We have known of her involvement with Spain for many months, but we had no proof.' He gave a wintry smile. 'Now she has committed herself in writing. We have the letter which speaks of a promised invasion from the Low Countries and the loyalty of many of her English sympathisers. It tells also of the plot to assassinate the Queen, which we have seen for ourselves and managed to foil, thank the Virgin, and the plans to deliver Mary from her imprisonment at Chartley.'

'How could she have been so foolhardy?' Maria whispered, dry-mouthed.

'When one is convinced the letter has been conveyed in deepest secrecy and written in code, one feels secure enough.' Sir Giles laughed. 'What she did not know was that the whole course of the message from messenger to receiver, even the method by which it could be managed, was evolved in the devious mind of our very dear Walsingham.'

Maria felt suddenly sickened. She had been horrified by the conspiracy, had almost lost her life at the hands of one of the perpetrators, but the means by which they had been trapped left a sour taste in her mouth. It had been necessary to save the Queen, and with her the very realm of England itself. She recognised that, had allowed the Secretary of State to use her in order to save Ursula Lester from the threat of torture, but she now felt like one of the executioners.

Sir Giles explained. 'Mary was supplied with casks of special ale from a particular brewer of Burton, which is near Chartley where she is imprisoned. Walsingham arranged for a special hollow tube to be placed within the corked cask bung. His own man, Gifford, was in touch with a man named Morgan, another malcontent. We have suspected Babington for some time, and some of the men he met with often.' Giles gave a short, barked laugh. 'The man was foolishly vain enough and so confident of the success of the venture that he insisted they all be painted together to bind them yet closer and as a memorial of the glorious plot. A sure way to pull the noose tight round the necks of all of them. We had no hard evidence, of course, until you happened to overhear them planning their next move at Lester's lodging. He, incidentally, was not one of the favoured six mentioned in Babington's correspondence with Queen Mary, but a mere tool used by the others because of his Catholic sympathies.'

'And Queen Mary answered Babington's letter?'

'Yes, she wrote of her approval of the very assassination plot.'

Maria fell silent. She thought of all those vainglorious foolish men, snared so easily by a superior antagonist, that quiet, dark, sardonic man in the shadows of Elizabeth's court, who waited and watched, and used all those who came into contact with him as he and Giles had ruthlessly used her. She shivered, despite the heat of the August afternoon.

Sir Giles said, reassuringly, 'It is all over. You've nothing more to fear. Lester can do you no harm, nor Tichbourne. I'd have dispatched him myself had I not been sure he will die a crueller death than I can devise.'

'Like your master, you are pitiless.'

'He dared to threaten you. How would you have had me deal with him?'

She averted her eyes, though her limbs trembled. How sweet it would be to allow herself to believe that Giles Norwood's ferocity sprang from love of her. But his pride of possession had been attacked, his Spanish prize of war, which belonged to him alone. For that assault on his honour he would wish Tichbourne to suffer, and horribly.

She shifted awkwardly and Sir Giles rose at once to his feet.

'I am tiring you.'

'No, no, I am well enough but—all this upsets me——'

He bent and formally kissed her hand once more. 'You are too tender-hearted, *querida*. Lester would not have spared you, had you stood in the way of his plan for the Queen's death.' At the door he made her a bow. 'I will come to you again very soon now, after you are rested. We must make our own plans.'

She forced a smile. Now was not the time to thwart his wishes.

She insisted on resuming her duties later that day. She was wryly amused to find how her companions had changed their attitude towards her. The curious glances she now found levelled at her held traces of unabashed admiration rather than the avid speculation she had become accustomed to over the weeks of her stay in the Queen's service. No one in her presence mentioned Ursula Lester's absence from their company. Catching sight of the opaque hardness of the Queen's dark eyes, Maria did not dare broach the subject of her friend's impending fate.

When Sir Giles presented himself, as he had promised, as escort for their customary walk in the palace gardens, she found courage at last to speak honestly of her doubts and fears for the future.

'Sir Giles, I know you wish me well. There has been much between us which might have excused your hard treatment of me, yet you honourably offer me your hand in marriage. I am truly grateful. I understand that you consider me compromised by my stay aboard your ship and wish to protect me. You appear to hold yourself responsible for me. Though my aunt in Northumberland has made a kindly approach, I cannot believe that she would now wish me to believe that I would be welcome there for anything but a temporary stay. Indeed, recent events at court concerning Catholics would mean my presence in her company could prove an embarrassment to her and her family. The Queen will not wish me to remain within royal service, I imagine. She has been very kind, but my presence will remind her constantly of her own nearness to death.'

Because what she had to say was difficult, she had lapsed into her native Castilian tongue. As he made to speak she hastened on in order to forestall him.

'You know that in Cartagena you feared that Don Luis, my betrothed, would not wish to ransom me. You were right. He resented the stigma of my mother's suspected heresy and the harm it would do to his ambitions.'

He nodded, his grey eyes resting steadily on her blue ones. 'You were never in love with the man?'

A little, bitter smile framed her lips. 'I think I came as near to hating Don Luis as I could, without endangering my mortal soul. No, you know I had no wish to marry him, but I have been thinking long and hard. There is no real place for me in England. The Queen of Scots' involvement with Spain and King Philip show that all Spanish subjects will ever be regarded with suspicion here. Always I will be "the Spanish woman" and an alliance with me could threaten your ambitions as it did Don Luis's. If—if it were possible, I would like to return to my own land, to my uncle's house in Cadiz.'

'But you said yourself, on board the *Gloriana*, that he would not receive you graciously.'

Again she smiled sadly. 'I'm sure I shall not be welcomed, particularly by my aunt, Beatriz, who will be shocked beyond all measure at the things which have happened to me.'

'Then what life could you have there?'

She drew a hard breath. 'I have considered that too. I could enter a convent. My inheritance would be more than sufficient to cover my dowry as entrance into the order.'

He frowned and there was a long silence between them. She waited, in an agony, for his reply.

He said, at last, 'I've no wish to force you, *muy doña*, into any course of conduct repugnant to you. And now, if you please, we will rejoin your fellow ladies.'

His tone was so stiff and unyielding that she was tempted to pour out her true feelings, of her terrible hurt at the knowledge that she had been deliberately placed in the Queen's service and used as a pawn by him and Walsingham, but did she detect in his manner just the slightest hint of relief at her decision?

He made no more reference to his proposal nor to her request, and that night she cried quietly to herself in the little room that seemed lonelier than ever without the comforting presence of Ursula in the truckle-bed beside her. Had she consulted Consuelo, she knew her duenna's face would have brightened with relief at thought of returning to Spain, and Maria could not have borne to witness her pleasure.

The Queen sent for her early next morning. Elizabeth was attired for riding in a green velvet habit, her matching hat perched atop the red wig, adorned with a monstrous plume of feathers attached to the cloth by a superb emerald which could only have been brought from New Spain by one of her corsair captains. The Queen abruptly halted her mannish strides about the chamber.

'How now, mistress,' she croaked harshly. 'What is this I hear about your rejection of Giles Norwood? Are you mad?'

Maria dipped in a nervous curtsy. Bewildered by the suddenness of the Queen's verbal attack, she struggled to think how best to counter it. Experience had taught her to remain silent during the Queen's rages. However, Elizabeth was intent on obtaining an answer and caught the girl's wrist in a punishing grip as she urged her to rise.

'Come, come, girl. You can see I am dressed for riding. Am I to wait forever for your reply?'

'Your Grace, I——'

'So you wish to return to Spain?'

'It is my homeland, Your Grace. I am a stranger here——'

'Have you any complaints concerning our treatment of you, chit?'

'No, Your Grace has always been most kind.'

'Indeed. I have received you, vouched for you, even gone to the trouble of finding a husband. How do you repay me? By threatening the life of one of my most trusted courtiers.'

'Madam, I would never——'

'Don't interrupt me.' The royal eyes flashed fire and Maria trembled. 'How dare you express a desire to be conveyed to this homeland you profess to love and which, incidentally, caused the death of your mother? Giles Norwood insists on returning you personally. How long do you think he would remain free after setting foot in Cadiz?'

'But surely that is not necessary, Your Grace?'

'What is necessary is beside the point. I could, of course, forbid him to leave England. He would disobey me. He considers it his duty to return you to the arms of your family, since he took you prisoner. No, Maria, if you insist on this ridiculous course, you will doom Giles Norwood. Is that what you want, your revenge, for his capture of you, his total ruin?'

Maria turned away, her eyes brimming with tears, her shoulders shaking with uncontrollable sobs. 'No, no, Your Grace. I wish Sir Giles no harm. I—I love him.'

'Ah, at last it is out.'

The Queen once more grasped her wrist less cruelly this time and drew Maria to the stool near her chair.

'Now, what is this nonsense? Why, if you love him, do you reject him?'

'He does not love me, Your Grace.'

'He's willing to marry you. What has love to do with it? Child, child, consider, what is there for you now in Spain? After all that has happened, your uncle will not wish to receive you, and for all your professed desire to enter a convent I tell you frankly, you are a fool. There are women who are born to the virgin state. You are not one of them.'

Maria stared up at the Queen wonderingly.

'I have loved two men in my life, Maria. The first one threatened my very existence and had to be sacrificed; the second,' she shrugged, 'threatened my reputation and security as Queen. I am one of those women who can embrace chastity and survive, but I tell you now, it makes a cold companion and must be chosen by one who has no other option.'

Maria dared not answer or look at the Queen. Nervously she pleated the silk of her overgown.

'What makes you think Giles Norwood has no love for you? He's anxious enough to take you and without dowry.'

Maria drew a hard little breath. 'They needed me for their purposes, Sir Francis Walsingham and Sir Giles.'

'Huh, what of it? My Moor would use his grandmother to further his own designs. You helped to preserve my life. Do you regret your involvement?'

'No, Your Grace, never think that.'

'Yet, you are, as you said, a daughter of Spain.'

'I am half English, Your Grace, and I have nothing but contempt for those who plot murder.'

'Well said. You've courage enough. I have watched you deal with those of my ladies who have been less than kind. Why not challenge Giles Norwood, tell him frankly what is in your heart?' Elizabeth rapped Maria's knee impatiently with two fingers. 'I'll not have this. Giles Norwood is a brave gentleman. He deserves better than a lifetime in the galleys, or, worse, a humiliating and fearful walk to the fire in some *auto de fe*.'

Maria's face contorted in sheer horror. Vividly she pictured him as she had first seen him, hair and beard matted, filthy, and him chained to the oar. A shudder ran through her frame as, again, she saw the rise and fall of that lethal whip. The Queen was right. He would, for honour's sake, land her safely in Cadiz harbour. She could not allow him to make such a sacrifice.

The Queen rose. For a moment her hand rested affectionately on Maria's shoulder. 'I'll send him to you. Think very hard of what you will say to him, for his sake, and your own.'

Maria sat hunched on the stool. The Queen had counselled her to tell Giles Norwood, honestly, what was in her heart. She could not. Centuries of breeding, as a proud daughter of a grandee of Spain, forbade her to risk rejection. She had tried to tell him once, upon the

Gloriana, the night before they had landed in England. She had gone to him, alone, and he had deliberately prevented her from speaking of her feelings. She could hardly risk such heartbreak again, yet she must urge him to remain in England. He must not land in Spain where he could be taken easily, and after his participation in the raid on Cartagena he was more deeply in peril. She could not go further, confess that she loved him with her whole being, ached for him——

He knocked and she croaked out such a whispered answer that she was afraid he would not hear her. She had risen to greet him and he stood by the door, waiting; those slate-grey eyes of his glittered strangely and a smile hovered around that mobile, bearded mouth. There was nothing of mockery in it. She could not determine his mood. He stood erect as ever, yet he appeared to lack his usual dashing confidence, seemed almost vulnerable.

'*Muy doña*, the Queen says you wish to speak to me. I am at your service as always.'

She blinked unhappily, as he made no effort to come closer. 'Sir Giles.' She plunged into impulsive speech, avoiding that very direct stare. 'The Queen informs me of—of your intention to sail back to Spain with me as passenger. That is out of the question.' Then, in a little rush of panic, 'You must not, cannot.'

'Why?'

'Why?' She echoed the word wonderingly. 'You will imperil yourself.'

'Does that matter to you? Am I not an Englishman and a dog of a pirate?'

'You are a very gallant English gentleman, Sir Giles, whose death I would—I would deeply regret.' She broke off uncertainly.

'So, there is some pity in that proud Spanish beauty who watched unflinchingly while they flogged the skin from my back.'

She advanced indignantly to confront him, her eyes flashing blue fire. 'You cannot believe that I wished it, enjoyed it. I have already explained—there was nothing I could do to prevent it. All that day I worried and grieved, and even now, in the night hours,' she shuddered, 'I see it all over again and—you cannot go back to Spain. Say you will not, please, I beg of you.'

Her eyes glistened with tears and he reached up and lightly touched the smooth wing of hair that brushed her brow.

'Then you *can* feel for me, my lovely Spanish prize. In spite of my roistering, piratical ways.' The tone was light now, bantering, yet she knew it was to cover his own weakness, his longing to reveal his over-mastering desire.

The barriers were down at last and each knew there was no longer need to speak.

He drew her close to his heart and pressed his lips on hers, gently at first, as if to seal their unspoken bargain, then passionately, hungrily. Her lips parted sweetly beneath his and her arms reached up to his neck. He was so tall she was forced to stand on tiptoe and he laughed and swept her up so she might tangle her groping fingers in the fair curls on the nape of his neck. She could not breathe. Her very soul seemed to fuse with his, so that they were one, and not even death could part them.

He put her down at last and, very gently taking her hand, led her to the window-seat. 'Say it,' he commanded. 'You are mine, you belong to me, body and soul.'

'I belong to you. I love you.' She spoke in English haltingly, and he laughed again in jubilation.

'And you will consent to become Lady Norwood and remain with me here in this cold, wet, unfriendly land?'

'It will not be cold or unfriendly when you are here.'

'Why did you reject me, *querida*?'

'I thought—that you asked for me only out of a sense of honour. On the ship I knew then—I tried to tell you— I—believed then that you did not want me. Then, when you placed me at court——'

'Walsingham forced me to do that and his reasons were so cogent, so overwhelming, that my duty forbade me to disobey. Since it was his wish that Lester should become interested in you, I was forbidden to declare my own love. Oh, my sweet girl, if you knew how I suffered

watching you with that young coxcomb and unable to
tell you what you meant to me. Then, when I knew you
were in real peril because of Walsingham's machi-
nations, I was ready to throw in my hand and defy him.'

'But the Queen was in deadly danger and needed both
of us.'

He nodded. 'That last night on the *Gloriana* I would
have spoken then, asked you to become my wife, but I
was still in Walsingham's service and I wished him to
release me before I could honourably come to you and
beg for your hand.'

'Because you had always been in his service against
Spain and was my enemy? Was that it? You came to
Spain to spy out the strength of King Philip's forces,
which might be massed against England?'

He nodded again. 'I am not ashamed that I was
Walsingham's agent. You have seen how the ambitions
of Philip of Spain threaten the peace of England and
the very life of its Queen. Yet I loved a daughter of Spain
and would not have her enmity. I needed to be free of
such service, having honourably discharged my duty and
seen that my sovereign was safe, so I waited, never
thinking that such a course would imperil *you*.'

'And now, you are free?'

'Yes, the Queen has granted me permission to
withdraw from court. If you will have me, I shall take
you to my home in Yorkshire. You will learn to be lady
of an English manor and all my folk will love you as I
do.'

'Oh, Giles, my dear love, I want that beyond anything, but...' She hesitated and he took her hand and
squeezed it.

'You wish our marriage to be blessed by your own
Church?'

She nodded tremulously.

'We will be married here, at court, as the Queen
wishes, and later I will find a way to bring a priest to
Askrigg. You asked me on the ship of my father's faith.
Have you not understood I am of the Old Faith, too,
and though I have seen its weakness in Spain, felt in my

own flesh its cruelties, I can never forsake it? Like many of my fellow Northern gentlemen I will refrain from church services, pay my fines as a recusant, yet remain truly loyal to the Queen, my dear sovereign, for she is the salvation of England.

'I bring you nothing,' she said, doubtfully, 'and because of me you will find it necessary to leave court where you can pursue your own fortunes. You have the Queen's favour, Giles.'

'But you are all I want. Do you think I forsook the ransom, left it without a qualm on the mole at Cartagena, without knowing then just how dear you were to me and always will be?'

She gazed up into those clear grey eyes of his, shining with love for her and hope for their future together, and cradled her head against his shoulder in delicious surrender.

They were married within the royal chapel. The Queen and Sir Francis Walsingham were both present. Elizabeth made Maria the gift of a single pearl on a long golden chain. Maria had wondered, not without some inner amusement, if the jewel had been rightfully returned to a Spanish owner and come into the Queen's possession, initially, as booty offered to her by yet another of her English corsairs.

A room was placed at their disposal inside the royal apartments and here Maria withdrew with Consuelo to wait for her husband. Consuelo assisted her from the elaborate court gown of heavy white silk trimmed with seed pearls and silver braid. After Maria had washed in scented water, she sat on a joint-stool while Consuelo brushed out the dampened tendrils of her shining brown hair, leaving it loose about her shoulders. Impulsively Consuelo hugged her charge and Maria clung to her as she had when she had been a small child.

'There is nothing to fear, *querida*. He loves you dearly, I know it, and even if he did not, you love him and have the power to make him love you. I told you, long ago, how easy that would be for you.'

Maria's lips quivered. 'You will not regret remaining in England?'

'Not if it is your wish, *niña* Maria. I shall be content.' She kissed Maria tenderly and slipped from the room.

Maria moved to the great testered bed, gazing wonderingly round at the luxuriously appointed room. From nearby she could hear the revelry of the guests at the small private banquet the Queen had given in honour of Sir Giles's wedding. He had promised Maria that he would see to it that there would be no noisy invasion into their chamber.

Was she afraid? Her mouth felt very dry. Yes, there was fear; not of pain, nor yet a dread of what the unknown initiation into womanhood would entail. It was fear that she might not please him. She had no skills, only basic knowledge. Consuelo had laughed at her fears when they had discussed her marital duties so long ago, it seemed, at the Residency in Cartagena, when she had been fearful of welcoming a very different husband to her bed. Consuelo had been so very confident that she was capable of making any man desire her. Now, Maria was not so sure.

Pale light flared from a sconce in the corridor then was blotted out by Sir Giles Norwood's massive form as he stood in the doorway. He pushed the heavy door to, and advanced towards her where she sat on the bed in her embroidered nightshift. He carried two beakers of wine.

When she would have refused one, he lifted the beaker commandingly to her lips.

'Drink it. Don't argue, woman. You are my wife now and must obey.' He spoke in English, almost brusquely, but the tone of his voice was not harsh with anger, but husky with desire.

She gave a great gasp as fiery fluid burned her tongue and throat.

He laughed in triumph. 'Rum has that effect. I should have warned you.' He drained his own beaker in one gulp, then he took her by one hand and lifted her to her feet. 'Let me look at you.' His eyes travelled the length of her all-revealing shift. 'Very beautiful—though, in truth, we needed no such garment, sweeting.'

She shook her head and he placed both hands around her face under the scented waves of dark hair which framed it and turned her chin towards the uncertain light from the single candlestick on the bedside table.

'God, how lovely you are,' he murmured, 'and all mine. No ransom could compensate for the loss of you. If Drake could see you now he'd admit that fast enough.' Her eyes were shining. He was not sure if tears glimmered on the dark lashes. 'Maria, you are not afraid of me?'

'A little, *señor*.'

'There is no need; I assure you, sweeting, this match of ours is not made in any spirit of revenge.' He could feel her body quiver against his own and he gave her shoulders a little, fierce shake of exasperation. 'Do you believe me, Maria, *querida*?'

'*Sí, señor.*' In her agitation, her English had deserted her.

'Yes, Giles,' he prompted firmly.

'Yes, Giles,' she repeated, and he smiled his pleasure at the quaintness of her accented use of his name.

He lifted her into the high bed and she waited while he hurriedly divested himself of his clothing and came to her side. When she would have extinguished the candle, he prevented her.

'No, sweeting. God has blessed our union. Do not be afraid to let me look on your beauty.'

She submitted while he undid the strings of her shift and drew the fine linen down from her shoulders to gaze on the splendour of her naked breasts.

'And to think Drake ordered me to sell all this for paltry gold.'

Her fingers reached up to his shoulders then slid down the muscled splendour of his back. 'These scars will always be there, reminding you of what you suffered because of my foolishness.'

'And of the gentle fingers which smoothed on the salve that finally healed. Even in your desperate fear you did that for me. Could I ever forget that?'

'I did plead with them to halt the whipping,' she said brokenly, 'and Don Esteban gave way in the end, though, by then, I think you had endured too much to know or understand. You fell fainting to the deck when they cut you down.'

'How your proud uncle must have hated that display, your open compassion for one of his galley slaves.' He gave a little, strangled laugh as his arms encircled her shoulder and he drew her close to his heart. 'He will be even more gravely displeased when he hears his niece has been abducted by this same slave and dog of a pirate, and, that, in the end, she gave herself to him in love.'

A little bubble of hysterical laughter threatened to surface as she thought of her aunt's disapproving countenance and of the gossip and innuendo her niece's disgraceful conduct would bring down upon that well-appointed household.

Then, 'Will your people not distrust and resent me?' she questioned fearfully.

'*Querida*, I have no family. As I explained, both my parents are dead and I have no brothers or sisters. My old nurse, who rules the household at Askrigg like a gorgon, will welcome you with open arms when she knows how deeply I love you.'

Maria was not so sure. Would this Englishwoman who, most probably, cherished her nursling as Consuelo did Maria, be so willing to give place to a wife, and a Spanish Papist to boot?

As if he read her doubts, he bent and kissed her reassuringly on her brow. 'Alice loves me and, because of that, she will love and accept you. It has been a thorn in her side for too long that I have brought no bride to Askrigg. Her only regret will be that she could not strew my bridal bed with herbs that ensure fertility.'

Maria's face and throat were suffused by a rosy blush and he laughed again.

'Will you not wish to bear our child, *querida*?'

'If God proves kind.'

'And you fear he will not?'

'I do not fear anything while you are with me, not even—that I will be unable to worship him publicly in the church. He knows I will do so in my own heart and I will bless him always that he gave me you to love. I pray that—that I can please you.'

'Do not doubt that, sweeting.' His voice was husky now with desire and her heartbeat quickened. Firmly he laid her back upon the bed and she gave a little moan of panic. He placed one finger gently upon her lips. 'You promised to trust me.'

'I do—but——'

He was leaning down above her, his weight balanced on his two hands placed squarely on either side of her shoulders. Those grey eyes of his, often so cold and distant, were warm now with love, the colour ever changing in the uncertain light of the candle from silver to soft green.

Her lips parted to receive his kiss, which was demanding yet still tender, lingering on hers. Her heart thrilled to the wonder of this strange joy which seemed to pass from each to the other. Her arms stole up again to enfold him, to draw him down, ever closer to her own eager body.

He was very gentle, as he had promised, his hands skilfully wooing her to respond, his touch light, teasingly caressing on throat, breast, thighs, bringing her patiently to the supreme moment of giving. She received him hungrily, welcoming the pain, and, with it, the ecstasy of consummation.

Afterwards she lay for hours utterly content, until the grey spears of dawn light entered the chamber from the high windows. He had drawn her close into his arms, her head pillowed on his shoulder. His eyes were closed and he slept, the sweat glistening on the golden hairs of his chest. She nestled against him, her whole body aglow with the delight of his lovemaking. Now, now she was his, and he, surely, all hers. If this wonder, this complete oneness, was sinful in the eyes of the Church, then she would gladly forsake all hope of heaven.

He moved contentedly in sleep, his arms tightening round her possessively, and she finally surrendered to her overweening longing to sleep.

They had ridden North the next day. The countryside had been glorious in full summer, but Maria had had eyes only for her husband.

The manor at Askrigg was a small, grey-walled jewel set in the lush Yorkshire Dales, and she had loved it at once, so utterly different though it was from her own Spanish *estancia*.

Giles's household had received her joyfully. Alice, his former nurse, showed no sign of resentment. If her dear Master Giles desired the stately dark beauty with eyes as blue as June skies, and she had brought him home again, Alice had no complaints. Maria had wondered how Consuelo would settle into this alien household, but the two women had found a bond between them. Each loved her own charge so dearly that to see them happy fulfilled their deepest desires.

For these last weeks Maria had lived cocooned from the world within the silken bonds of love. Today Giles had left her to go to Masham. His favourite horse had gone lame and the blacksmith there was well known for his skill. It was the first time since their homecoming that they had been more than an hour apart. A messenger had arrived soon after Giles had left and Maria had felt a stirring of vague alarm. Surely the man had not brought a summons for Giles to return to London.

She walked the scented garden restlessly and turned eagerly when she heard Giles's step behind her. Even in the blackest of nights she would recognise it and sense his nearness.

For once she saw, even in the gloom of dusk, that he was unsmiling, though he caught her two hands within his own with his usual ardour and raised them to his lips.

'My Lady Norwood should not be lingering in the autumn evening. It's already beginning to get quite cold.'

'Is all well?' She halted in their walk to stare at him intently.

'Aye, sweetheart, the smith assured me Roland will soon be right again.'

'There was a messenger.'

'Aye, he brought news from Walsingham.'

Her heart leaped with sudden fear and she uttered a little, alarmed gasp and he squeezed her hand more tightly.

'There is nothing to fear.'

'He does not demand that you return to court?'

'No, no, he sends me news of the plotters.'

'They are all taken?' she whispered. 'Father John Ballard, too?

'Aye, sweetheart. It is all over, for all of them.'

'Tell me,' she commanded.

He looked away from her to the purple and grey of the distant hills. 'Walsingham began rounding up the conspirators soon after we left the city. He arrested Ballard on grounds of being a disguised seminary priest. There were fourteen in all. Ballard was found guilty of treason and suffered with the rest.'

Maria gave a heavy sigh. She remembered how kind the Jesuit priest had been to her.

'The Queen was in vengeful mood and even demanded of Burleigh that something more terrible than quartering should be devised to despatch the traitors, an example to all onlookers. He managed to persuade her that—that there could be no worse fate.'

Maria drew her hand free and pressed it tightly to her lips to suppress a little whimper of distress and pity.

'Babington was taken on August the fourteenth. He was in the first batch of prisoners to be despatched in extreme agony. By the following day the Queen was more merciful and the others died at the hands of the hangman, spared the indignity and horrifying terror of the later butchery.'

Maria's lips were very stiff as she tried to frame the question. 'And William Lester? Did he...?'

'Lester died in the Tower before being brought to trial. It seems his tormentors had overestimated his limit of endurance.'

'The Virgin be praised he was spared that humiliating and shocking death. And what of Ursula? Dear God, Giles, what of Ursula?'

'Walsingham writes that Ursula Lester has been released and delivered into the care of a cousin who has a manor in Kent. She will be held in close confinement for a time, but, some day, she may be allowed to ride north and you will see her again here.'

Maria's eyes brimmed with tears of joy. Ursula, at least, had been saved from the remorseless slaughter of the conspirators. She would pray constantly that her friend would eventually find some measure of contentment, as she herself had done.

'The business is not concluded yet. The Queen of Scots has been arrested at Tixall where she had been hunting in Sir Walter Aston's park. Her apartments at Chartley have been searched and it can be but a matter of time before she is tried and brought to book.'

'But surely they would not dare to execute her. She is a crowned and anointed Queen.'

Giles shook his head. 'Walsingham will not have her escape the block. He laid his plots well and he holds the damning letter to Babington speaking of her approval of the assassination attempt. That will doom her.'

'But will not the Queen save her? They are cousins——'

'The Queen will not be pleased to shed royal blood. That comes too close to her own position of power, but she knows, as we all do, it is for the good of the realm that Mary should die. She will squirm against the necessity of signing the death warrant, but she will sanction it in the end.'

They had reached the herb garden and the low, declining autumn sun had turned the windows of the manor hall to molten gold. Maria felt suddenly chilled. Giles was right. Winter, now, was very close. She pitied the royal prisoner, who all said was a martyr to aches in the joints, in the damp confinement of her prison quarters.

Before entering the house, Giles turned Maria to face him, his two hands firm on her shoulders. 'We must put it all behind us, the pain, the heartache.'

She nodded soberly. The events of the summer would never be forgotten. In this year she had become a woman, and one whose hopes and desires were fulfilled. They had each other and were greatly blessed.

The house loomed before them, the pride of Giles's heart. The gold he had brought back from the expedition to Cartagena would go some way to refurbish and improve it, as he wished. The manor had become neglected since the days of his grandfather's misfortunes. Together she and Giles would see it come to full splendour as he hoped. Among her jewels which Consuelo had brought her aboard the *Gloriana* was the string of rose-coloured pearls which Don Luis had given her most unwillingly. She would present them to Giles when she thought the time was ripe for her to do so. They were extremely rare and beautiful and would, in part, repay him for the ransom he had left upon the mole at Cartagena and provide a small dowry for his penniless Spanish bride.

He held out his hand as she lagged behind him. 'Of what are you dreaming? I thought, now this Babington affair is over for us, we would ride north soon to Northumberland and visit your aunt. If we delay much longer it will be too late. Winter comes early on the Borders.'

Her face lit up. 'Oh, Giles, that will be so pleasant. She has written so many times that she would like to see me.'

His heart almost stopped, as it always did, when he witnessed the glory of her happiness. He stooped and drew her into his arms, careless of any servant who saw them. Her lips parted to receive his kiss and, laughing, he drew her into the house.

The other exciting

MASQUERADE
Historical

available this month is:

MADEIRAN LEGACY

Marion Carr

Brought up in an orphanage in Cornwall, life was stark for Coriander May, but her bright vivid personality refused to give in.

So when a mysterious stranger from Madeira came, claiming to know her background, Coriander was intrigued. Raul Beringer told of an inheritance awaiting her, and that he wanted to buy her out. But the lure of a family, at last, was impossible to resist, and Coriander insisted on travelling to Madeira with Raul – into danger, and deceit . . .

Look out for the two intriguing

MASQUERADE *Historical*

Romances coming next month

DEEP WATERS
Victoria Aldridge

Trapped in a small enclave of Swedish whalers on the nothern tip of New Zealand, by the death of her adoptive parents, Jara Perrault knew it was only a matter of time before she was drawn into an unsavoury life.

The providential arrival of Captain Kit Montgomery, looking for a crew to sail to Macao in China, gave Jara her chance. Persuading Kit to take her on board as the cook was reasonably easy. Discovering the crew were violent convicts was something else – only Kit's protection could save her.

But Kit harboured secrets, and their destination proved a revelation in more ways than Jara expected!

JEWEL UNDER SIEGE
Polly Forrester

Constantinople, 1097 – the Crusaders were at the gate – but refused admittance to the besieged city!

On starvation rations, Emil Selest, a poor Frank intent on making his fortune, made it into the city – only to injure himself in Elena Rethel's garden. Looking death in the face, he was astounded when Elena secretly harboured him from danger. And was further shocked to realise she ran her dead husband's business – women never interfered with a man's work!

Divided in so many ways, courting danger at every step, Elena rued the day she allowed compassion to rule her . . .

Available in August